The Bay of Angels

ANITA BROOKNER

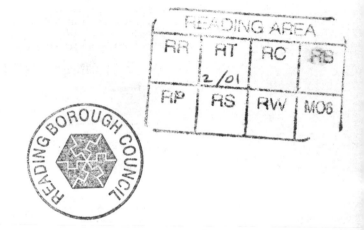

VIKING

VIKING

Published by the Penguin Group
Penguin Books Ltd, 27 Wrights Lane, London w8 5tz, England
Penguin Putnam Inc., 375 Hudson Street, New York, New York 10014, USA
Penguin Books Australia Ltd, Ringwood, Victoria, Australia
Penguin Books Canada Ltd, 10 Alcorn Avenue, Toronto, Ontario, Canada m4v 3b2
Penguin Books India (P) Ltd, 11 Community Centre,
Panchsheel Park, New Delhi – 110 017, India
Penguin Books (NZ) Ltd, Cnr Rosedale and Airborne Roads,
Albany, Auckland, New Zealand
Penguin Books (South Africa) (Pty) Ltd, 5 Watkins Street,
Denver Ext 4, Johannesburg 2094, South Africa

Penguin Books Ltd, Registered Offices: Harmondsworth, Middlesex, England

First published 2001
1

Set in 12/14.75 pt Monotype Bembo
Printed in Great Britain by
Clays Ltd, St Ives plc

A CIP catalogue record for this book is available from the British Library

ISBN 0-670-89662-4

I read the *Blue Fairy Book*, the *Yellow Fairy Book*, and the stories of Hans Andersen, the Brothers Grimm, and Charles Perrault. None of this was groundwork for success in worldly terms, for I was led to think, and indeed was minded to think, of the redeeming situation or presence which would put to rights the hardships and dilemmas under which the characters, and I myself, had been labouring. More dangerously, it seemed to me that I need make no decisions on my own behalf, for destiny or fate would always have had the matter in hand. Although I was too sensible, even as a child, to believe in a fairy godmother I accepted as part of nature's plan that after a lifetime of sweeping the kitchen floor I would go to the ball, that the slipper would fit, and that I would marry the prince. Even the cruel ordeals undergone by the little match girl, or by Hansel and Gretel, would be reversed by that same principle of inevitable justice which oversaw all activities, which guided some even if it defeated others. I knew that some humans were favoured – by whom? by the gods? (this evidence was undeniable) – but I was willing to believe in the redeeming feature, the redeeming presence that would justify all of one's vain striving, would dispel one's disappointments, would in some mysterious way present one with a solution in which one would have no part, so that all one had to do was to wait, in a condition of sinless passivity, for the transformation that would surely take place.

This strikes me now as extremely dangerous, yet parts of this doctrine seemed overwhelmingly persuasive, principally because there were no stratagems to be undertaken. One had simply to exist, in a state of dreamy indirection, for the plot to work itself out. This was a moral obligation on the part of the plot: there would be no place for calculation, for scheming, for the sort of behaviour I was to observe in the few people we knew and which I found menacing. This philosophy, the philosophy of the fairy tale, had, I thought, created my mother, whose strange loneliness was surely only a prelude to some drastic change of fortune in which she need play no active part. I therefore accepted as normal that she should spend her days sitting and reading, engaging in minimal outdoor activity, for surely these were the virtuous prerequisites for vindication of some sort, for a triumph which would confound the sceptics, whom I was also able to recognize. She was a widow; I was hardly aware of the lack of a father, for I accepted that the road to validation was in essence one of solitude, and rather than engage in some productive occupation I preferred my mother to wait for the solution to her situation to be presented as none of her own volition.

I was thus aware of her unhappiness but able to bear it, with the help of the knowledge and indeed wisdom I had culled from my reading. As a child I did not perceive her longings, which had been cruelly cut short by my father's premature death. Nor was I much interested in him, for he belonged to prehistory; I had no image of him other than as a face bending over me, and a photograph of a slim young man in an academic gown. Even the photograph conformed to my belief, for it showed someone who was not quite grown up, and therefore a fit companion for my mother who was not quite grown up either, a woman in embryo whose maturity was still far off. This made me comfortable with my own position, a fit descendant of a couple on the verge of existence who were merely undergoing some form of trial and who were surely approaching some beneficent outcome which would make even my father's death assume acceptable proportions. He had died, and my mother had survived his death. Her unhappiness, I was confident, would be overturned, as any term of trial must be. It sometimes seemed to me that my father's disappearance had merely prepared the way for a story very much like the ones I was so fond of reading. I was not then aware of the universal desire for a happy ending: I would not have understood such an abstraction. But I did know, or was convinced, that our story would have a happy ending, not realizing that there is no proper ending in human affections until time provides an ending to which all must submit.

The fact that we were of the same species (even my absent father contributed his very real silence to our own relative silence) merely emphasized the gulf that existed between ourselves and the harsher world outside our flat in Edith Grove. At least I assumed that it was harsher: how could it not be? When my mother walked soundlessly from one room to another, sat reading in the quiet afternoons, or carefully watered the plants on our little balcony, I was not aware of any lack or discrepancy in our lives, or not until some outward agency disrupted our slow peaceful rhythm. Our street was nearly silent, almost abandoned by the late morning: I could be trusted to make my own way to school. After I had done my homework in the evening I would take up my position at the window. I liked to watch the lights go on in other houses, as if preparing for a wayfarer's return. My reading had conditioned me to think in terms of wayfarers, so that footsteps on the pavement gave me an agreeable sensation that the stories contained enough authenticity to justify the fact that I still read them.

No visit disturbed our evenings, nor did we wish for any. It was only at the weekends, when my mother said, 'Better put your books away. The girls are coming,' that I resigned myself to a lesson in reality which would be instructive but largely unwelcome. I feared this lesson on my mother's behalf; I knew instinctively that her good manners were inadequate protection against the sentimental tactlessness of our visitors, who surely thought their presence something of a comfort to my mother and even to myself. 'They mean well,' said my mother. 'They are good women.' But we both knew that this was a lame excuse.

'The girls', as opposed to 'the boys' (their husbands, twin brothers in the hotel business), were as devoted as two sisters might have been, although they were not related. Rather it was my mother and I who were related to them, through my great-grandfather, who had married twice and had raised two separate families, one eventually resulting in my father and the other in the boys, who did not accompany their wives on these visits, although they might have done, on some vague grounds of consanguinity. What family feeling there was seemed to be in the gift of the girls, Millicent and Nancy, who faithfully kept up with my mother, whether through charity or genuine interest. It seemed to intrigue, even to excite them, that a woman of my mother's age could live without the presence of a man; they regarded her with pity, with anxiety, but also with curiosity, as if in her place they would have gone mad. They had little self-control, were obtuse, and kind, but also avid. Neither had children. Their days seemed, to hear their anec-dotes, full of activity: shopping, maintenance, which was of a high order, visits, and then back home to the boys for dinner and an evening of bridge, at which they would complain incessantly, their beautiful complacency fracturing slightly to reveal a perhaps unguessed-at discontent.

Despite their physical perfection, which impressed and unselfishly delighted my mother, they were women whose very real innocence was but one feature of their glossy appearance, nurtured solemnly, and thus providing a fit basis for compli-ments. Drawn together by the accident of their marriages, they remained devoted to each other by virtue of an extraordinary

4

similarity of temperament. They were sensuous, but not sensual, felt relieved that neither one of them was entirely satisfied by their husbands' company, took refuge in material comfort and busy social arrangements. Marriage was no less than their right; it was also their alibi, protecting them from any form of censure, and may have been entered into precisely for that reason. My mother was well aware of this, as they may not have been; I deduced this from her kindness, which had something protective about it, as if they needed to be sheltered from certain realizations. I accepted them as a fact of nature. Their anxiety, unusual in very handsome women, was directed towards my mother, for whom they felt genuinely sorry. Their visits were mercy visits, in the sense that there are mercy killings, with the same admixture of motives.

I disliked them because they interrupted our peaceful lives, with their incessant suggestions as to how my mother might improve her solitary condition. I disliked them because these suggestions made no provision for myself. She was urged to, in their words, socialize, and offered the occasional invitation to their parties, which she attended with a martyr's stoicism. I was also aware that they discussed her, deriving some comfort from her sadness, her obvious inactivity. I could see that they meant well, since their visits were occasions of lavish generosity: boxes of cakes were produced, a beautiful pineapple, and cartons of strawberries brought up from the car by Millicent's driver; at the same time I was puzzled that their real kindness gave them no legitimization in my eyes. My favourite myths did not apply to them, for I could not in all conscience see them as the Ugly Sisters. I simply perceived that they had not waited, and therefore had not been rewarded, as my mother would surely be rewarded. It is not impossible that they perceived this as well.

'You both look splendid,' said my mother with a smile. This fact at least was incontrovertible. The girls habitually looked splendid since most of their time was devoted to that end. Millicent in particular was immaculate; her beautifully manicured hand frequently patted the upward sweep of her imposing coiffure, which was cared for every day by a local hairdresser who had no objection to sending one of his juniors to the house in Bedford Gardens to brush away any imperfections that the early morning might have wrought. Millicent was the younger of the two, plump, wide-eyed, expectant. Nancy, by contrast, was tough, imperious, a heavy smoker, granted seniority by virtue of having lived abroad, in various of the brothers' hotels, mainly in the region between Nice and the Italian border. I saw that she could be relied upon to look after Millicent, but that neither of them would look after my mother. Once, when some malaise or illness had kept my mother at home, they had sent a deputy, 'poor Margaret', who had been adopted as a child by Nancy's parents and who performed the valuable function of looking after both girls. She lived in a flat in Nancy's house, which was conveniently situated in the same street as that occupied by Millicent and her husband Eddie. I disliked Margaret even more than the girls, since I sensed that she was willing to break out, could hardly be constrained, in fact, and only conformed to others' plans for her because she was too lazy, or perhaps too fearful, to strike out on her own. In this she differed from my mother, who, though passive, had not altogether forgone courage, as I, and perhaps the girls, were obliged to recognize.

'If only you'd learn to play bridge,' lamented Millie, to which Nancy rejoined, 'Leave her alone. How do you know she hasn't got a secret life?'

This was taken as a risqué remark, although it would have been quite in order for my mother to take a lover (I thought 'a suitor'), in which case they would have been shocked, and even disappointed. They did not suggest that she get a job. In the 1950s it was thought quite reasonable for women to stay at home and live a peaceful semi-detached semi-suburban life. The great awakening, which was supposed to benefit my generation, had not yet taken place. My father had left a little money, the remains of a legacy, which was supplemented by a small annual cheque from some investments: we lived frugally but decently, unlike the girls, who served mainly as showcases for their husbands' success. This too was thought quite normal at the time, although they seemed to me idle and pampered. Their discontent, which they would furiously have denied, came from purposelessness. In any event, although enjoying the spectacle of their prosperity, I preferred the propriety of our own circumstances, which seemed to fit in with the preordained plan which I knew from my early reading. I did not know, nor, I think, did my mother, that circumstances can be changed, or at least given a helping hand. There seemed to be something natural, even unavoidable, about our lives, which may be why they were so peaceful. Any dissent, any criticism, came from the girls, fascinated as they were by our unmanned condition. Our function was to set their own lives on course, to bring their many advantages into relief. My mother played her part. I merely looked on.

'What eyes that child has,' said Nancy. 'Has she nothing to do?'

'She reads a lot,' said my mother. 'We both do. Zoë, have you thanked the girls for the strawberries?'

It was true that I read a lot, but by now I had graduated to adult reading. Dickens had my full attention, for surely in those novels he was telling the same story of travail and triumph. The additional benefit, apart from the eccentric characters, with their eccentric names, was that many of these travails were undertaken by young men of peerless disposition. This was welcome proof that such life experiences were universal, and, more important, could be, and usually were, brought about while suffering an initial handicap – wicked step-parents, an indigent family – which the heroes (for David Copperfield and Nicholas Nickleby were undoubted heroes) could circumvent with little more than their own blamelessness to guide them. This struck me as entirely beautiful, and convinced me that one must emulate their efforts, that one must never be discouraged by the unhelpfulness of others. Not that I had ever experienced such an obstacle at close quarters: what I took for wickedness was in fact worldliness, as my mother explained to me. The unapologetic presence of our visitors, their peculiar blend of restlessness and complacency, which was discordant, was essentially harmless, though it occasionally sought relief in imprecations, in disapproval of others, principally of my mother and myself. I saw – in Nancy's hoarse smoker's laugh, in Millicent's delicate hand smoothing her hair – a quality that was alien to our own lives, faintly undesirable. Sometimes my mother's eyes had a look of tiredness, and she was obliged to turn her head away for a brief moment, as suggestions for improvement, or rather self-improvement, came her way. These visits, which I now see were undertaken for more merciful reasons than mere curiosity, were in essence a form of female solidarity before that condition had been politicized. They were concerned for any woman living on her own, with only a child for company. At the same time they were fearful that such ivory-tower isolation might be catching. They wanted my mother to be reinstated in society for their sakes as much as for her own. They genuinely pitied a woman who had no status, but they also translated this lack of status as failure in the world's terms.

What distinguished my mother was a form of guilelessness which they had, perhaps regretfully, laid aside. This was what I saw: they had exchanged one condition for another, and may not have been entirely compensated. My mother was their crusade: they also usefully saw her as a pupil. When they rose to leave, the frowns disappeared from their faces, the concern evaporated, and their embraces were genuine. They were glad to get back to their own orbit, with its comprehensible distractions, glad to have done their social duty, even if the results were so sadly lacking. My mother, shaking cushions after their departure, would be more silent than usual, and I somehow knew I should not intrude on her thoughts. I reflected that Nancy and Millie were characters, no less and no more, and that any confrontation – but none had taken place, nor would take place – would be unequal. My mother was bound to succeed, for she was untainted by the world's corruption and thus qualified for remission from further ordeals. This was slightly less affirmative than my previous beliefs. I comforted myself that even David Copperfield had had moments of downheartedness.

On the whole I was happy. I liked my school, I liked my friends; I liked the shabby charm of our flat, from which a light shone out in winter to guide me home. I liked our silent streets, the big windows of the houses in which artists had once lived: I liked its emanations of the nineteenth century. The only difference was that I no longer thought in terms of wayfarers; such people had now become neighbours, or, once I was out of their orbit, pedestrians. That we were somewhat on the margin of things did not disturb me, although the girls, making their way by car from Kensington, complained of the distance, as if they had been obliged to cross a frontier, or to go back in time. It is true that our surroundings were a little mournful, perhaps unnaturally so to those habitual shoppers. I, on the other hand, cherished them as a place of safety. The street lamp that shone outside my bedroom window I accepted as a benevolent gesture on behalf of the town council, the man who swept the leaves in autumn as a guardian of our decency. I was hardly aware of the sound of cars, for fewer people drove then. Even footfalls sounded discreet and distant, and the clang of an iron gate was sometimes the only sound in the long afternoons.

This struck me as an ideal state of affairs. But as I grew older I began to be aware that my mother was less happy than I was. Her eyes had a distant look, and she turned her head slowly when I spoke to her, as if she had momentarily forgotten that I was there. She was still a young woman but she was slightly careworn, as if her thoughts were a burden to her. She was also more silent, nursing what I later came to understand as grief. She was entirely lucid, had devoted her life without complaint to a child who may not have been rewarding (but I did not think that then), and by dint of suppressing almost every healthy impulse had maintained both her composure and her dignity. Hence her silences, her very slight withdrawal from myself. Her survival depended on a control which had not previously been in default. For the first time I began to wish that my father had lived, but selfishly, as young people do, in order to leave me free. I knew, with my increasingly adult perceptions, that it was not in my gift to deal with such a deficit, that my mother's loneliness was acute, that regrets, long buried, had begun their insidious journey to full consciousness . . . My mother was a good woman, too good to give way to self-pity. This austerity of behaviour denied her close friends. I think she exchanged only the most obvious pleasantries with our neighbours, keeping her most painful thoughts fiercely to herself. To voice even one of them would have constituted a danger.

Her sadness, I thought, was brought on by the knowledge that life's opportunities had definitively passed her by, and also by virtue of the fact that the redeeming feature, or presence, had not manifested itself. She was thus cast into the category of the unwanted, the unsought. I perceived this on certain lightless afternoons, when there was no joyous voice to greet me when I returned from a friend's house, from noisy friendly normality. I perceived it, no doubt correctly, but it burdened me. I wanted no part of her passivity. I was young and not notably unfeeling, but I did not want to be a partner in anyone's regrets. Had I been of an age to understand the full implications of this dereliction I should have resented it strenuously. As it was I began to see some virtue in the girls' remonstrances, though in truth they had little but themselves to offer by way of compensation for her solitude. Therefore, when I put my key in the door one afternoon and heard Millie's festive voice exclaiming, 'Now, I'm counting on you, Anne. There'll only be a few people. Nice people. I know you'll like them,' I was inclined to add my own encouragements to hers.

My mother murmured something placatory.

'Nonsense,' said Nancy. 'You have to make a bit of an effort in this life if you want to get anywhere. And as far as I can make out you're not getting anywhere.'

'Six-thirty,' said Millie. 'I'll send the car for you.'

After that it would have been difficult to back down.

My mother's expression, after they had left, was bemused, resigned, even cynical. I took it as a good sign that she went into her bedroom and opened her creaking wardrobe door. Everything in our flat creaked, a sound I found friendly. Now I saw, perhaps for the first time, that it was rather gloomy, that my mother's room was in perpetual shadow, too conducive to nostalgia, to introspection. On her dressing-table was the photograph of the young man in the academic gown whom I did not remember. His face was steadfast, obedient, not quite up to the task of growing up, certainly not of growing old. I regretted his absence, as I had not done when still a child, with my mother to myself. Now I had her to myself, but was no longer a child, was beginning to feel a hunger for wider experiences, for a life outside the home, even one as well ordered as ours. Perhaps precisely for that reason.

'Do I look all right?' asked my mother, on that next Friday evening.

I thought she looked beautiful, in her simple blue dress and jacket. She was plainly agitated, and had it not been for the car being sent would have thankfully abandoned the whole adventure. When Tom, Millie's driver, rang the bell, we were both in a state of high concern. It was almost a relief when she left, and I was thankful for the hour or two I could spend on my own before her return. I thought of her among those nice people and hoped painfully, not that she was enjoying herself – that would have been too much to expect – but that she was not feeling too lonely. For a woman as shy as my mother social occasions on which she was unaccompanied were a nightmare. That was why Millie's pressing invitations, offered, or rather insisted upon for entirely defensible reasons, were, more often than not, gratefully refused.

But she had not refused this one, and it was at Millie's party, on that Friday evening, that she met her second husband, my stepfather-to-be, and thus changed both our lives.

2

My mother's fate having been settled according to the archaic principles of natural justice, and the conditions for her redemption having thus been met, I was now free to cast off on my own. I was sixteen, nearly seventeen, and the timing was providential. I had no doubt that we should all be entirely happy. I loved Simon, who, at our first meeting, embraced me with Jewish cordiality, making no distinction between my mother and myself. It was my first contact with genuine expansiveness and I warmed to it. Standing in our flat in Edith Grove he revealed its shabbiness, and thus deducted much of its charm. He was a big man, who seemed to smile all the time, delighted to have found a woman as unspoilt as my mother. He later told us that he too had had to be prevailed upon to attend that epochal party, for, although naturally gregarious, he was aware of the lack of a companion in these most public of circumstances. He was a widower, who, since the death of his wife, had devoted his life to business, or rather to 'business interests', as he termed them. He exuded a pleasant air of health and viability, which did something to mitigate the fact that he was rather old: he was self-conscious about his age, which he dismissed as 'nearly the wrong side of seventy', but he was so obviously fit, and so benignly energetic, that I soon overlooked this fact.

I knew that he could be relied upon to take care of my mother, which seemed to me our prime concern. By this stage I knew, or suspected, that she had money worries: the tenancy of our flat had only another year to run, and after that we should have to move into more restricted quarters or take out a loan from the bank. Both were problematic, but the problem was solved by the fact that Simon occupied two floors of a large house in Onslow Square, into which he was anxious to transfer my mother as soon as possible. He also possessed a house in France, which I thought much more interesting. Over dinner our fates were swiftly settled. My mother would live in Onslow Square and I would stay on in Edith Grove until the lease ran out, after which Simon would buy me a flat of my own. 'Look on it as a wedding present,' he smiled. 'There's no reason why you shouldn't share in my good fortune.' This easy generosity was very difficult to resist. Besides, none of us had a desire to live under the same roof. My mother thought it would be unfair on me, even indelicate, to live at close quarters to a late marriage, particularly between two people of different ages, and Simon was naturally fastidious, anxious to hide the evidence of his years – 'my advanced years', he joked – from critical eyes. As for myself I had no desire to see his pills in the bathroom, to witness his laundry arrangements, or be present at his intimate life with my mother. This, I thought, should be kept as secret as possible.

Something in me shied away from the thought of his making love to her, for this was the flaw in the arrangement. Later I understood this as a primal scene, the kind infants fantasize, or even register, as taking place between their parents. If my mother had met someone more like herself, or even like the young man in the photograph – modest, trusting, steadfast – I should have had no further qualms. It was just that Simon, so obviously a good man, was foreign to our way of life, our settled habits. His bulk filled our flat whenever he visited us, as did the smell of his cologne. I could not quite get used to his habit of humming under his breath, or his restlessness, which might just have been an expression of his insistent physicality. He had the good taste to make no allusions as to what was to come when my mother would live with him. As far as I was concerned he was a sort of Santa Claus, a provider, to whom giving was second nature.

I felt a deep relief on my mother's behalf and also on my own; I should now be able to begin my David Copperfield progress towards my own apotheosis. I never ceased to feel this with regard to Simon: he was a facilitator, an enabler, and the unlikely outcome of his attending a party, a tiresome social engagement to which he had not looked forward, and which he intended to leave early, was, I thought, beneficial in the way that only unexpected rewards are beneficial. He was, quite literally, our gift from the gods.

Whether my mother thought this or not was another matter. I was old enough to understand that she was preoccupied with the business of having to find another flat for us both, and perhaps tired of pretending that she was entirely satisfied with her way of life. Perhaps the example of those visitors, the girls, with their talk of holidays, had made more of an impression on her than she was willing to concede. She did not envy them their entertainments, but she did envy their security, and even their unthinking acceptance of their husbands' indulgence. Although sincerely shocked by their entirely natural delight in this state of affairs, she was made wistful by the presents that the chauffeur brought up from the car, wishing that she had it in her gift to endow others in the same manner. The fact that these presents always consisted of things to eat merely reinforced the impression that some fundamental discrepancy existed between the sort of woman she was and all the others, who had made a better job of marriage and extracted from it satisfactions that were almost edible, certainly tangible. I now see that even the most saintly of women can ponder the difference, and although we both deplored these gifts – the cakes, the strawberries – we were forced to admit that we enjoyed them. Only we enjoyed them rather thoughtfully, as they made their incongruous appearance on our dinner-table. Some days our evening meal consisted almost entirely of these offerings, and I firmly believe that the sight of a chocolate éclair on my plate, in lieu of something more sensible, made her reflect that this would not do, that none of this was appropriate, and that if it were too late for her to start again the same need not necessarily be true for myself.

To do the girls justice they were both delighted. 'I must remember to thank them,' laughed my mother. But she was almost serious. She thought herself inadequate in the light of such good fortune, and needed stronger personalities to maintain her resolve. The girls' fretful attention was now directed towards my mother's appearance: the car arrived punctually to bear them all off for an afternoon of shopping, and she would return home with bags from Harrods and Harvey Nichols, complaining of a splitting headache. I detested the clothes the girls made her buy, or had thrust on her as presents, and so did Simon. 'We'll find something in France,' he said, his big hand pushing aside a silvery skirt which had no place in my mother's life. 'You can leave all this stuff here, or give it away.'

'They meant well,' said my mother.

'Of course they did. Their intentions were of the best. But they wanted you to look like themselves.'

'And to be like themselves,' said my mother to me after he had left. 'And I don't think I can be.'

'He loves you for your own sake,' I said stoutly.

'Yes, he does. He does seem to. Isn't that extraordinary?'

I suspected that the girls had tried to indoctrinate my mother in the ways of acquisition, paying no attention to the fact that appropriation was foreign to her nature. They may have been sincerely shocked by her attitude of modest dependency, for she almost at once, and instinctively, began to behave like a wife to Simon, thus once again earning the disapproval of the girls and furnishing them with an agreeable subject of conversation. They hated, with some reason, her life of lowered expectations, and always had, fearing the comparison. Her celibacy had been abhorrent to them, and now that this was at an end they found it difficult to come to terms with the fact of her brighter eyes, her more frequent smiles, even her rare but now occasional laughter. Feelings were disguised, but not entirely successfully. I began to dislike the girls, and was grateful that their patronage would be no longer needed. They had never had any time for me, nor I for them. I foresaw that we should shortly be separated by circumstances and was secretly relieved.

Now that I am so much older I see that this new opportunity was not one to be missed, but embraced perhaps a little less than wholeheartedly. This was not first love, which my mother must have experienced for my father, however remote that must now have seemed. This was a prudent arrangement which had been entered upon almost by accident and which was to retain an air of absentmindedness, of not quite willed satisfaction. It was providential: all seemed to agree on that point. If it gave my mother any joy it was a joy she expected to reveal itself in the longer term, when she got used to her new life and was able to take a fuller part in it, when she would come to accept her new dignity (but never to exploit it), and when she learned to be as expansive as her new husband, a task for which she was singularly ill-prepared.

I shied away from the prospect of my mother's physical life, for I was as contained as she was. Simon had perfected the agreeable business of kissing us both, with the same obvious affection, in the short interval my mother spent in our flat, with me, before moving into Onslow Square. Of course I missed her, but as Simon insisted that I see her every day I did not mind too badly. This was helped by the fact that I felt more at home in our old flat than in Onslow Square, and also because

I had a great deal of studying to do, for I was soon to go to university. My prolonged childhood seemed to have ended rather abruptly, and I felt unsettled by this: at the same time I recognized the fact that it was over and that in future I should have to rely on my friends for company. I was momentarily in demand, as newly-fortunate people are, and the fact of having my own flat added to my prestige. Simon made me an allowance, but told me not to spend it on clothes. 'We'll get you something in France,' he said, as he had said to my mother. 'You can leave your ordinary clothes here.' Thus, once again, the transformation scene was being prepared. Truly those fairy stories had proved themselves to be prophetic.

My mother was married at Chelsea Register Office in a ceremony that was rigorously secular. This seemed to me entirely appropriate, for, despite the almost miraculous manner in which it had come about, this union did not have the appearance of one blessed by God. It looked, unfortunately, as if advantage had been taken by both parties, of wealth being exchanged for comeliness, as in some dire Mannerist allegory. Simon wept copiously, which was something I had not anticipated; my mother, on the other hand, seemed composed, almost abstracted. Though there was undoubtedly love of a sort it was not the sort that made an appeal to one of my age, for although it satisfied the requirements of legend it made me aware of what all the stories left out, namely the facts of what happened next. The stories had ended on the highest possible note, whereas what they should have indicated was the life that followed. The nuptial arrangements made me slightly uneasy, as did the wedding itself. It was not that I objected to its sparseness: that was acceptable. Anything more elaborate would have been unwelcome. My contact with religion came mainly from services in the school chapel, and I instinctively rejected all the warnings, the penalties and restrictions, as well as the childlike petitions for forgiveness and the equally childlike promises of rewards, always postponed. If I sometimes felt unconsoled, in a strange uncomfortable way, it was because not all changes are welcome; even in the midst of our good fortune I had a feeling of loss. I knew that I would never lose my mother, but I also knew that she would not be at home to greet me in the early evenings, and that I should have to rely on my own company for a good part of the time.

The physical emptiness of the flat I had left that morning did not frighten me, nor did I dread going back to it, but I began to see it in a new light, was struck anew by the loneliness my mother must have felt, a loneliness compounded by the silence of the street and the yawning creak of her bedroom door, when, tired of standing at the window, she would rest on her bed in the afternoons, for the sake of the relief she would feel when the interval for such matters was safely past, and she could make tea and prepare for my homecoming. Now she would have a different home and there would be a different kind of preparation. I was a little disturbed by this vision, for my mother's previous life had been so singular, in all senses of the word, and so dedicated, that it had left its trace on my own conduct, and for a brief moment of sadness I wondered whether I should now be obliged to take my leave of a certain way of life which had hitherto seemed to me to be lacking in nothing.

The austerity of the wedding ceremony was emphasized, even thrown into relief, by the hilarity of the girls, and even of the boys, whose acquaintance Simon was and who thus fortuitously provided the link between all the participants. The boys were hearty and extremely enthusiastic, having adopted a manner which probably served them on all social occasions, particularly those in which the protagonists were not too well known to them. The girls were, of course, splendidly turned out, but their hands brought out delicate handkerchiefs at the right moment, and all in all provided the scenic change that turned the whole thing into a rite of passage. The wedding breakfast took place in Onslow Square, where a hired butler and waiters moved suavely among the guests, obliging them all to be on their best behaviour. Simon and my mother were to spend the night at the Ritz in Paris, a convention already out of fashion, and to go on to Venice, where they would stay for a fortnight, returning home by way of France. This would be my mother's first introduction to his house, some miles inland from Nice: it would be a politeness to show her what would be her future home, to greet the *gardienne*, Mme Delgado, to give a few discreet instructions, and to keep the visit tactfully short. Two nights at the Negresco were to follow, and then they would be home.

In some strange way I did not altogether believe in this homecoming. The champagne at the reception had left me with a headache and when I returned to Edith Grove I was newly aware of absence. We were now physically separated by more than a few streets, and soon she – they – would be out of reach. 'My home will be yours too,' Simon had said, but this was difficult to believe. I could not find the requisite image by which this future could be called to mind. I was landlocked, had only been abroad on school trips, had valued the fellowship of my friends rather more than my surroundings, and was indeed vaguely frightened by the prospect of a new life, however desirable. My mother had come to the door with me and said, 'You've got all the telephone numbers? And the girls will look in on you to see that you are eating properly.'

'I am seventeen,' I had reassured her. By this time we were both in tears.

'I know, darling, I know.'

'Anne, the car is waiting,' Simon had reminded her. 'No more tears, now. This is a new life starting for all of us.' A wallet of money found its way into my pocket.

'Goodbye, dears,' sang Millie. '*Bon voyage!* We'll take you home, Zoë. Unless you'd like to come back with us? Yes, that might be best.'

But no, I had said. I'd been invited out. This was untrue. I wanted to see how I would fare on my own, promising myself a hot bath, my dressing-gown, routine comforts. This would be my first experience of what might be a tremendous ordeal, as I knew it to be for others, neighbours of ours who turned out bravely for unnecessary errands, aware all the time of their return to an empty house. On this particular evening I was too tired to feel anything but gratitude for the quiet street, for the dark flat, even for the sound of a recalcitrant tap dripping in the kitchen. My mother had seemed to think that I needed comforting: perhaps I did. Even a happy ending cannot always banish a sense of longing.

3

All this changed during my first summer in France, the last of my school years, before I was due to begin university in the autumn. Truth to tell I was initially alienated by Simon's house, Les Mouettes, a white stucco villa with a flat roof and a protruding central feature which was midway between a conservatory and a glassed-in terrace. The absence of a skyline disconcerted me: the vogue for Art Deco had not yet got under way. I believe it was photographed for a magazine in the early eighties, by which time it was no longer ours and had long ceased to be. Nor was it, as Simon had said, a few miles outside Nice: it was a few miles from the centre of Nice, but still on the outskirts of a recognizable suburb. I did not even much like Nice, with its roaring traffic along the coast road, but I went into town every day on the bus and wandered about rather uncertainly until I found a place I thought I could call my own, the small garden of the Musée Masséna, frequented by children parked there by their Swedish or Danish au pairs. I looked out for them both, the children and the nannies; both became my friends. The au pairs, seeing me as a safe pair of hands, could leave their charges with me and decamp to a café on the front. One such child showed a touching confidence in me. Like most French babies he looked overworked, even careworn, and in moments of low spirits he would sit beside me and lean his head against my arm. At such times he looked older than his age; he was, I was told, just three, having recently celebrated his birthday, which may have explained his air of exhaustion. The girls were equally accommodating; they introduced me to their boyfriends, when I met them later in town. In this way I was able to enjoy one or two adventures, which was a great relief to me. I was allowed total freedom to come and go as I pleased, and took to spending the day on my own, away from the house, knowing that Simon and my mother trusted me, even when I returned late, sometimes arriving only for the evening meal, and going out again soon after that.

France seemed to me a country of various liberties. I admired the way all the men seemed to be able to work with a cigarette in their mouths; I admired Mme Delgado's dashing speed on her moped, on which she arrived every morning at seven to make our coffee. She sped off again in the late afternoon, having taken care of the rudiments of our dinner. And if I was never quite at home in Nice I was at home with the fierce light, a revelation after the gloomy, shadowy surroundings of my earliest years. The sun is God, said the painter. I accepted the truth of this as I wandered in the pitiless afternoon glare, disdaining the long rest I was advised to take. When Simon and my mother retired to their room I slipped out of the house into the glorious cloudless blaze, took the bus into Nice, was momentarily glad of the shade and silence of the Musée Masséna garden, and sat there with my book until Honoré, my particular three-year-old friend, greeted me before going off to play. This little community delighted me: the girls were friendly, easy-going, emancipated, and I practised being the same. For a time my efforts were rewarded, and I saw myself in a new light, as someone with the same manners as the young people around me. My appearance improved, as did my clothes. I could see what I must become, and did not have to struggle very hard to be that person. Though I was never taken for French, I no longer looked like the obedient schoolgirl daughter I had been until that moment.

Simon was kindness itself, although with my new sharpness of vision I saw him for the old man he truly was. His place at table was surrounded by remedies, mysterious French pills prescribed by Dr Thibaudet, his neighbour, who looked in sometimes in the early evening for a glass of wine on his way home. The formality of this arrangement amused me; there was a Mme Thibaudet but she stayed behind unless summoned to dine with her husband. Thibaudet and Simon would vanish into another part of the house for a spot check on Simon's blood pressure, while my mother made desultory conversation with Armelle, Mme Thibaudet, a placid sweet-faced woman of no great pretensions but able to put on a massive dinner when we were invited back in our turn. I did not know my abstemious mother amid all this catering; I was merely glad to see her looking so well. I never told her much of what I did during my free time (but all my time was free), though I think she was reassured when I mentioned the little children in the garden, as was Simon. 'And how was Honoré today?' he would ask, and I had no trouble entertaining them in a way they found entirely acceptable.

My mother seemed unchanged to me, or perhaps I merely wanted to see her that way. She was quiet, but she had always been quiet: she said little but watched Simon tenderly as he took his pills. Both seemed in excellent health. I believe she settled down cautiously into married life, although I found it difficult to believe her entirely comfortable in that light, a light that searched out imperfections, the wrinkle of a collapsed neck, a slightly drooping mouth, both of which were visible in her husband. If she had hoped for a more romantic lover she gave no sign of disappointment, though I think she feared turning into Mme Thibaudet, who acted as a nurse and guardian to her own husband, and who had indeed once been a nurse in the clinic in Nice of which he was the director. The only thing I noticed about my mother that gave me pause was that she too liked to be out of the house. As my afternoons were spent some distance away I was for a time unaware that she sometimes went off on her own, much as I did. I assumed that she spent her time in a famous garden near by, sitting quietly, as she had always done. But as she was always there when I returned I did not see anything untoward in this. She had always preferred her own company – and mine, of course – to that of women friends. Whatever the age difference between Simon and herself, I think she was grateful to him just for being a man.

That first summer was the happiest time of my life. As well as the familiarity of my mother's presence I enjoyed a form of social acceptance, even popularity, that I had never known before. At home I was used mainly as a confidante by more adventurous friends. In France I was learning the attractions of carelessness, of frankness. I was something of a success with the young men who joined the girls and myself for an apéritif before we made our way home. Everyone was, or seemed to be, intelligent, purposeful. I was at ease, whether chatting to Mme Delgado in the kitchen or soothing Honoré through one of his frequent crises of disenchantment. Nice still seemed to me a blatant charmless sort of place, but I was part of a group, persuaded that love and friendship were common currency and that one need never be without either. The cars still streamed past the café where we met for our *apéro* but I had got so used to the noise that I hardly noticed it. I took it for granted that everyone moved quickly: no wayfarers here. Somehow I had put all those fantasies behind me; they remained in London, in Edith Grove. Here I was driven out of my earlier self by the power of the light. Even when I made my way back to the house in the early evening I retained an after-image of the blaze. By the time I was due to go home, alone this time, for Simon and my mother were staying on, I saw that I should never forget that first summer, and that I would return, was indeed expected to return, until, with all my meagre experience and my new-found enthusiasm, I was accepted as part of the landscape.

4

I hesitate, even now, to assign to the gods of antiquity full responsibility for the mismanagement of human affairs, or for human misapprehension. Such fatalism goes against my earlier belief in a more benign mythological providence, which, if fallacious, or at least misleading, is no more misleading than other mythologies, which promise much, but deliver little.

I took a last walk down Edith Grove very early one dark Sunday morning in February. In truth it was to be a walk I had taken a year earlier when the lease on our flat had expired. I had managed to negotiate a further year's grace by dint of paying an increased rent, but clearly I could not continue to do this. The estate agent had proved surprisingly conciliatory, especially when I told him that I could move out at very short notice: the flat that Simon had bought for me was ready and waiting. 'Oh, you'll like it there,' the agent had said. 'Quite a Mediterranean feel to it.' He was presumably alluding to the fact that the flat was situated in a courtyard and had wooden floors. I knew better, remembering my holidays in the sun.

I disliked the new flat, was reluctant to leave the old one. That I was able to be so careless in this matter owed everything to Simon's generosity. He had decided that he and my mother were to live in France, and had sold his property in Onslow Square, saying that they could always rent a house if and when they returned to London. In the event they never did. On the conclusion of the sale he had opened accounts at his bank for both my mother and myself, so that as far as I was aware I had no anxiety with regard to money.

This gave me a feeling of great freedom, as well it might. I

26

did not question the sources of his income, for he gave such an impression of wealth and ease that I had accepted from the start that he was a very rich man. I saw no reason to doubt this, or to question his decision to live in France, which seemed to me eminently sensible. Besides, I had grown used to being on my own and to arranging my own affairs. I had graduated to independence and was finally relieved. I was also quite glad to have them at something of a distance, for I doubted that my mother would quite approve of my new friends, of one in particular, with whom I spent most of my time. Indeed my cavalier attitude to both my flats proceeded from the fact that I was rarely in either. I had finally arranged for my furniture – our furniture – to be moved on the following day, and even this did not seem momentous. I was acting with a speed and a certainty I had come to accept, though it was not really in my character to do so. Something of those holidays in Nice, which were now regular occurrences, and particularly the first one, had left me light-hearted. I see that this was the ideal basis on which to conduct a love affair, which was why my own was going so well.

On this particularly gloomy Sunday, which I knew would be my very last in this quiet place, I patrolled the street, trying in vain to revive the affection I had always felt for it. But it was dispiritingly dark, silent, even forlorn. There was nobody about. I imagined a thousand dusky bedrooms, a thousand supine bodies entwined in musty duvets. I did not blame these sleepers, but I disapproved of them. The working week should not lead to this abject collapse, which was accepted as some sort of entitlement. Later, much later, cups of tea would be made, and taken back to bed. Waking would come slowly, rising even more slowly. Then there would be the reading of the newspapers, another ritual, until, perhaps in the afternoon or early evening, the morose desire to go for a walk, or perhaps to visit a parent, an obligation shouldered reluctantly but undertaken with a remnant of filial obedience. By the evening spirits would be low. After Sunday, Monday morning, though held to be a nightmare, was in fact something of a relief.

In Edith Grove the air was not enticing, having about it something of the staleness of the previous night. The only sign of life was the motorbike parked in the forecourt of the strange church opposite our flat and the light I could see dimly shining from its interior. This building had always intrigued me, its extreme ugliness seeming to defeat its purpose, which I took to be encouragement, uplift, harmony. Yet it was well attended, even in that secular decade, and we had seen large ladies and even the odd unaccompanied man making their way in on Sunday mornings and Wednesday evenings for a celebration of what was announced as fellowship. These were truly valiant souls, willing to spend their free time in that flat-faced red-brick building, which had something rather too democratic about it, as if it intended to defuse both mystical feeling and any expectations of a transforming experience which the congregation might have entertained. Indeed so downbeat was it, yet so determinedly cheerful were its female congregants, that we had decided, my mother and I, that we were disbarred from receiving its particular message by some quirk of character which others could discern at a glance. We warmed to the ladies, but not to the incumbent or celebrant, who would appear briefly on the threshold in ordinary working clothes, and looking as if he had just got out of bed himself. The motorbike was presumably his. When my mother passed him in the street he would nod his head very briefly, as if noting her reservations. No word was offered; he consigned her to her fate. Her salvation was not his concern.

In this terrible Sunday morning gloom our building retained a modest air of Edwardian decency. I supposed that I should look in on the new flat to which I had the keys, had had them for some time. I was reluctant to take possession: I had not chosen the flat and did not like it. The Mediterranean feel that the estate agent had described did not extend beyond the windows, which let in very little light, and that of poor quality, owing to the courtyard effect, which had been designed not for the tenants' amenity but so as to cram as many flats as possible into a restricted space. In order to see the street I was obliged to imagine the intervening buildings out of the way. At the same time it was noisy. When I had looked in one evening I could hear the light being switched on in the bedroom on the other side of the wall. I had not met any of my new neighbours, had not yet said goodbye to any of the old ones. They were used to seeing me going in and out, but would not worry unduly if I no longer did so. 'You're young,' one woman had said to me enviously. 'It's easy for you. Here today, gone tomorrow. When you get to my age it's a different matter, as you'll find out.' I did not want to hear this, for nothing surely could deprive me of my freedom, my lightness of touch. My expectations.

My clothes were packed, and my suitcases were in the bedroom of which I had seen so little recently, for most nights were spent in a large dilapidated house in Langton Street which was owned, or partly owned, by the man of whom my mother would not approve, Adam Crowhurst. She would not approve of him because she was of the wrong generation to understand so extremely uninhibited a personality. Middle-aged women, those who did not succumb to his outrageous charm, looked askance at his conquests and consoled themselves with their hard-won dignity and the knowledge that they were safe. I was an unlikely partner for him, since I was docile, and, I thought, uninteresting. But I had managed to win his friend-ship, which presumably other women scorned as a consolation prize for the total possession which he withheld. Prince Charming must have had the same effect on those whom the slipper did not fit. Was it possible that some part of me, the most archaic, the most unreconstructed part, still remained faithful to that schema, to that belief? If so I am ashamed to this day of my touching credulity. The gods, with whom at that time I was barely acquainted, were ready with their punishing gifts of caprice, of unaccountability. Their behaviour was in all cases unforgivable, yet those in my situation were persuaded of their power, since all depended on their favour. Thus two opposing interpretations fought for precedence, not only in my situation but in the world of quite sensible men and women, women in particular, hoping for a successful outcome to hopeless love affairs, convinced that there must be – *must* be – a reward for virtue, yet seeing all around them evidence of expectations unfulfilled, and worse, their own bewilderment turned into a joke that others might enjoy.

I had no idea what to do with my day. The evening, fortunately, was taken care of: I was to dine at Adam's house, together with an elderly couple who were friends of his parents, up in London for a week of theatres and sale-rooms. I thought this auspicious: I hoped they would take away with them a good report of my suitability. Adam had asked me to supply a few items, avocado pears, olives, nuts. He was an excellent cook, would take care of the main part of the meal. I had done my shopping the previous day, and stowed the bags in what remained of my kitchen. I added some of my mother's dishes, for it pleased me to blend my effects with his. All was ready for the evening, which merely left the rest of the day to fill.

In this curious February half-light it would be difficult to see where the day ended and the evening began. I felt tired. Perhaps I was not as prepared as I thought for any sort of change. Indeed I felt so tired that I abandoned any thought of further exercise, sat down in my mother's old chair, which, on the following day, would take its place in the removal van, and fell into a doze, predictably waking with a start when a light went on in the house opposite. I thus found that I had slept in this manner for a good part of the afternoon.

I now see that this was prophetic. At the time I merely went into the bathroom and washed my hair, regretting that I had not done so earlier. There was just time to make a cup of tea and to change. I set out with my carrier bags for Langton Street – no distance from Edith Grove – and as luck would have it the lowering sky dissolved into a heavy shower of rain. My hands were not free; in any event I had no umbrella. My still-damp hair was thoroughly wet, but no real harm was done: Adam would lend me a towel and I would repair the damage. I did not think I had to make a glamorous impression on his parents' elderly friends, but simply to behave naturally, in accordance with my mother's precepts and example. Apart from the knowledge that I was not looking my best, and remembering that the removal men were due in Edith Grove at eight o'clock the following morning, I was not too concerned. My faith would move mountains, though at that stage I was unaware that there were mountains to be moved.

'What on earth have you been doing?' said Adam on opening the door. 'You look wrecked.' He was annoyed with me, hated anything less than a favourable appearance.

'Just let me use your bathroom. I shan't be a minute.' I made for the stairs.

'Don't go up there,' he said quickly, but I had my foot on the first step. I think I had no suspicion, even then, that anything was wrong. In retrospect I still see myself at the foot of the stairs. I got no further, for coming down to meet me was a girl whose tousled hair had obviously made contact with a pillow.

I stared, as a droplet of water made its way down my neck. Adam gave a laugh that was almost a groan, but recovered more quickly than either this unknown girl or myself.

'Do you know each other?' he asked smoothly. 'Zoë

31

Cunningham, Kirstie Fellowes. Kirstie is a physiotherapist,' he added.

'Oh, yes, I know all the wrinkles,' said Kirstie Fellowes, whom I observed to be in a state of post-coital triumph. She laughed loudly. Adam looked at her with dawning disfavour.

I put my bags in the kitchen. I am ashamed to say that I behaved extremely well. When she joined me a few minutes later, brushing her hair vigorously, I simply said, 'Oh, please, not here.' My lips felt stuck to my teeth, which made entertaining Adam's guests, the Johnsons, rather problematic. They in their turn were disconcerted by the presence of Kirstie Fellowes, for we were five at table. 'Are you staying?' Adam had asked her as I brought in the avocadoes. 'Of course I'm staying,' she laughed. Helen Johnson understood the situation at a glance, and remained as silent as I was. Her husband kept up a determined conversation with Adam, but even that began to falter. Kirstie Fellowes contributed a great deal of enthusiastic laughter. Without her we should have been almost mute. But then without her all would have gone on as before. 'Coffee?' I inquired.

In the kitchen Adam hovered. 'Don't look at me like that, Zoë. It's no big deal. We all know the score.' I said nothing. 'I'll drive you home if you'll wait a bit.'

'I'll walk,' I said.

The Johnsons were leaving, discomfited. The display of intimacy had offended them. I was able to wish them a pleasant goodnight, and then I left. I walked home, the rain flattening my hair once again, the pathetic fallacy working overtime. In Edith Grove I fell into a black sleep. Some time during the night I was aware of the telephone ringing, but could not extricate myself from sleep long enough to answer it. In any event I knew who was calling.

What stayed with me when I surfaced on the following

morning was a feeling of acute shame, even horror, at the memory of my dilapidated appearance. I could see myself with my wet hair, and my two bulging plastic carrier bags: I could still feel the droplet of water making its way down my neck. On such details do our fortunes depend. I did not for a moment blame Adam for his defection, for it seemed to me that I had provoked it. Memory should have told me that this was not the case, that I had chanced upon a matter that I had not been meant to witness, that this incident, though clandestine, had been entered into spontaneously on both sides, that I was, if anything, the intruder, unwelcome, and the more unwelcome because I had discovered Adam to be at fault. For this I blamed myself. In addition to my unfortunate appearance I had cast a shadow over two people's innocent enjoyment. For I could not see it as particularly reprehensible. The ethos of the age had dismissed loyalty, constancy, fidelity as disqualifiers for successful guilt-free relationships. Such old-fashioned beliefs were dismissed as hang-ups, a cute unserious term for what was in effect a reversal of the established order. I myself had known no guilt when exchanging one partner for another during that first summer in Nice, but somehow that was different, affectionate, as if we were all children accustomed to harmless play on whom the shadow of the adult world had yet to fall. The sun, the sun! In London's perpetual dusk the incident looked clumsy, badly managed, graceless. At the end of a dark day it took on an air of undeserved finality. The only conclusion to be drawn was that I had been defeated by an adversary whom I could not have anticipated, and had almost sealed my fate by appearing in such an unflattering guise, as if to emphasize my unsuitability for any role other than the one I had come unwittingly to fulfil. There was an inevitability about this scenario that absolved the other two protagonists from blame. I alone, with my wet hair and my plastic bags, was deserving of censure.

The removal men arrived sharply at eight, and I made tea for them. I had thought that the transference of my furniture would take a mere half-hour, but this was not the case. When I emerged onto the pavement the woman who had congratulated me on my youth and warned me of its inevitable demise was standing there with a suitcase.

'I'm off to warmer climes,' she informed me. 'Marbella. You're leaving, then?'

I was leaving, I confirmed.

'Give my regards to Mrs Cunningham. Mrs Gould, I must remember to call her.' She laughed, as if my mother's marriage were a fantasy. 'Good luck, then. All the best.' Like many others she meant well.

This evidence of other lives proceeding normally was a useful indicator that the world had not come to an end. My feeling of shame had given way to a more settled regret, which was compounded by the unkempt and unfinished appearance of my new home. Until that moment the flat, which I thought of as 'the other flat', had seemed temporary, unreal. Now as I went into the much smaller kitchen to make more tea for the men I could see my actions mirrored by a figure exactly opposite. The lights were on in nearly all the kitchens so generously exposed to my view across the central well of the building. It was four o'clock in the afternoon and already growing dark. When I shut the front door on the removal men I turned reluctantly to the bedroom, the darkest room of all. Its one advantage was concealment. I was not anxious to be seen. To my decrepitude of the previous evening was now added a layer of dust from the day's activities. I wished it were later than it was, time to take a bath and go to bed. As it was I telephoned my mother.

'Darling! What a lovely surprise!' Her voice sharpened with anxiety. 'Are you all right?'

It was not our usual day for telephoning. Saturday evening

was when we usually caught up with each other's news. 'Is she all right?' I could hear Simon asking in the background.

'I'm fine,' I said. 'I just wanted to remind you of the new phone number.'

'As if I needed reminding! Was it a terrible day? Did the men come when they said they would?'

'Everything's fine,' I repeated. 'It's all done. It seems a bit strange, that's all.'

'You'll soon come to terms with it. But moving is always a melancholy business. I expect you're tired.' There was a pause. 'You're sure you're all right?'

This was how our conversations tended to go when we had been separated for any length of time. I'm all right. Are you all right? Are you sure you're all right? I had never confided in my mother. There were things she did not need to know, nor did she wish to know them. My private life was as guarded as hers was, and we were both obscurely glad of this.

'What did you do yesterday?' I asked.

'Well, we had an early lunch at Queenie's. You remember; we took you there once.'

'I know it.' I had in fact been there many times with my friends but did not remind her of this.

'Then we came back here. Simon had his rest, and I went out for a walk.'

'Where did you go?'

'Oh, round and about. You know I love to walk.'

I did not know this. She had never gone out much when we lived in Edith Grove. In France, however, she evidently liked to be out of the house, on those mysterious afternoons when others slept. I suspect that she found it difficult to remain at close quarters with a man she still regarded as a miraculous stranger. I also suspected that she was not entirely at home in Simon's house, though there was nothing to dislike except its unfamiliarity, and perhaps the fact that he had lived in it with

35

his first wife. This fact, once mentioned, had not been referred to again by either of them.

'Then the Thibaudets came to dinner.'

'What did you cook?'

'Gazpacho. Roast chicken. Lemon sorbet, which we bought in town. Armelle seemed to think it a very light meal, but we had a pleasant evening.'

'What's the weather like?'

'Mild, a bit damp. What's it like where you are?'

'Pouring.' I had no need to look out of the window. I could hear the rain splashing onto the forecourt.

'You'll be in college tomorrow. You'll feel better then.'

I supposed that I would. My work was interesting, my tutor well disposed. He had once asked me to check a footnote for him, and seemed pleased by my ability to do this without asking further questions. I reminded myself that I had yet to unpack my books, which were still lying about in cartons. I felt acutely lonely.

'It won't be long before you're back with us. There was a definite feeling of spring in the air this morning.'

'I'll ring you on Saturday as usual.'

'Is there any food in the house?'

'Not much.'

'Then you'd better go out shopping. And make up your bed. I expect you're longing for it.'

'I am rather.' I was. 'Love to you both. Until Saturday.'

I went out, bought bread, cheese, the makings of a salad, a battery for my radio. I was surprised to see people in the streets, although all seemed cowed. A disconsolate crowd had gathered at the bus stop, though no bus seemed to have passed within living memory. I did not want to go home, was subjected once again to the image of the previous evening. I knew that what had taken place was not very grave on the scale of human misdemeanours, and that I should have to come to terms with imperfection. The shocking encounter now began to fade, although the after-image of those two flushed faces did not. I returned to an awareness of how unequal I must have appeared. I knew that however successful I might be in later life (for now was a time of failure) I would never entirely eradicate the memory of that episode. My own embarrassment had been nothing compared with the embarrassment on Adam's face; in a mysterious way he was as humiliated by our fall from grace as I was. And my abrupt departure had added to the confusion. Yet any discussion, should there be an opportunity for one, would simply make matters worse.

Though now burdened with yet another plastic bag I went on walking. I was sorry that I had telephoned my mother, who would now imagine that something was wrong. Nor was I much consoled by the image of her felicity in a different place. She should have been here, with me! Simon should have taken care of me on this dreadful day! Yet I had frequently felt relief that I did not live under their scrutiny. I knew that it made them comfortable to contemplate my life from a distance. They were sentimental and must therefore be shielded from all sorts of unwelcome realizations. I also knew that their happiness was more apparent than real, and that it consoled them to cherish an image of a family that had nothing to do with the truth. They must be protected, for I now saw that theirs was a hazardous enterprise. I thought that friendship should be lifelong, and not cemented on the spur of the moment. In many ways I enhanced their association, or had done during that first summer in Nice, when I behaved so naturally that they were charmed and emboldened to do the same. Subsequent visits had never quite recaptured that feeling of ease. At the time I had been aware that words and smiles had to be ever so slightly exaggerated to convey a conviction of happiness. And my mother's afternoon escapes from the house that she could not quite consider her own were an indication that loneliness can be felt even in the most ideal of circumstances.

By the time I got home I knew what I must do. Humiliations, though ineradicable, must be repaired before they take root. I should do my best to allow Adam to consider himself forgiven, so that we could go on as before. We knew each other too well to cancel our friendship. Without unpacking my shopping I went to the telephone. 'My new number,' I said. 'Write it down.' There was a scratch of a pencil on paper. 'And do come for a meal. After all, it's your turn to come to me.' Profuse thanks. My last remark slightly spoiled the exchange, but on balance some kind of resolution had been achieved, and for this I was absurdly grateful.

5

It seemed an endless seamless passage of time, one that embraced the flat, the street, the whole city. I got up early to write my essays, having spent the night which should have been set aside for them with Adam. In the dark mornings, with the light on, I dispatched them as soon as I could, anxious to be out, to see whether new buds had appeared on the trees, or new flowers in the gardens. I was aware that I was not working well, and that examinations were approaching. I was not brilliant, like Adam, who had been promised a great future, not least by himself. I could only aspire to a run-of-the-mill degree, but once again I had proved myself to be a safe pair of hands: Dr Blackburn, my tutor, suggested that I might find work on other people's manuscripts, checking their grammar, their footnotes. I could do this work at home, or in the libraries with which I was already familiar. I accepted this idea, for I was unwilling to break entirely with a past which had otherwise proved so accommodating. Yet when I sat in the kitchen on those early mornings, when the sky lightened infinitesimally, and so slowly, and my eyes ached after a sleepless night, I wished that some more radiant escape were in sight, one in which I could make my mark and make others proud of me. I had no idea what this future might be. I only knew that it contained Adam Crowhurst, whose favour it was still important for me to seek.

I asked my mother, in the course of one of our Saturday telephone calls, whether I might bring a friend when I came down at Easter.

'Of course, darling. Who is it? Mary? Verity?'

These were the friends of my youth.

'Adam Crowhurst. A friend from college.'

'Yes, I suppose so. Though it might be a good idea if you were to write Simon a note first.'

'Why? Is he likely to object?'

'Not really. But he is of another generation. And it is his house.'

It was indeed his house, the one from which my mother seemed eager to escape. There had been no further talk of their coming back to London, though despite the attractions of the climate and the surroundings there was little for them to do in Nice. This suited Simon, who was relieved to be there, doing nothing. Not so my mother, her duties taken care of by Mme Delgado, her days idle. Simon liked to have her with him at all times, in the same room, if possible. I found this both tiresome and desirable, for no such domesticity was likely to come my way. Adam's possessiveness was in his own gift, and might at any time be diverted either to myself or to other women who had aroused his interest. I do not know what kept us together. That we were still attached was due mainly to my own assiduity. I studied him with the care I should have given to my books, made allowances which shamed me. Yet in between his lighthearted infidelities he returned to me. I was too fearful to do more than accept this.

He was like the man in Chekhov's story 'The Lady with the Dog', a cynic who is nevertheless touched by his mistress's tears and converted into a belated acknowledgement of love. Not that I wept, unlike Chekhov's heroines, who seemed to weep all the time, from guilt, from ecstasy, from remorse. Another of these stories, 'The Darling', should have taught me the dangers of excessive compliance. Olenka, the darling, marries one man after another, simply because they ask her, and grows old in widowhood after they have died or left her. She ends her days looking after the young son of one such man, and this is where the story hurt, for I could see in her devotion to the child something of what I might feel for a child of my own. I was young; there was no need for me to feel such wistfulness. Yet the feeling was present, for I knew that I would be denied any expression of such a wish. That is why stories are so important: they reveal one to oneself, bringing into the forefront of one's consciousness realizations which have so far been dormant, unexamined.

There was no possibility that Adam would ever accede to my wishes rather than to his own. There was an aura of success about him, of brilliance, which made no allowance for my docility. I was compliant, like Olenka, and he was Gurov, the cynic who fell in love with the lady with the dog, but reluctantly, and only when his hair was turning grey. I was a feature in Adam's life, yet his frequent silences left me with far too much time for speculation. Women were easily attracted by his ease, his considerable beauty, attracted too, it must be said, by his fearless bad manners, his unapologetic licence. The conditions for being accepted by him, of being allowed to share his leisure hours, could be met only by total capitulation to his rules. For there were rules: no questions, no reproaches. I had come by this knowledge the hard way, and from time to time it seemed too hard even for me to bear. But, like Chekhov's darling, I never seemed to learn. Simply, I was unhappy because I could not trust him. That is to say I could trust him when he was with me, but not at all when we were apart. I kept my feelings to myself, in accordance with his rules. I wanted him in my life for ever, whatever the price I had to pay.

We saw each other as often as he wished, had travelled together, and in small hotels, out of season, becalmed, had got on easily and well. I had been invited to his parents' house in Dorset for a weekend, and had been impressed. His parents seemed relieved that I was financially independent: this seemed to be something of a ticket of admission to their society. I did not like them, could not entirely come to terms with their indifference towards a guest. I now see that this was because they had had so many guests like myself, with expectation written large in their anxiety to please. I thought them a cynical couple; they automatically assumed that we would want to share a bedroom, which shocked me slightly: I should have preferred a little more hypocrisy. My attempts at carelessness were never entirely convincing. I see that now. At the time I merely resolved to do better, to try harder. That this was not what was expected of me was no impediment. As far as I was concerned it was up to me to change, to become adaptable, even when I could see that such adaptability would have to encompass a large cast of people – Adam's friends – whom I could never entirely admire. Therefore it seemed imperative to invite him to Nice, which I thought of as my home ground. I thought that contact with two transparently good people, my mother and Simon, might reveal another part of him, even to himself. I think I saw us refashioned as innocents, as I had been with my earlier friends of that first summer. I remembered the children in the garden, my clear conscience in their company.

In that small hotel in Spain, where we had spent our Christmas vacation, he had seemed so much more accessible, and I in my turn had warmed to his accessibility, reclaiming something of my earlier confidence. Not that I was ever entirely confident when I was with him: I was a spy as well as a lover. As he lay on the bed in our cheap room, his eyes distant, I watched him, safe in the knowledge that we knew no one in this tiny place, and that in the evening, as in the evenings that had gone before, we should walk along the harbour wall, and I should feel his arm around me. That holiday, which he later dismissed as rather boring, had convinced me that the episode must be repeated as frequently as possible. That it was not possible had to be put down to Adam's extremely crowded social life, and his dislike of having anything decided for him.

An accomplished escape artist, he justified his unavailability with elaborate generalizations about men and women, which I found annoying and unconvincing, but have come to accept as obvious.

'The more a woman falls in love with a man the more he's going to back off. It's natural. Women lose their power when they fall in love. Men get irritated by this, don't like them so much.'

'Does this always happen?'

'I reckon so.'

'Does it happen to you?'

'Something like that.'

He had the grace to look slightly ashamed. He too was young, and not as cynical as he liked to appear. But his liberty mattered more to him than whatever affection he might have felt, and it was in a spirit of making amends that he agreed to come to Nice.

The visit was a disaster. My mother was bewildered by the freedom Adam felt in a house in which freedom was held at bay by rules which were in fact imposed by an elderly man. Simon hated him because he was young and careless. Adam would put his arms round Mme Delgado when she arrived in the mornings, bestow smacking kisses on her stern face. Clémence, he called her. I could see that she loved it, loved him, the bad boy who enlivened her austere days. My mother was barred from her own kitchen by this strange complicity, and sometimes breakfast was extremely late. But Adam in the kitchen was preferable to Adam in the salon, where he sat with his legs wide apart and an expression of amusement on his face. Simon's attempts, initially at least, to make him feel at home, were unnecessary: Adam was at home, in a way that caused them great anxiety. They had given us separate bedrooms, but Adam made no pretence of staying in his, and came to me every night, although this caused me anxiety of a different kind. I could hear Simon's steps in the corridor, patrolling his domain. Sometimes these steps slowed down outside my door: there would be a creak as I imagined him bending down to listen for illicit sounds. This horrified me, put him momentarily beyond the pale. I could not understand how he could behave like this. I did not know anything about the sexual jealousy of the old, who realize that their powers have gone for ever. I did not know the bitterness of this realization. My mother, so much younger, was aware of it. This made me angry and sad on her behalf, giving me an unwelcome insight into their private life. Fortunately Adam slept through that breathing, that unconscious humming, on the other side of our bedroom door. I, as ever, was wakeful, keeping watch. In the end they were as anxious for us to leave as we were to go.

'Funny chap, your father,' said Adam.

'Stepfather.'

'Whatever. I must say I'm rather glad you're not related. Though I hardly see how you could be. He's an old man.'

'Not so old. On the wrong side of seventy, he always says.'

'Seventy-five if he's a day, even more, if I'm any judge. I feel sorry for your mother.'

So did I. And it was the secret knowledge of what must have been my mother's discomfort that drove me away from them for a while. The explanation for her absences in the afternoons, when Simon would expect her to lie down with him, now suggested itself to me. I resented the fact that I was thus made a party to their intimate life, though of course nothing had been said. I pitied my mother fiercely. Nor did I ever forgive Simon for introducing me to this fierce pity. I felt deep shame on my own behalf for the failure of the visit, though I did my best to counteract this by suggesting that we go on somewhere else. On the move, and safe from prying eyes and ears in modest hotels, we were once again comfortable and even happy. We went to various towns in the Rhône Valley, making our way towards Paris. When we arrived it seemed almost like summer. The chestnut trees were in blossom, the sun was shining, although the wind was still cool. We stood blinking in the sunshine after our night in the train. I felt happy, relieved to be away from Nice, romantically happy to be in Paris. It was in every sense conventional, but it promised much. I looked forward to spending these few days with Adam, walking, drinking wine, looking at pictures, buying books, before we had to return to London and our real lives.

'Fix up somewhere for us to stay, would you? I'll meet you back here for lunch. Twelve, no, twelve thirty. That should give you enough time.'

'But where will you be?'

He said that he had promised to see a friend, though I was saddened by this announcement, as I had been by the way he slipped off to make telephone calls, even in Nice, even in Simon's house, until discouraged by the latter's disapproving silence at lunch. These calls were always unexplained: they seemed to be occasioned by my presence, for although we were happy together, he was, I think, exasperated by the constancy imposed on him. I accepted this, as I accepted everything. Besides, I was filled with shame at the memory of Simon's watchfulness, his resentment at Adam's presence in his house, and the easy way in which advantage was taken of its amenities. He even resented Adam's familiarity with Mme Delgado, for it was clear that she was all indulgence for him. The teasing that Simon could not help but hear enraged him even further.

My mother looked on helplessly, refraining from comment. Yet she did not like Adam any better. Something in her took fright at his feral nature, and it did not help that he was amused by this. It was clear that she thought him dangerous, but I was no longer touched by such simplicity. Her blamelessness, which I had always taken for granted, now appeared unduly

45

prolonged: she should, I felt, have grown used to the ways of the world, as I had. My dislike of Chekhov's virtuous heroines now extended to my mother. Such ludicrous innocence! Then I remembered those afternoon flights of hers, those voluntary escapes, those perhaps hopeless attempts to get back into character, away from Simon's loving tyranny. For I had no doubt that by this time she was made to pay for his indulgence. I myself was now at the risk of his displeasure, for I had introduced an unwelcome reminder of his age and incapacity into the house he had thought of as a safe haven. Suddenly our lives were darkened with discord, with various incompatibilities.

I was in no position to effect any kind of reconciliation, since none of this was in the open. But I resolved to spend less time in Nice, to let my love for my mother take second place. This had never happened before. But Adam would now fill my horizon, though I knew that this was not in his plans. I shrugged. I had managed so far. I had indeed managed so well that his inconstancy was now part of my life. This accommodation removed me even further from my mother's way of thinking. But perceiving the imperfect nature of her own happiness merely reinforced my instinct that we would be better apart, at least for a while. And Adam was the cause of this, though no blame could be laid at his door. His very freedom, and the unapologetic use he made of it, would have invited censure even in less constrained circumstances. At close quarters, the uneasiness, which had to do with sex as much as with age or even good manners, was too apparent to be ignored.

It had nearly all gone wrong. The situation had been rectified, the danger just averted, by our decision to leave. The time thus saved would be spent away from unwelcome vigilance, a vigilance which we had brought into being. I was now free: we were both free. Freedom seemed to me the only worthwhile objective. I wondered whether Simon's insistence that he and my mother live in Nice sprang from a desire to isolate her as much as possible from her few friends, even from those generous but intrusive patrons so anxious to remove her from her solitary life. He was clearly opposed to any form of closeness that did not approximate to his own. That was why an occasional look of distaste, of suspicion, at my activities was so difficult to ignore. At the same time I had to remind myself that without his financial indulgence I should not have been able to pick an hotel in Paris which was so much more expensive than the ones we had formerly chosen. There was a certain amount of defiance in my acceptance of this. I wondered whether thoughts for my future had played a part in my mother's acquiescence. But I dismissed this thought as being unworthy even of myself. The compromises I had learned were of a different order of magnitude to those of two solitary people who had found an approved form of company. At least, that was what I told myself.

In the three perfect days that followed I even managed to feel a little sorry for Simon and his makeshift family, for he seemed to have none of his own. This was now threatened by defection by at least one of its members. He had wanted us to remain as we had been initially, undemanding, grateful, appreciative. Instead we, or rather I, had been perceived as restless, seeking gratification outside the fastness he had arranged for us. He saw that even his wife, whom he surely loved, preferred to be out of the house, although I was sure that she looked after him carefully, entertained his elderly neighbours, played her part as conscientiously as she had played her part with me in our days in Edith Grove.

'You talk a lot about your mother,' said Adam, sprawling on the bed.

'Well, she is my mother.'

'I don't go on about my mother, do I? I know where she is. That's enough.'

'Don't you want to know that she's happy?'

'Good God, no. That's her business, not mine.'

And yet he had all the hallmarks of a successful upbringing. I had not liked his mother, had been uncomfortably aware that she had not much liked me. My upbringing too had been successful, but perhaps our straitened lives had left their mark, had made us careful, in a way that Adam could not recognize. That was why he took his freedom for granted, as I could not quite manage to do. I could not even understand the freedom to behave badly, which he exercised without remorse.

'Did you manage to see your friend?' I asked casually.

He smiled, and swung his legs off the bed.

'Where shall we eat tonight? Did you manage to find somewhere half-way decent?'

We wandered out into the beautiful greenish dusk. Despite our hunger we were not in a hurry to sit down in a restaurant, with all the other tourists. We walked in silence through glamorous streets, far from regular students' haunts. We felt pleasantly in harmony, all tedious discussions left far behind. I think that this was the best time for both of us: the cool evening, the stately streets, the passers-by, subdued, like ourselves by the majesty of the darkening sky. Although we had a little time left I knew that it would be an anti-climax. I had a fateful sense of things coming to an end: at the same time I knew that this memory would never fade. We progressed as if in a dream, not caring where we went, and it was only when we felt the chill of the air that we turned back. That night we both slept.

We awoke on the following morning knowing that the holiday was over. Instinctively we packed our bags, paid our sizeable bill. On the way to the Gare du Nord Adam held my hand; again there was no need to speak. The journey passed in that way. At Victoria we parted, again with few words. We kissed, and I went back to the flat.

Even London looked presentable. There was light, there were leaves, even flowers. I wondered if my so-recent happiness had brought all this into being, but once at home I was forced to realize that nothing had really changed. Adam had gone back to Langton Street without a word about our next meeting, but I was supposed to be used to that. I made coffee, unpacked, took another bath. On the other side of the party wall I could hear my neighbour's dog bark. The barks faded, and could then be heard in the street. I could count on half an hour of quiet reminiscence before they returned.

I telephoned my mother to tell her that I was home. I had not much looked forward to this call, which was why I had preferred to send postcards – 'Love to you both' – while we were travelling. But this could no longer be postponed. I did not want to think of Nice, of that house, of those people, for whom I felt a certain exasperated impatience. Even my mother seemed old, out of touch. In future I would reserve my time for Adam, despite the fact that he might not want me to do so.

The telephone rang only once before it was picked up.

'Darling! Where have you been? We were worried.'

'Still in France, working our way home by stages. I'm back now.'

'We were disappointed that you left so abruptly.'

'I felt it wasn't going too well,' I confessed. I did not tell her of the footsteps in the corridor, the breathing and humming outside our door. She may have known about this, but it would not be discussed.

'It's true that Simon was a little shocked. He still thinks of you as a little girl. He couldn't quite get used to the idea of your friend being with you.'

Your friend. Not Adam.

'I'm afraid he will have to come to terms with it.'

'Look at it from his point of view, Zoë. He is of a different generation. As, I suppose, I am.'

'That argument doesn't hold water. All women are in the same boat now. The Women's Movement . . .'

'Yes, I have heard of it,' she said drily.

'We're free now,' I went on. 'We don't have to respect men, be grateful to them. It's their turn to respect women, to allow them some space . . .'

'Oh, yes, I've heard of that space. What will you all do in it, apart from complain?'

'Your generation didn't complain enough!' I said furiously. 'I wonder if you realize that?'

'Of course I do. But really opportunities for change are so rare. I was brought up to admire men, to be grateful to them. I may have wanted freedom, but I also wanted protection. Support and protection. I hope you never find out what it is to live without either.'

It seemed as though we were having an argument. Her voice was slightly raised, her indignation unmistakable.

'And are you grateful?'

'Of course I'm grateful. Simon has given me more than I expected, certainly more than I deserved.'

'There you go again. Deserved!'

'Yes, deserved. There was no way, as you would say, that I could otherwise have entertained hopes of living in the sun, with a man who is kindness itself.'

'Why didn't he like Adam? Why was he so rude?'

'He wasn't rude, darling. He was shocked. And really your friend (still my friend, not Adam) was quite rude himself.'

'It was because he felt unwelcome.'

'That's unfortunate, certainly. But I don't think he had any thoughts of that kind. He just found us very dull. Not what he was used to, perhaps.'

'You didn't like him either.'

'I did, in fact. I could see he was attractive. But Simon was so put out that I had to take his part. You and I are his family, after all.'

'Why has he no family of his own?'

'I believe there is a nephew somewhere, but they seem to have lost touch. Now he has only me. And you, of course. Come back and see us soon, darling. Don't be upset. We love you; we love to see you. You know you can always invite one of your other friends.' She meant my girlfriends, or, as we were now trained to say, women friends.

'I'll think about it. In any event I've got exams soon. I've got a lot of revision and so on.'

'Yes, of course. We'll talk on Saturday. And it would be nice if you had a word with Simon. He does miss you, you know.'

I nearly asked her if she were happy, but realized in time that this would strike her as ill-mannered. Besides, I had no further wish to know. The subject was closed. As Adam had said of his own mother, her happiness was not his affair. I could never achieve his degree of insouciance, which I privately considered astonishing. But as my ambition now was to resemble him as closely as possible, I left the matter of my mother's happiness unexamined.

6

My studies ended – satisfactorily, to my surprise – and my working life began. Almost immediately I was given a thesis by a Japanese professor to work on: the grammar needed checking, hesitant English to be tactfully corrected. This would keep me in London for the rest of the summer, for which I was oddly grateful. Between Nice and London there reigned an air of embarrassment, even of constraint. My mother, while continuing to assure me that they both longed to see me, was equally anxious, or so it appeared, that another visit on my part might be postponed. I surmised that she knew about Simon's watchfulness, was shocked both on his behalf and on mine, and no doubt also on her own. I doubt whether she ever brought this matter into the open, but I did not doubt that she knew about it, may even have witnessed it. I preferred not to understand what may have passed between them on that night, which I now viewed with horror. She would have had to be very skilful: they were both too disinclined for a confrontation for one ever to have taken place. Instead, she told me on the telephone that she was trying to persuade him to take her on holiday: Venice, she said, where they had spent their honeymoon. To judge from subsequent telephone calls this holiday was still on the horizon, always a possibility, but a possibility never quite brought into the foreground. She was sure I would understand if I postponed my next visit until Christmas.

This suited me well, or well enough, for I too had reason to feel embarrassment. Adam had a new friend. 'This time it's serious,' he said, with that charming carelessness which had drawn me to him in the first place. I shut the door of Langton Street behind me for the last time and wandered back to the flat in the early hours, suffused with a blush which I thought would never fade. Again I blamed myself. So deep was my shame that I was grateful to the unsuspecting streets for sheltering me from the public gaze. I registered failure in the one area of my life in which success meant most to me, and I knew that I could never speak of it, least of all to my mother. Simon, I knew, would be delighted, for she would certainly tell him. What else did they have to talk about? For a time indignation on my behalf would wipe out the memory of his conduct. He could be, and would be, self-righteous, producing as justification his distrust of Adam, his fear lest I be hurt. It would be a useful way of defusing a situation which had made them both uncomfortable. My mother would have been shocked out of a complacent acceptance of their apparent harmony. I should be performing a service if I played the part of a heartbroken girl who looked to them for support. Perversely, perhaps, I refused this role. My own feelings were so overwhelming that I could not consider those of my nearest and dearest. Besides, they had ceased to be the people I considered closest to me. Their compromises, their adjustments removed them from the tragic single-mindedness which was to be my lot. They retreated into the background of my life, where I desired that they should stay.

Within a few weeks, it seemed, the fixed points of my existence had revealed themselves to be untrustworthy. My reaction was to withdraw from those who knew me, to sit at home in the flat with my dictionaries and my thesaurus, to ignore the sun outside my kitchen window, and to work as though I intended work to fill my existence. The unworthiness that a rejection confers on the one who has been rejected was almost palpable. I preferred not to be seen. In the late afternoon I would go out to the park, and walk, my head bent, seeing nothing. Friends telephoned and suggested a drink, a meal. Sometimes I accepted, but such occasions were not a success. I had little to say for myself, could hardly talk about my dull work when such details were supposed to furnish conversation. And in comparison with real work – or what I thought of as real work – my efforts seemed nugatory. In that way, surprised, they began to think me uninteresting, for I had nothing to offer them, no confession of a broken heart which they perhaps suspected I was harbouring. They too would have been lovingly indignant on my behalf, and sometimes I wished that I could be entirely honest, but not for long. Uncensored behaviour seemed to me unbelievably dangerous, and like the Spartan boy with the fox under his shirt I preferred to suffer. I suffered so well, both for my unhappiness and for my silence, that I felt reduced to wordlessness, and relied more and more on my dictionaries to supply those words to which I felt I had no right.

Of course I could have behaved differently. I could have acted the part of a friend, even to Adam, whom I would have questioned delightedly, as if I were on his side. But I could not be on his side in this of all matters. I could have joked about him with my other friends, who were surely aware of the situation and who were too kind or too tactful to ask me how I felt. I had the disagreeable suspicion that everyone knew my business, for surely everything was out in the open? My silence was, if anything, held against me as a form of abstention that was not natural. Thus I failed to pay my dues to friendship, persuading myself that in time I should do what was expected of me and offer up my broken hopes for their scrutiny. I refused this role, just as I refused the daughterly role of confiding in my mother. The time for confidences had passed, belonged to the relative innocence of schooldays. The elaborate exchanges between women which were supposed to be a hallmark of my generation had never appealed to me. I thought that the details of a love affair should be secret; all the more reason, then, for no allusion to be made to the fact that the affair no longer existed. The appetite for such details struck me as unwholesome, although I knew that they were normal currency.

Behind my back – terrible phrase that sums up the whole situation – I knew that speculation was rife. My friends stood by, loyal but disappointed, waiting for some kind of breakdown. Alone in my bed I too waited, for it seemed as though this sadness must have some violent outcome. Yet by the morning I was subdued again. The most terrible thing about my dilemma was my acceptance of it. I told myself that in this way I should somehow regain my independence, and perhaps I was right. But I also knew what it was to be unconsoled, to go through days which were somehow not on record because they were not witnessed. Work was both my alibi and my disguise. Concealment was imperative, and my excuse was my work. I did work, conscientiously and well, and was thanked. More work materialized, and it seemed as though my course was set. 'I can assign you a researcher,' I had heard Dr Blackburn say on the telephone, in response to some academic inquiry. I was the researcher, it appeared. I accepted this and tried even harder in an attempt to appease the fates. The fates had now taken over from those earlier agencies from whom I had confidently awaited a good outcome. Even the gods had lost some of their power. That power, which was the power to make mischief, now appeared to me all too human.

Gradually I grew less constrained, but never really felt at ease in my own life. In the last warm days of a remarkable autumn I spent more time in the park, occasionally ate lunch at a nearby café. It was quiet, the children had gone back to school after half-term, and students were once more in their libraries. I was unsettled by the fact that there was no real need for me to leave the flat, for I had no office to go to. My time was no longer articulated by the academic year, and this made a considerable difference to my perceptions. I felt rootless and invisible, and the invisibility, which had initially suited my purpose, was no longer an advantage. I began to leave the flat more often, but at unusual times of day, the very early morning, or the late evening. I rehearsed the welcome I would give to Adam if I met him in the neighbourhood, the genuine friendliness I would feel if such a meeting were to take place. In a strange way such imaginary conversations became something of a comfort. I would return home just as my neighbour, Mr Taft, was going out with his dog. 'Nice to see a smiling face,' he once said. This too I should have to watch.

It was after all a banal disappointment. My unhappiness became routine, my secret dialogues with an absent Adam ceased to ramify. In other words I managed. I even thought that I managed rather well. I knew the extent of the damage, but I also knew how to hide it. I went out again, saw my friends, 'circulated', 'socialized', as those two eager visitors had once urged my mother to do, and was assimilated once again into a group of men and women of my own age, all of whom seemed glad to see me. In this way I could call on a little company if and when I felt the need of it. But I never entirely lowered my defences, and was thought of as something of an enigma. Men found this intriguing, women less so.

The news from Nice grew more animated the longer we were apart. Since the ritual of the weekly telephone call was so firmly established, and since there had been something of a breach of trust, we relied on gossip, on current affairs, to fill out our news bulletins, which were becoming a little threadbare. My mother in particular played her part as valiantly as she had played all her other parts. Thus I got to know about Dr Thibaudet's retirement, and the splendid dinner Simon had given them all at Le Chantecler. Armelle, I was told, was thrilled to have 'the doctor', as she called him, at home all day. Even more thrilling was their projected visit to their married daughter in Philadelphia, long planned, and, unlike my mother's putative holiday in Venice (still a subject for discussion), likely to take place in the near future. This talk of retirement was locally unsettling, for Mme Delgado was giving advance warning of her own. My mother, in a parody of genteel concern, wondered how they would manage without her. Maybe you'll come home, I suggested. Maybe, she agreed. This wish seemed to me sincere. The adventure in Nice was over, for my mother as well as for myself.

'Of course, I haven't said anything to Simon. Not yet, anyway. I have to be tactful about this. After all, the house is his. And you know how he loves it.'

I did indeed know this. He was rarely out of it. Those visits to the Thibaudets seemed to me his only excursions. The trip to Venice was thus in the realm of unexplored possibilities. This was a matter we were not anxious to disturb.

I remembered how she had said, 'I have to take his part.' She had little choice but to do so. What in fact did she know of him? She had responded to his kindness as only a lonely woman could, feeling a timid wellbeing that cast the world in a rosier light. Simon's first visit to our flat in Edith Grove had created such an excellent impression that it would have seemed churlish and impolite to question it. He had seemed not only prosperous but open, indeed the acme of accountability. We never elucidated those 'business interests' to which he had alluded: my mother had simply said, 'Property, I believe. He has tenants, or so I understand.' There was the nephew with whom he had lost touch, but on the other hand there were the respectable bank accounts which he had opened for my mother and myself, and without which the modest sums I earned would have been inadequate. He was, and always had been, extremely good-humoured, yet the single incident of his voyeurism made me question his secret life. The incident may have affected my mother rather more than it had affected me. It would not have been mentioned, but it would have had a witness. Simon was an old man, and the old are undignified. Had he really been inspired by care for me, or did that unconscious humming outside the door signify some sort of excitement?

There was now no doubt in my mind that Adam's defection was in some way connected with this incident. He may have been more wakeful than I knew, may even have noticed signs which had escaped me. Adam had not even pretended to like Simon, had felt sorry for my mother. I now had ample time to ponder these matters, and my horror grew. The little family I had thought to exhibit was in any event as nothing to set against his own endowment of natural parents, of brothers and sisters, of relatives all firmly settled on ancestral acres. I was modestly proud of Les Mouettes, which I accepted as my own birthright, whereas in fact it was merely an unusual house to which my mother had acceded by accident and in which she was not quite at home. The care with which she had set down dishes before Adam's place at table was the care of a visitor, not of a hostess. She was unused to dealing with guests, was intimidated by more confident personalities. Long years of reclusion had made her diffident, and she was alert to her husband's disfavour. The dislike he so clearly felt for Adam, and which he hardly bothered to disguise, had affected her. At the same time she wished Adam out of the house, so that he could cause no further disruption. No wonder he preferred Mme Delgado, with her reluctant smiles, her responses to his teasing, to his strong arm around her waist.

In contrast my mother had been kind, polite, but clearly not at ease, not only on Simon's account but on her own. Life had not prepared her for the introduction of her daughter's lover. I think she envisaged my life as closely resembling her own: years of pious simplicity crowned by a gift from the gods. But gifts from the gods are usually qualified; conditions are attached, the gods' indulgence never to be taken for granted. Adam's presence, which no one could ignore, struck her as boastful, whereas it was merely confident. But without his being in any way at fault he had introduced into their settled lives the subversive notion of sex, and, worse, sex which knew no formal boundaries. In their world, certainly in my mother's, such behaviour had no place in other people's houses. The difference was that she would have felt not indignation at a breach of good manners, but sadness that I was being seduced away from those standards of modesty and propriety which she had upheld with such difficulty for so many years.

Simon would have needed no such pretext for denouncing Adam, but he would also have been fascinated. For here was a man whom Simon could never have resembled, a man who took his own facility for granted, and who pleased himself in all circumstances. Simon clearly had a right to criticize Adam's manners; in objecting to his youth and beauty he was on shakier ground. It was clear from his generosity, his fussy care, his desire to maintain the fiction that we were all devoted, and happy to be so, that Simon had never enjoyed licence. Adam's liberty of behaviour was an affront to his whole way of life, for he too, it seemed, had been lonely and virtuous. He was old, he had grown heavy: it was impossible to ignore the contrast between them. And Simon was also rather vain, took a pride in his appearance, which was nevertheless that of a man 'almost on the wrong side of seventy'. Faced with the sight of Adam every morning he found it easy to imagine the preceding night. All of Adam's nights, whether known or unknown, would have offended him. And now there was no cure for the years of good behaviour, for age had dealt with them in a fashion against which there was no redress.

Adam's fault was to understand this long before I did, so that I was concerned merely to smooth over difficulties which had to do with incompatibility, or so I thought. I was more worried about Adam's feelings than about Simon's, although I realized that it was a matter of some urgency to separate them. I had not, I realized, made sufficient allowance for Adam's distaste, the distaste one might feel at having a deviant in the family. My mother's position would have been undermined by both of them, for, left to themselves, virtuous women can entertain harmless fantasies about young men, whom they see as the sons they never had. But she was obliged to ally herself with her husband, whose elderly habits were not perhaps entirely to her taste. While Adam and I were in Paris reproaches were probably mildly voiced on either side. My mother would not have been surprised by Simon's vehemence, for her instinct had supplied explanations not consciously taken into account. The detail of his voyeurism would be remembered when the cause of it had moved on to more accommodating prospects.

I was too sad at the irreparable effects of this on my own life to feel much sympathy for Simon, or even for my mother. Both were ill-equipped to deal with modern behaviour, because they still obeyed harsher and more rigid rules. They were now beginning to understand that they too might have enjoyed their youth had they been differently taught, or less frightened of their own wishes. It was as if the Bible had been spreading false doctrines, and although neither of them was in the least religious they bore the marks of a sententious upbringing, in an era when obligations were more important than entitlements. Their incomprehension had something pitiable about it as well as ludicrous. And the embodiment of their confusion was so sincerely unapologetic that he made nonsense of their careful constraints and of who knew what disappointments they might have kept concealed.

What was clear was that they had been made unhappy, that my mother, in particular, was less happy now than she had been in the past. In the course of my next telephone call I asked if I might come to Nice for Christmas, professed a longing to see them which was sincere, for it seemed to me to be up to me to persuade them that nothing had come between the three of us. My mother's response was so eager that I was glad of my impulse to gratify them. Other irreconcilables I would deal with on my own. If the way ahead for all of us was to be through reconciliation I was ready to play my part. My austere way of life had given me a longing for some kind of comfort, wherever it was to be found. I resolved to reserve my pity for others. For I was not altogether unfamiliar with the harsh imperatives of a doctrine which was in many ways not negotiable. I smiled with exasperation at my earlier version of a happy ending, saw belatedly that some form of ordeal was inflicted on every character in literature, and that even the gods had to make do with fairly limited powers, and were allowed only the satisfactions of caprice and rarely those of reciprocity.

The people whom I knew to be good somehow remained good in spite of themselves. Such were my mother, and possibly Simon, who gave money when he could give nothing else. The harm he had caused me had proceeded from a dreadful, because forbidden, curiosity, and from the unbearable presence in his house of someone whose behaviour he could only imagine. He too must have experienced shame, but I had little sympathy with him on that account. What made me genuinely sad was the knowledge that with the best will in the world one can still fail the test that the world sets, a test easily surmounted by those with more variable standards. I still wanted life to be conducted justly, honestly. But what if honesty brought into the open unpalatable truths, tendencies, compulsions? Honesty could hardly be its own reward in those circumstances. How strongly should one condemn a curiosity which had, perhaps, never been satisfied? The well-behaved may have many regrets, have realized too late that they might have had a more amusing time had they only seized other opportunities, precisely the opportunities from which they had obediently averted their eyes.

I now felt pity for those two people, whose moral education had been so rigid, even absurd. I considered myself to be wiser than they were in many respects, though I was in a position to measure the danger of complete enlightenment. *Tout comprendre, c'est tout pardonner*; I beg to differ. Total forgiveness in all circumstances seemed to me to be nothing less than hazardous, for I understood both Simon and Adam and could forgive neither of them. I understood them, that was all. This did not automatically confer indulgence but was directly responsible for my pity. One feels pity for those who are unprotected, at risk, those whose high ideals have not been met. Therefore, in some strange way, I was bound to cherish Simon and my mother, not because they were my family, or what passed for one, but because they relied on me to cement their partnership, to bring them joy. They longed to be restored to themselves, after the irruption into their lives of a person whom they saw as lawless. That this could only come about by virtue of a fantasy was of course regrettable, but it would do no harm, and possibly some good, to be lenient.

In London the days grew darker, colder. I no longer walked in the early mornings: that phase of my life was past. The streets made an attempt to be festive: Christmas decorations had been in place since October. I was almost glad to be leaving for the holidays, although I knew that re-entry would be difficult. It was the time of the year that I most dreaded. And even Easter, which would surely come, would promise little in the way of true warmth, but perhaps something more in the way of hope. Holidays would be planned: I could even take a holiday myself, but I had no use for such limitless time. I was used to being left to my own devices, though I now saw how inadequate these were.

There were crowds at the airport. What I retained from that

moment of departure was a feeling of solidarity, of rightness. On the plane we congratulated ourselves on having got away on time, joked, were conversational as we might not have been at any other season of the year. We applauded as the plane landed safely, bestowed good wishes on our neighbours, prepared to confront whatever arrangements remained to be made. The man in the next seat promised to telephone me, for we were the only two people travelling alone. He handed me over to Simon, whose uplifted arm signalled me from the airport lounge, with a certain regret; with Simon so insistently present there was no room for anyone else. He seemed to me, in the instant of recognition, much older, and also more anxious, as if much time had passed since our last meeting. And also as if he had doubted that I would ever return.

My mother too seemed older. She was taking on some of her husband's elderly characteristics. They scrutinized me timidly, lovingly, and with excessive care. I was irritated by this, but also touched by it. Who could not be? When my mother showed me the new bedspread she had bought for my room she expressed tentative hopes that I should be pleased. They were out to woo me, as if I might desert them for other pleasures, as I had before. The Thibaudets were coming to dinner, my mother told me, lingering by the bedroom door as if reluctant to let me out of her sight. They were looking forward to seeing me, she said.

'You won't be too bored, darling? You know you don't have to be with us all the time. You are entirely free, you know that.'

I assured her that I should be quite happy, said that I might look up some of my former companions. She approved of this. I was to be what I had always been, someone they could trust, young, carefree, without attachments.

'Come down when you're ready. We're longing to hear all your news.'

In fact they were not eager to hear any of it, fearing revelations of further liaisons. Simon, in particular, seemed to have placed an embargo on any questions, pre-empted any possible outpourings with a running bulletin of his own. His eyes sought mine constantly, but looked away when I returned his glance. He seemed ashamed, even fearful, relaxed only in the presence of the Thibaudets, who supplied any conversation that might otherwise have been lacking. Fortunately their forthcoming trip to their daughter in Philadelphia was pretext enough. Without this to look forward to, confided Armelle, she feared the doctor might have found time hanging heavy. Not that he missed his work – he was glad to be free of it – but he missed the structure that his work had previously given to the day. Had Simon felt like this on retirement? she asked. No, said Simon, I have everything I want here. His face cleared, and the look he gave my mother seemed filled with sweetness. Sweetness and gratitude. It was obvious that his own gifts to my mother had been more than reciprocated.

The two weeks passed quietly enough. I spent a lot of time out of the house, walking in the mild air. There was nothing much to do, for which I felt relieved. I was just a little concerned for my mother's changing looks, her air of pleading concern.

'Are you quite well, Mama?' I asked her, as the time came for my departure.

'Of course I am, darling. Never better. Why do you ask?'

'You look a little thinner. Is everything all right?'

It was the nearest I ever came to soliciting information, and, as I hoped, none was forthcoming. We were both content to leave matters in abeyance, aware that to do so was the prime concern. Simon, in particular, was as benevolent as he had always been, apart from the anxious darting looks which I put down to the wariness of old age. Indeed the day could not be far distant when his age would no longer be notional but a very real factor in their lives. I saw his efforts as he got out of

64

his chair, the determined bracing of his shoulders. But he did not impress me as infirm. We were all on our best behaviour, and we were all grateful for the harmony thus restored.

I telephoned when I got home. 'We so enjoyed your visit, darling,' said my mother quaintly. 'When do we see you again? Try to come before Easter. You know you are always welcome.' This was taking politeness too far. Was this how we were now expected to communicate? 'Simon wants to say a few words. I'll hand you over. Goodbye, darling. Until Saturday.'

Simon was touched by my thanks, as if he did not deserve them. 'If there's anything you need, Zoë, let me know. No need to worry your mother.'

He meant money. I assured him that everything had been taken care of, and thanked him again.

'Goodbye, darling. Come back soon. We are lonely without you.'

This was clearly true. I had not been able to ignore their loneliness, so much greater than my own. I sat down and wrote a loving letter which was completely sincere. I should be back soon, I wrote. In the meantime they were to take great care of themselves. I ended it as I ended all our conversations: Love to you both.

7

What happened next had to be pieced together from several unreliable narratives; those of Mme Delgado, Dr Thibaudet, Armelle Thibaudet, and my mother, when she could finally speak.

On the telephone, rather earlier than her usual Saturday call, my mother, determinedly cheerful, told me that they had had a bit of bad luck: Simon had slipped on the terrace, fallen, and sprained his ankle. Dr Thibaudet had very kindly bound it up, though that was not, and never had been, his job, had given him strong painkillers and something to help him sleep, and advised him to rest. They were quite all right, she assured me; there was no need to worry, and certainly not to interrupt my work and fly out to see them. A sprained ankle was not an illness, and Simon was being very sensible, blaming himself for not being more careful. They both sent their love and would telephone as usual in a week's time.

That night, Simon, no doubt confused by his sedatives, had got up, had gone into the bathroom, had trodden heavily on his injured ankle, had fallen again and cracked his head on the marble floor. My mother had heard him fall, had followed him, and had been unable to rouse him. Frightened, she had telephoned Dr Thibaudet, who had come at once. He had seen what she had not seen. He had retreated into professionalism, and into French.

'*Il est condamné, Madame*,' he had said, indicating the soiled floor. '*Voyez-vous, les sphincters se relâchent.*'

She had either not understood him or had taken no notice. She had entreated him to get Simon back to bed, where she would look after him. Mindful that the Thibaudets were to catch their plane the following afternoon, she had thanked the doctor, assuring him that after a night's sleep Simon would be recovered. Look, she had said, he is almost asleep already. Thibaudet had shaken his head and had told himself that she would be more rational in the morning. He would look in again before they left for the airport, for he knew what had to be done. He had told her to sleep if she could; in any event he would be there when she awoke.

Mme Delgado, arriving to dust the bedroom, gave a shriek of horror when she saw the dead man in the bed, with my mother lying faithfully beside him. She ran downstairs to find the doctor already approaching. He already knew what she had to tell him.

Then the telephone calls began. The body was removed, the smeared sheets bundled up, my mother, with some difficulty, placed in a chair. She did not appear to understand what had happened. There was no possibility of leaving her alone in the house. Thibaudet, with an anxious glance at his watch, arranged to have her transferred to his clinic in Nice, where she would be under the supervision of a colleague, Dr Balbi. He called me in London to say that this had already been done, gave me the address of the clinic, and said that he would be back in three weeks' time. I was to stay as calm as possible. He had discussed my mother's strange torpor with Dr Balbi, and they had decided to put her into a deep sleep, from which she would awake in a few days' time. Until then it would be unwise to attempt to disturb her, but I would of course want to be at hand. Dr Balbi was an excellent man, and the chief nurse, Marie-Caroline, would be in her room at all times.

'Simon is dead, then,' I said slowly.

He sighed. '*Un ami de toujours.*'

Before leaving London, I in my turn made telephone calls, one to Dr Blackburn, asking him not to send me further work, and one to *The Times*, asking them to print a brief notice in the Deaths column. I caught the next plane to Nice, rigid with shock. My main imperative was to get to my mother. In Nice I took a taxi to the clinic and was directed to her room. I was met at the door by a nurse, presumably Marie-Caroline, who said I might look in, but no more. In the bed I saw a motionless figure attached to a drip. I was told that there were to be no visitors for the foreseeable future, but that I should telephone every evening. She promised to give me a full report, smiled, and told me not to be alarmed: they had had significant successes with this type of cure. If I could telephone the following morning I might be able to speak to Dr Balbi. In any event by the end of the week she was sure that my mother would be able to speak to me herself.

I took another taxi back to the house, then went down the hill to Mme Delgado's *pavillon*. She was relieved to see me, as she had no intention of working any longer at Les Mouettes. After twenty years, she said, wiping away a tear. But the shock had been too great. In her quiet way she had been devoted to Simon, '*un brave homme*,' she repeated. She seemed to care less about my mother, or was perhaps relieved to learn that she was in the clinic. They would take care of her there, she assured me. Since the clinic was something of a luxury, to which she herself could not have aspired, she assumed that all cures there were guaranteed. There was no resentment in this, but on the other hand only a routine kind of sympathy. Sleep cures were for the rich, was the implication, and for foreigners who could afford them. She herself had always lived simply. I took the hint, and gave her money for her wages. Then we shook hands, and she saw me to the door. When I turned round to wave goodbye the door was already shut.

In a way I was relieved that death had dealt with Simon swiftly, if not cleanly. I had foreseen a long decline, after which I imagined that my mother would return to London, leaving

Les Mouettes as a holiday house to which she would return two or three times a year. Or perhaps not. The house had never really suited her, was too eccentric, too formal, and always too hot in the summer months. Her great adventure, for that no doubt was how she saw her marriage, had involved too many changes for a person of her settled temperament. I had always known her as cautious, even timid, certainly prudent. A life of luxury, as she laughingly described it, was not quite to her taste. Hence, I supposed, her desire to wander in the afternoons, in search of a place she might call her own. She had never found such a place, had returned to her duties, trying to persuade herself that she was still the modest housewife she had been ever since her first marriage. No word of complaint had ever reached my ears. Yet as I settled down uneasily in my old room I could see that my own present discomfort was as nothing to what she must have felt at the sight of the uncompromising white building, with its air of pride, of artifice, even of arrogance. There were no hidden corners, no shadowy alcoves: everything was blatantly modern, or rather 'moderne', in a style which disconcerted her. I myself had appreciated it, but then I had always been a visitor, free to leave when I so wished. My mother was a captive, and like all captives yearned for liberty.

I slept badly. I had not eaten, and I had given most of my money to Mme Delgado. This would be a problem. With great reluctance I searched Simon's dressing-room and found a cache of notes, current household expenses, I imagined. I looked for, but did not find, an address book on his desk. This left me perplexed. If there were no private papers I did not know how I was to proceed. I should have to postpone all inquiries until my mother woke up and was able to tell me what to do. It did not occur to me, at that stage, that she might not know either.

I was not familiar with the life of the body, except my own, did not know how it could betray, implode, or alternatively be put into a deep sleep and survive. In dreams my mother always appeared intact, upright, smiling gently. I could not identify her with that silent figure in the bed. Her condition appeared to me anomalous, for I had never previously seen her asleep. I knew that accidents could happen, and accidents were, of course, in the gift of the gods, my old enemies. Marie-Caroline continued to meet me at the door of my mother's room, barring access, refusing me entry. My questions were met with the politest of refusals to acknowledge that anything might be wrong. I was told that I should have to see Dr Balbi, who, unfortunately, was at a conference in Marseilles. He was expected back any day now; if I cared to wait he would surely see me. She indicated a chair in the corridor, and repeated that there was no need to worry. These cases looked alarming but were in fact routine. She smiled again, and shut the door quietly but firmly in my face.

I spent a day in the corridor, listening for the sound of approaching footsteps. This was the third day of our ordeal, which I had been told might last for another four or five. I had no desire to go back to the house, was quite happy to sit and wait and listen. Several times footsteps approached, but they belonged to nurses bearing piles of towels. Once or twice a woman in a dressing-gown, supporting herself on a stick, and accompanied by yet another nurse, would make her way slowly in my direction, would steady herself, then thankfully retreat, the nurse's hand under her elbow, their voices falsely cheerful. The sheer weight of encouragement needed in order to survive this process depressed me: there was no one to whom I might have recourse, no one who could help me. With the Thibaudets away I was even deprived of information. I missed them acutely; in particular I missed Armelle, who had thought to post me their telephone number in America. I would not use it, I told myself, except in an emergency. What that emergency might be I refused to think.

I rose unhesitatingly at the appearance of a dapper man with polished hair and twinkling shoes who conducted me to his office on an upper floor. Seated behind his desk he looked like the sort of doctor who attended conferences rather than one who looked after patients. I was numb with waiting, could not rouse myself to ask the questions which any novice should have been able to command. I sat in a chair on the opposite side of the desk and waited for him to tell me what I wanted to know. In all this ordeal I had managed to remain calm, or maybe I too was in shock. Events had moved so swiftly, and I had left London in such a hurry that I had lost my bearings. It seemed to me vital to endure until this particular episode was concluded. I was grateful that my mother had been removed from the house to this quiet place, grateful to Marie-Caroline, to Dr Balbi, to whom I failed to put a single question.

'Your mother is quite safe with us,' he assured me in excellent English. 'We are very well known. I dare say this is all quite strange to you.'

I cleared my throat and acknowledged that it was. The atmosphere was dangerously sympathetic. To my shame I burst into tears.

'Please do not cry. It will not help your mother if you break down. She will need a great deal of support when she wakes up.'

'When will that be?'

He looked dubious. 'The cure itself might last for five or six days, during which she will be fed artificially. Then, of course, she will need to be rehabilitated. We will keep her here for a minimum of three weeks.'

'When will she be able to talk to me?'

'Very soon. The time no doubt seems long to you.'

I bent my head. The tears flowed again.

'You have somewhere to stay in the meantime?'

'Their house. My mother's house, or rather my stepfather's. Simon . . .'

I could no longer speak. The pathos and the ugliness of Simon's death oppressed me now as it had not done when I had heard of it on the telephone. This was not a death that could feature in a sentimental anecdote. In England I should have known what to do. Here I contented myself with the fact that I had not seen the body. The excellent Thibaudet had arranged for it to be cremated; I had given it no further thought. In my mind I saw him lying on a marble floor in perpetuity, the evidence of his mortality only too visible, his poor body rendering up its substance as it can do only when every control is lost.

'Ah, yes, Les Mouettes. A fascinating example. You are interested in architecture?'

'No,' I said, 'not particularly.'

'I am a great admirer of the period, which I believe will one day come back into favour. Indeed, I have made something of a hobby of photographing such buildings, and now have quite an archive. One or two colleagues have expressed an interest, have suggested a lecture on the subject. I am considering it. You will continue to live there?'

'I live in London,' I said.

'I meant your mother.'

I supposed she would continue to live there, for the time being at least, but I did not see her there in the long term. I imagined that she would come home, for she always referred to England as home. This matter would have to be settled sooner or later, and perhaps sooner rather than later, for she would not necessarily want to stay in a house which held such horrifying memories. Dr Balbi may have seen something of my calculations. His sharp eyes had not left my face.

'There is no need for you to worry about costs for the time being,' he said. It was his way of reminding me that eventually a bill would be presented. I had no idea how large this would be, or whether my mother had any money with her. I had none. I should have to go back to London to clear my account, and my mother's too, if that were possible. If I left the following day I could be back by the weekend to resume my vigil.

I said something of this to Dr Balbi. Did I detect some slight relief in the alacrity with which he stood up and guided me to the door? When I got to know him better I was not entirely surprised at his occasional lapses. He had risen from the ranks by sheer assiduity, had acquired his polished manners along the way, together with his interest in period artefacts. At that stage I was pathetically grateful to him simply for having put in an appearance. My own lamentable performance would have to be improved at subsequent meetings.

I told him that I should be absent for two or three days, which he accepted as entirely reasonable. I may have said something about the bank. He patted my arm and told me not to worry. It was unlikely that my mother would be completely awake when I returned, but her progress would be monitored with extreme care. He could vouch for the vigilance of Marie-Caroline, and for the night nurse, Marie-Ange. Even at night my mother's sleep would not be natural. It was true that she was a healthy woman, and that no harm could come to her in this place. But the whole of Nice was now inimical to me. I longed to be back in my ugly flat, with its reassuring noises, the water in the pipes, the barking of Mr Taft's dog. Once my mother had recovered I would stay with her at the house until she was well enough to make her own plans. She was not old; her life was not in danger. I reassured myself in this way as I made my way down the stairs. I told Marie-Caroline that I should be back at the end of the week. Smiling, she put down her magazine, and permitted me to approach the bed. My mother looked deathly pale, her lips bloodless. She seemed stern, even judgemental. I placed a light kiss on the hand that was not connected to the drip.

Back at the house I poured some wine into a mustard glass and drank it off to give myself courage. I regretted my earlier tears: nothing less than grim determination would see me through. Yet I felt immeasurably sad, the weight of Simon's death more palpable as my eye encountered the objects of which he had been fond. These were not imposing, but like all relics made their own mute statement: his paper knife, his ashtray, unused since he had given up smoking, the spare key to the terrace. In his dressing-room I should find his clothes, his brushes, his shoe-trees, which I should leave untouched. My mother would no doubt want to see them when the time came for her to make the house her own again. Except that it had never been her own; in an odd way I had settled into it more happily than she had done. When I had my first sight of it, so white and uncompromising in the brilliant light, it had signified the beginning of an adventure, the door closed on my childhood, and I had willingly exchanged loyalty to our shadowy home for this alluring strangeness, into which were built all manner of references: the sea, the beach, the holidays which need never end.

But my feeling now was one of alienation. I dreaded the silence of the rooms, even of the kitchen, where Mme Delgado had hung up her dusters to dry. The house was now the domain of those who had departed, whether through choice or through necessity. When my mother returned I would urge her to make some changes, though I knew she would refuse. The house had always been to her a museum in which she was the main exhibit.

Curiously I examined this theory, which would once have seemed to me outlandish. Now I perceived her loneliness, which I had never taken into account, for I was used to her solitary dignity, had grown up with it. It had been the climate of my childhood, yet when the rescuer appeared, when the providential arrangements were made, and all was changed, it did not occur to me that a certain settled sadness might be more rooted than the upheaval of new opportunities, and that when the excitement and the romance had faded she might find that she missed her half-life in a way she had not anticipated. For we had been happy, too fiercely fond of each other to tolerate outsiders. That Simon had been such an outsider I did not now doubt. Our life at home was our secret, the secret we shared only with one another. Yet it had been for my sake as well as her own that she had made her decision. And the stark white house bore witness to the courage this had taken, and must at times have seemed the outward embodiment of such courage.

Darkness had fallen, and the wine was making me sleepy. I was to leave for London in the morning, to visit the bank, then to take another flight back to Nice. It occurred to me that I was the wrong person to be entrusted with such tasks. I was sober, certainly, practical, but deeply uninterested in financial details. I did not even know how much money there was in my account, let alone how much was needed. And there might be a will. Surely Simon had left a will? Without such a document nothing would be possible. Reluctantly I went back into the study, tried the drawers of his desk, all but one of which were locked. The unlocked one contained more sad relics, including a photograph of Simon taken some thirty years previously, to judge from his slimness, and his hair. His disarming smile reminded me why I had once loved him, and why my mother had found him difficult to resist. There was no will: how could there be in that unguarded place? In the waste-paper basket, which Mme Delgado had not emptied, there was an envelope with an English stamp. I removed it, was disappointed to find that it was empty, but for some reason noted the superscription: 'Redman and Redman, Solicitors', and an address in Seymour Place. These people knew Simon, knew his address in France, must surely provide the kind of support I was seeking, even if they had no idea who I was. Suddenly everything made a little more sense. They knew me at the bank: there was no problem there. And Redman and Redman could furnish some of the information that was so badly needed. I went to bed with my confusion a little relieved. All I had to do was seek advice. This was what was lacking in all this terrible affair.

Back in London, and in the flat, I looked round with surprise. I could make no connection with the person who actually lived there. Who had supplied that clock, that kettle? On the table my dictionaries were as I had left them. I allowed myself a brief half-hour before undertaking the business of the day. I felt a vague indignation on my own behalf, for I saw that in the future my loyalties would be divided. I too had felt relief on handing over my mother to Simon. Now she was in my care, for ever, it seemed. Either she would recover completely and live at Les Mouettes, with another version of Mme Delgado, whom she would have to engage, or she would, as I suspected, want to return to London. In which case I should have to find a flat big enough for the two of us. At the moment my own flat seemed highly desirable, probably because I saw that I should have to leave it. I could not see my mother in a flat of her own, alone and unprotected, and no doubt bearing the marks of what had happened to her. For the shock of Simon's death, which she must have registered, if not consciously, would undeniably affect her for some time. And her subsequent way of life would, except for myself, be unaccompanied and definitively altered.

There was an old copy of *The Times* on the dresser. I looked at the property advertisements with horror, for there was nothing we could conceivably afford. Surely Simon had left some money in trust? That was what wealthy men did, and there was no doubt that he was wealthy. I picked up my keys and went to the bank. This, I thought, must take priority. Then I must telephone Redman and Redman and make an appointment to see someone conversant with Simon's affairs. The suspicion that these might be well concealed visited me only briefly.

I walked to the bank in Sloane Street, glad of the time it took me. It was February again, as it always seemed to be in that area, but the same old ladies were shopping at the supermarket, the same old men walking their dogs. Had my time been my own I should have lingered, bought some milk, another newspaper. But I had to be purposeful, to come to terms with the fact that I had obligations to meet. I turned into the doors of the bank regretfully, thankful that there were other people at the information desk. What was ineluctable was the knowledge that such problems would in future accompany me throughout life. Until . . . But this could not be envisaged.

I explained to the girl behind the desk that I wished to close my account. She expressed disappointment, that of a parent with a disobedient child. I asked her humbly how much money I possessed; she mentioned a sum which seemed respectable but inadequate to meet further costs. I then said I should like to close my mother's account. That would not be possible, I was told; her permission would be needed. Or power of attorney, she added. In any event she thought it unwise. Wearily I explained the situation. After some discussion we agreed that it would be better not to disturb my mother's account. My own money would have to suffice for current expenditure. In time, when my mother was recovered, she would no doubt want to take charge of her own affairs. I agreed to this, because I already had an uncomfortable amount of money in my bag.

With this I should have to pay bills at the clinic and buy my ticket back to Nice.

Redman and Redman, in Seymour Place, sounded remote, until I explained that I was acting for my stepfather, Simon Gould, who had sadly died. The voice at the other end of the telephone softened slightly: oh, yes, Mr Gould had been a client, and they had been very sorry to read of his death in *The Times*. Mr Clifford Redman would certainly see me, but unfortunately he had no free time before the following Friday morning. I made an appointment for the Friday morning, wondering why everyone I needed to see was so busy. I remembered my day spent waiting in the corridor of the clinic, and the pure gratitude I had felt at the sound of approaching footsteps.

In the interstices of a crisis there is nothing much to do. I telephoned Nice for news (there was no change) and told Marie-Caroline that I should be back shortly. The French voice induced a pang of nostalgia, not for Nice or the clinic but for the days of easy exchange, a long time ago. In a strange way I was imprinted by that first visit, just as I was imprinted by Adam, and our days in Paris. A peculiar innocence was gone for ever. By innocence I really meant ignorance of the world's demands. I had been blessed, I now understood, and my present situation was the common consequence of unsought responsibilities. Though I was not yet old I felt old, for I was now to be my mother's guardian, a parent to my own parent. Later I came to understand that this too is the common lot. And yet I longed for my freedom. Deliverance was no longer possible. Even envisaging my mother's total recovery required an effort I could no longer make. And my own recovery? That, I feared, would have to be postponed indefinitely. It would be safer, and wiser, to assume an endless vigilance. The motionless figure in the hospital bed was now all my future.

8

Mr Redman impressed me favourably. A large mild man with a soft voice, I identified him with the brothers Cheeryble, those benevolent men of affairs who disposed of a cottage at Bow to house the helpless Mrs Nickleby and her daughter Kate. I hoped he might do the same for me, until I remembered that such felicity occurs only in Dickens.

Even more reassuring was the interesting decrepitude of his establishment. In the outer office a lady in advanced middle years was working at an upright Royal typewriter which I instantly coveted. There was a smell of coffee and a sense of order which only initiates could understand. Seymour Place had alarmed me: it had seemed severe, metropolitan. The office, such as it was, breathed a kind of dusty informality which formed a sharp contrast to the silence and efficiency of Dr Balbi's clinic. Apart from the noise of the typewriter this place too was silent. I wondered if Mr Redman had any clients at all, apart from Simon. It was possible that men of immense wealth preferred to entrust their affairs to this diffident affable man, but I was not convinced that he would be able to control the ramifications of their interests. Perhaps there was an invisible stratum of discreet millionaires who preferred to keep their activities from the public gaze. In which case no better guardian could have been found.

Mr Redman stood up slowly to receive me, as if I were a bona-fide client, albeit one without resources. I was grateful to him for his courtesy, his almost complete lack of curiosity. He indicated a chair and asked me if I should care for coffee. I assented eagerly: I seemed not to have eaten for some time.

He went to the door of the outer office. 'Scottie,' he said, 'could we have some coffee?' and to me, 'You will find Miss Scott most helpful with inquiries. She has been here almost as long as I have. Which is a long time,' he added, with a smile which took in myself as well as Miss Scott, a woman whose rectitude was evident from her unpainted face, her bleached dry hands, and her martial activity at the typewriter.

I longed to work in such an office, to turn up every morning with a handbag and a briefcase, to hang my coat in a cupboard, and to be only dimly aware that outside the window a whole area of activity, in which I would have no part, would be keeping others working in offices just like this one. At the end of the day I would retrieve my coat from the cupboard, pick up my bag and my briefcase, and go out to take my place at the bus stop. I should make my peaceable way home to an outer suburb where no further tasks awaited me. Or I might meet a woman friend, one of long standing, for a meal and a chat. This would take place no more frequently than once a fortnight. We should both exchange views of our employers, in whom we took a maternal interest, and profess to look forward to the weekend, when we might visit relatives. Our consciences would be crystal clear, our clothes seemly, chosen for their quality and their suitability. On Sunday evenings we would not be depressed by the thought of the working week. By the same token we should be quite ready for retirement, when we planned to move to the coast. We should miss the company, of course, but would always cherish the memory of the small party given to mark our last day at work, and of the presentation of the cheque which would take care of at least some of the arrangements. On that day our walk to the bus stop would be more pensive than usual, but we were made of sterling stuff and were determined there should be no regrets.

'Very sorry to read of Simon's death,' said Mr Redman,

breaking into this agreeable fantasy. 'We go back a long way. He was a friend as well as a client, you know.'

I was relieved to hear this. Scottie's excellent coffee, and the biscuits she produced, woke me up from my reverie, focused my woefully unfocused thoughts.

'Heart attack, was it?'

An accident, I replied. A fall. He shook his head. 'None of us is safe,' he remarked. 'How did your mother take it?'

'Rather badly,' I told him. She was at the present time in hospital, and I should soon be on my way back to her in Nice. I thought of Nice with loathing. 'I just wondered whether you had Simon's will. I should be very grateful if you could tell me something about his affairs. I shall have to deal with the arrangements until my mother is well enough to do so for herself.' I had no idea when that would be.

'I have his will, of course, which I will open, since you are here.'

He went to a large iron safe and brought out a file. How wise those millionaires were to trust him! Everything was under lock and key; there were no other parties, no officious underlings to scrutinize these documents. I was prepared to love Mr Redman for the rest of my days. In his hands I was safe.

'He leaves his money to your mother, Anne. That is quite straightforward. The money is in a Swiss account, in the BNP in Geneva. Rue des Bergues,' he added.

'Is there . . .' A lot, I wanted to say, but did not.

'There is not as much as there would have been a few years ago, I'm afraid. He had been spending rather freely.'

'Where did the money come from?'

'He owned commercial properties in Walthamstow. Warehouses. Two he sold to finance the purchase of a property in Onslow Square. The sale of Onslow Square, when property prices were up, was advantageous. Then, against my advice, he sold two of the remaining properties and opened two new bank accounts.'

'For my mother and myself.'

'Quite so. Well, now, there is one property remaining, which I should advise you to sell.' He smiled. 'This sounds more complicated than it is. You will find a purchaser without difficulty.'

'Can I leave this with you? I must be with my mother in Nice, until she is quite restored.'

'I can give the appropriate instructions, certainly.'

I prepared to go, searched for my bag. 'Then there will be enough for her to live on? That is really what I hoped you would tell me.'

'She will have to be prudent. For instance she will need to look for somewhere to live. I should advise London rather than Nice. You should be able to afford a small flat, though not in the centre. Wandsworth, perhaps. Balham. Tooting.'

'That won't be necessary. She has the house in Nice, and if she decides to sell, which I'm sure she will . . .'

He took off his glasses and laid them on the desk.

'That will not be possible, I'm afraid. The house would not be hers to sell.'

I stared at him. 'But it was Simon's house. Surely there is no question of ownership?'

'Indeed there is. Simon did not own the house. It belonged to his first wife, Margaret Spedding. Her will, which I also possess, specifies that he should enjoy it for his lifetime. That now, sadly, has come to an end.'

'But could he not have sold it?'

'Not without breaking the terms of the will, which would have been contested.'

'By whom?'

'By the man to whom the house now rightfully belongs, Anthony Spedding, Margaret Spedding's nephew.'

The nephew with whom Simon purported to have lost touch . . .

'He will certainly want to take possession. Your best plan would be to rent it from him, if he is willing to let it in the short or long term. Long term might pose a few problems. But I'm sure you will be able to come to some arrangement.'

'Do I write to him? Have you got his address?'

'I have an address, certainly, but it may be an old one. He may have moved. I should get in touch with his bank; they will follow it up. And they will know more than I do at this stage.'

'So the house never belonged to Simon?'

'No. And it was probably not a good idea for him to occupy it. He should have bought a property of his own, as soon as he was able to do so. It was foolhardy to expect that he could stay there indefinitely. But he was an optimist, you know.' I nodded. 'He obviously made no attempt to get in touch with Anthony Spedding. He may even have hoped that Mr Spedding would not bother him.' He shook his head. 'I take it that Mr Spedding was in ignorance of his second marriage. Was that announced in *The Times*, by the way?'

'I'm not sure. I don't think so.'

'That might account for his silence in the matter. Poor Simon. Delightfully impractical. And generous to a fault. Apart from the legacy to your mother there are no other assets. He had no other home? In London, perhaps?'

'I don't think so,' I repeated.

'Your mother will have enough to live on, but not in the manner to which she has been accustomed.'

'Actually she never liked that house.'

'No? It is a valuable property. I'm afraid there is no possibility that you will be able to buy it from Anthony Spedding. Your best plan is to meet him and discuss the matter fully. It may

83

well be in his interest to have your mother as a tenant. I believe he is quite a wealthy man. Property interests, you know.'

'Like Simon. That might have brought them together.'

Mr Redman smiled. 'I'm afraid Simon's business interests were on a much lower scale. Those warehouses in Walthamstow were in pretty poor condition. But it's all big business now, and that area has been pretty keenly surveyed.'

'So there's nothing left?'

'There is one remaining, which you should sell. And there is the account in the rue des Bergues.' He rose from behind his desk. 'I hope this has been helpful. It is always preferable to know the worst.'

'Is it?'

He smiled kindly. 'Have faith, Miss Cunningham. All is not as bad as it sounds. You will be able to rearrange your lives accordingly. Life is a process of adjustment, you know.'

It was no doubt what he told all his clients after giving them the bad news.

He saw me to the door. 'I shouldn't advise north London,' he said. 'North London is becoming very expensive.'

'I'm sorry?'

'For your next purchase. Go south, is my advice. Sydenham, I believe, is quite attractive. Or of course you could go further out. Bromley. Petts Wood.'

'You say the money in the Swiss bank will be enough for my mother to live on?'

'If she is very careful, yes. As for the property in France, I think you should reconcile yourself to some sort of an arrangement with Mr Spedding. He may be glad to have a tenant *in situ*. I believe he travels a lot himself. America, and so on. You will be able to reassure him about your own future in a face-to-face discussion. Write to him at the bank. They will know of his whereabouts.'

I did not see how Anthony Spedding could refuse my

request. My mother would be an excellent tenant, although, knowing her dislike of the house, my next task would be to persuade her to live there. I thought it highly unlikely that she would consent to a temporary tenancy or lease, but as we could not afford to buy the place there was no alternative. I thought it wiser for the time being not to inform her that the house was no longer hers. If I could disguise from her the details of my discussion with Mr Redman, or indeed with Anthony Spedding, when I finally made contact, she might be quite content to live there until she was strong enough to learn that other arrangements would have to be made, were indeed actively under discussion. I could not see her in Tooting or Petts Wood. Her unvoiced desire to return to London was, I knew, connected with her life in Edith Grove, as if the brief residence in Nice (and I was shocked when I realized how brief it had been – just a few years) were merely an interruption, after which her existence would be as it always had been. She would need to be eased out of this assumption, made to see the necessity of forming other plans. Life is a process of adjustment, I would tell her. Yet all the while I doubted whether she were capable of contemplating exile to a remote suburb, where she knew no one. Surely she would see Les Mouettes as a preferable alternative?

It would also suit my work, and no doubt my future life, if we were to live apart. Neither of us had lived at close quarters with another woman since her marriage, both believing that it was natural for a woman to live with a man. The desirability of this arrangement had always been obvious to both of us, despite our intense fondness, and I have no doubt that it would have been a consideration in her decision to marry Simon. It would suit me to know that she was in a place that was familiar, if not entirely to her liking; it would suit me to pay whatever rent Anthony Spedding required, knowing that if circumstances changed we could terminate the lease. This might not be for some time, not until I myself were settled. For I too might claim a life of my own, might marry in my turn, might have a husband or partner to advise me. This, I knew, was my dearest wish, not just for my own sake (that involved another type of reasoning, or rather of magical thinking) but for my mother, who would surely assent gladly to advice from a man. My mother belonged to an era when men made all the decisions. I had been obliged to make my own. And yet without the flat that Simon had bought for me I should have had great difficulty in assuming my independence. I was determined to keep the flat, which would ensure any future partner of my respectability. The flat advertised my availability as a free agent. It was therefore a matter of urgency to get in touch with Anthony Spedding, so that my mother's future could be assured.

In the outer office Miss Scott raised a hand in valediction when I thanked her for the coffee. Mr Redman, no doubt relieved that I had not made a scene, promised me his support. I was to keep in touch; he would of course oversee any agreement on which I might require advice. Another bill, I reckoned. It could not be helped. Indeed nothing could be helped. I thanked him, and he patted my arm, just as Dr Balbi had done. Such kindly gestures were my reward in this matter.

An urban child, I had always considered London my birth-right. My conscientious mother had taken me, when young, to all the obvious places: The Tower, the Houses of Parliament, Westminster Abbey, the National Gallery. Later, with my schoolfriends, I had explored Oxford Street, the King's Road. I looked back on these excursions with indulgence. The home to which I had returned then was more stable than any I had known since. My present flat was more than a temporary refuge: it was the temporary refuge from which, once more, I should have to depart. I knew that this was unthinkable, but was forced to think of it. I wanted, like so many others before me, for things to remain the same, or rather as they had been before the time of change. I also knew that I should give up my freedom if it made my mother comfortable to have me near at hand. Yet I was lonely, made lonelier by the prospect of life as a caretaker, for that is what I would become if my mother proved too shaken by her experiences to face life on her own. The alternative scenario was much more appealing: a temporary sojourn at Les Mouettes, which could be prolonged indefinitely, a full explanation of our situation, and a considered appraisal of what options remained. It was entirely possible that Anthony Spedding was a reasonable man whom this arrangement would suit well enough. He travelled a lot, Mr Redman had said, had property interests, would eventually wish to retire. At this point we should be obliged to leave, but that might not be for some years, by which time my putative husband would take matters in hand. That my mother might be opposed to this arrangement could no longer be a deciding factor. Les Mouettes would have to house her for the time being, and she would have to accept that this was how she must live. When I thought of that figure in the hospital bed, her hair flattened, her lips bloodless, I tried not to think of the implications of her appearance. In a day or two she would be roused as if from the dead, and when asked, like the character in *A Tale of Two Cities*, whether she cared to live, might reply, like that same character, 'I cannot say.' That was when I should be needed, and I should play my part. For until she was safe I would know no peace.

I decided to spend the weekend in London. I had letters to write, one to Mr Redman, thanking him for his time and promising to keep in touch, and one to the bank, requesting Anthony Spedding's address, or, failing that, an understanding that they would forward any letters addressed to him. Then I would have to write to Anthony Spedding, care of the bank if necessary, asking for a meeting. These letters seemed to me to take care of all eventualities, but I put off the task of actually writing them. I wanted only to sit at the kitchen table with a cup of tea until it got dark, and then to go to sleep in my own bed. When I heard *The Archers'* signature tune from the flat upstairs I sighed, got up, and rang the clinic. There was no change, I was told. I explained that I should be back in Nice the following week. This was received without comment, as if it were the most natural thing in the world. I was grateful to the clinic for passing no judgement on me. At the same time I must reserve all monies, actual and potential, for payment of the bills. The costs had not been mentioned so far, but I had no doubt that the charges would be considerable. The presence of Marie-Caroline alone must figure on an eventual bill.

At no time in my reflections did I think to blame Simon. I set the shadowy Swiss bank account beside the reality of the remaining warehouse in Walthamstow. Both would somehow supply our needs, as he had no doubt intended. In his own eyes he had acted honourably, and, more important, as a lover should. He had endowed the pretty widow with all his worldly goods, including those he did not quite possess. There was no doubt that he had loved my mother, had generously extended that love to include myself. And so ardent had he been that we had not thought to question his generosity. There had been no ponderous male relative to advise caution, to investigate his affairs. We had taken him at face value, as he had desired to be taken. And we had profited: of that there was no doubt. Women will always urge marriage on one of their own, particularly if there is, or seems to be, a splendid new life in the offing. Our mistake was not to have looked a gift horse in the mouth. But who does? A stroke of good fortune is taken to be the work of benevolent guardians, not of those capricious gods who may withdraw their gift at any moment, or indeed transform it into something else. Take a chance, we urge our friends, when an alluring prospect beckons. Nothing ventured, nothing gained. And once the chance is taken there is no way of turning back. And Simon had been so happy to supply the happiness of others, so loveable in his enthusiasm, his extravagance . . . I saw him as benefiting from an immense illusion that would ensure our comfort for ever. Perhaps it was fortunate that he had died before fuller explanations were due. In that way his death was in tune with his whole life, an airy delusion of wellbeing that had endured until those same guardians had precipitated his fall onto a marble floor, leaving the entanglements which he had concealed to be dealt with by others.

It occurred to me to wonder how much of this my mother knew, how much she had sought to query. I dismissed this out of hand: her status as a new wife would have imposed on her a discretion which she would not have thought to breach. Simon had been attracted to her by her innocence, an inno-cence almost unknown in those years of liberation. That innocence, I now saw, was entirely faulty. She had accepted his endowment as the gift he had intended it to be, and in that way had contributed to his general feeling of gratification. She would now have to be told the facts, which would come to her as a shock. I did not even know if she remembered the scene that had determined her removal to the clinic. Now she could no longer be spared. At some point, presumably when she was fully awake, I should have to tell her, or to remind her, that Simon was dead. She would then have to undergo a period of mourning, during which time I should have to be entirely supportive, and, more than that, sympathetic, when in truth I would be longing for her to take charge. Dr Balbi had said that she would be in the clinic for three weeks. And during those weeks I should have to be at hand, gently reconstructing for her events which she might have no memory of having witnessed.

I got up and went out, thinking that a walk in the dark

streets would prepare me for a night which would be sleepless. After a day of mild sunshine, in which it had been possible to think of spring, the weather had turned cold and damp. Those streets which had witnessed my childhood now seemed to me to be infinitely kind. Even the darkness was welcome, for it concealed me. I walked through the drizzle for about an hour, without paying attention to where I was going. There were few passers-by, only the odd car sizzling on the wet road. In the windows lights were on behind undrawn curtains; dinner was being eaten, or children being put to bed. These images of other people's domesticity affected me; I longed for such a setting for myself. These happy people would get up in the morning assured of a day of leisure. It would be Saturday, a day for shopping, an evening for dinner parties. That reminded me that I had not eaten. Small shops were still open: I bought bread and cheese, butter and coffee. That would have to do. The idea of sitting down to a full meal in my present predicament was somehow inappropriate.

I hoped most strenuously that my mother somehow knew that Simon was dead, and that the long sleep would not have wiped her mind clear of memory. I thought it preferable that she should suffer shock than that she should continue to enjoy that ignorance that had sustained her through life. I would have her ravaged by grief rather than comforted by an illusion that at any minute Simon would resume his existence. I knew that, without prompting, she would prefer to luxuriate in the kind care of Marie-Caroline, postponing for ever the questions she would need to ask. I should have to be tactful, but I should want to be brutal, harsh. I now intended to bring matters to some sort of conclusion, however fearful or horrified I might feel. I had heard from Mr Redman how bad things were, or might be, and I recognized that it was up to me to bring order out of present chaos. My mother, in the meantime, would slowly come to terms with my decisiveness, and perhaps recognize this as the protection she had always sought. I was determined that this should not happen.

My home, when I reached it, seemed to me to be infinitely welcoming, and, more important than that, discreet, tactful, asking no questions, respecting my right to be there. I made coffee and ate my bread and cheese. I wrote my letters, stamped them, and even did a little work: this too I should post off in the morning. In the stillness of the night, for it was now very late, I felt it important to show good will, to establish my credentials. Aware of the task that awaited me, I wanted others to think well of me. I even felt a slightly shaky sense of wellbeing, no doubt brought about by the food and the coffee. I had done as much as possible in the time at my disposal. Now it was for others to take up the burden.

Despite my exhaustion I slept fitfully. My dreams were fragmentary but vivid. In one my mother appeared, looking dishevelled, as she had never done in real life. She carried her possessions in two plastic bags, and her face was as I had seen it in the clinic. In another fragment I was in some sort of chemist's shop, staffed by two men of outstanding beauty. I hesitated to interrupt their conversation, for they were clearly in love with one another, grabbed the first thing that came to hand, laid my money on the counter, and left silently, so as not to disturb them. I could make no sense of this dream, although the other was all too clear. I had two days left in which to come to terms with my situation, though I knew that a whole lifetime might not be sufficient.

9

I had no desire to return to Nice. So great was my reluctance that I did not catch a plane until the early afternoon. I knew what awaited me, the multiplicity of arrangements that it would be my task to oversee. I even lingered at the airport, was tempted to buy a magazine like an ordinary tourist, and to sit on the beach, lazily, not even thinking. If I had to think I wanted to think of myself and of my own inclinations. The stay in the flat had altered my perceptions: within the flat I could lead a peaceable existence until a good outcome presented itself. This was now very imprecise, no longer had the lineaments of unnatural good fortune as I had once believed. I wanted to live a life like that enjoyed by everyone else, with only normal duties and demands to fulfil. I wanted a settled domesticity, or, failing that, a life of quiet study, and the privacy such a life would provide.

Privacy and protection: perhaps the sort of life my mother had once known, until removed from it by the gallant stranger. That this had once seemed a good outcome was now seen to be incorrect. No woman of my time was allowed to think in terms of total withdrawal from the world, although this was now my dearest wish. On a more practical level, when I was capable of constructive thought, I resolved to hand everything over to Mr Redman, who was already in charge of our financial affairs. I would telephone him from Les Mouettes and inform him, no, instruct him, to deal with us as he dealt with his other clients, to make any decisions that had to be made, any letters that had to be written, any negotiations that would invariably present themselves. This decisiveness relieved me somewhat. I was unequal to these complications: I was even unwilling to go to the house, to the clinic. I wanted to be in the sun, with the money in my bag all to myself. Time and inactivity seemed the greatest endowments any woman could enjoy. This heretical thought was also an unconvincing one. Nevertheless I found time to look around me, to gain one more sight of the golden spoilt city. I settled into the taxi as if for a peaceful drive, yet my feeling of unpreparedness was, I believe, prophetic, my desire to idle away the time the last revolt of which I felt capable.

I entered Les Mouettes by way of the kitchen, as I always did, and was alarmed to hear a radio in one of the upstairs bedrooms. I looked around me, bewildered, at the paraphernalia of food on the table, noted several bottles of Simon's wine brought up from the cellar. I was disturbed by a scowling dark-faced woman who appeared from the scullery that also served as a utility room. 'Who . . .?' I began, but she merely jerked her head and said, 'In salon.' This was my reintroduction to the house I had so recently thought of as my second home, and yet I was not surprised. I had expected something like this since leaving London: my idling, my dawdling, took on an interesting significance, as if all were known in advance, before the evidence had been produced.

In the salon I found a man and a woman sitting in chairs whose positions they had altered and nursing large tumblers of whisky filled with clinking ice cubes. The man sprang to his feet as I came in and held out a large damp hand.

'Hi,' he said. 'Tony Spedding. This is my wife, Tina.'

Tony and Tina. Names from a television game show. Like most contestants for large prizes they had the insistent smiles that would assure them victory, and behind the smiles the naked gaze of acquisitiveness.

'You must be . . .?'

'Cunningham. Zoë Cunningham. You've taken possession, then?'

'Well, you can't leave a house like this empty, can you?' said Tina. 'Anyone could get in.'

Tina was already dressed for the Riviera, in white trousers, a white shirt, gold necklaces, two gold bracelets, and a great deal of asphyxiating scent. She also wore a full make-up, such as is usually seen on television presenters, blue eye-shadow, and exceptionally long nails. 'Is there a decent hairdresser around here?' she asked. I was vaguely frightened of her.

Tony too had dressed the part: officious navy blazer, and tan-coloured trousers. They seemed to be entirely at their ease. Tina had not stood up when I appeared.

'I shall have to stay here for the time being,' I said. 'My mother is ill in hospital . . .'

'Not our affair, is it? The house is mine, always has been mine.'

'I'm afraid I don't understand how you come to be here.'

'She doesn't understand,' said Tina, rolling her eyes.

'If the house was always yours, which I doubt . . .'

'Oh, there's no doubt about it. I've tried to take possession in the nicest possible way. I felt sorry for the old man, though I never much liked him. So I wrote, suggesting that he leave the premises.'

'Where did you write to?'

'Here, of course. He never answered my letters. I had to break into his desk to see if he'd kept them. No dice. And I wrote to his place in Onslow Square. No answer from there, either. I was about to put my people on to it, which could have been nasty, I can tell you, when I saw the notice of his death in *The Times*. Pure chance, I might say. I usually read *The Telegraph*. If I hadn't had a lot on my plate all this would have been taken care of a long time ago.'

'We found the place in a terrible state,' said Tina. 'Conchita had to clean it from top to bottom.'

They both frowned, their faces darkening. I was filled with shame, not for myself, but for my mother, and above all for Simon.

'Simon had a fall that killed him,' I said. 'You must understand that I have been too anxious about my mother, who is quite ill . . .'

'Nothing to do with me,' said Tony, whose smile was no longer in evidence. 'Don't drink any more,' he told his wife sharply. 'I want this settled now.'

He was a slightly menacing figure, despite his short stature. Round his expanding waist he wore a lizard-skin belt. The smile, I felt, would not be resumed until he judged it necessary. He had nothing in the way of ordinary politeness, which he probably thought redundant. He was clearly angry, as was Tina, who, despite her husband's warning, had poured herself another drink. Simon's bottle of Glenlivet, half empty, was smeared with their fingerprints. They seemed an uneasy couple, who left traces everywhere. The scent that rose from Tina was mingled with a faint smell of sweat. Tony too was slightly damp about the forehead; a large silk handkerchief was applied from time to time throughout this interview. Tina flicked back her hair, peered down into the depths of her shirt. Their anger was habitual. Mine was of the once in a lifetime variety, building up to an explosion which would destroy us all.

'So, if you'd like to collect your things,' said Tony.

'That will not be necessary. I shall have to stay here until I can make other arrangements.'

He took a couple of steps towards me, and smiled pleasantly. 'You've got fifteen minutes,' he said.

I was tempted to strike him, to kill them both. Instead I turned on my heel and went up to my mother's bedroom, which they had now made their own. Her clothes had been removed from the wardrobes and dumped in the corridor, together with two large suitcases. In the offending bathroom, in which the aroma of Tina's scent was strong, there was an array of pungent and expensive cosmetics. My mother's modest effects had been either hidden or thrown away, probably the latter. Of Simon there was no trace.

I filled the two suitcases as best I could, though I knew I should have to leave behind most of our clothes. I remembered, even in my anger, to pack a couple of nightdresses, a thin silk dressing-gown, two trouser suits, and the dresses we usually wore when dining with the Thibaudets. Two pairs of shoes, which should have gone in the bottom, went on the top. I could not find my mother's hairbrushes, her nail scissors, or her slippers. These I should have to buy in town. In the bureau which had been hers and was now Tina's, to judge by the smell, I found tights and some underwear. One suitcase was now full. Into the other I crammed a light coat, a jacket, three sweaters, a tweed skirt, and two silk shirts.

Tina appeared in the doorway. 'Taking all that, are you?'

I ignored her. 'You can send on the rest,' I said. 'I'll give you my address in London.' This I took time to do, sitting at my mother's desk. 'And if you'd be good enough to telephone for a taxi . . .'

'I dare say Miguel could take you in the car, if you'd like to hang on until he's off duty.'

'I would not like to hang on, and I have no intention of doing so. I have to find somewhere to stay.'

'Yes, well . . .'

'So, if you would be kind enough to make sure that your man is available . . .'

'No need to take that tone.'

'I'm afraid there's every need. I perhaps expected more in the way of tact . . .'

She laughed harshly. 'We're practical people. Tony hasn't got where he is today by being tactful.'

'And I dare say you won't even live here.'

'We'll use the house. Don't think you can come back. Conchita and Miguel will be here all the time.'

'Have no fear,' I said. 'And now if you'll excuse me? Perhaps you could help me with that other suitcase.'

I knew that if she had been alone she would have opened it to see what I was taking. As it was she clattered down the stairs in front of me, empty-handed.

Tony was standing guard by the front entrance, which we rarely used. In the wide semi-circle of gravel that served as a drive stood a man lazily polishing an unfamiliar car. 'Miguel,' said Tony. 'Take the lady to the railway station. You can find a cheap hotel there,' he told me. He held out his hand. 'All the best,' he said cheerily. 'No hard feelings, I hope. After all, what's mine is mine, no doubt about that.'

'You'll be hearing from my solicitor,' I said. 'You have taken many of our possessions.'

He laughed coarsely. 'That fool, Redman? I can deal with him, no bother. I think you'll find, Miss Cunningham, that I know what I'm doing.' He shot his cuff and consulted a large and expensive watch. 'I think we've spent enough time on this, don't you? I'll leave you with Miguel. He'll know where to take you. You needn't tip him,' he added gallantly. 'This is on the house.' He waved, as if to go back inside, then thought better of it. He was still there when the car moved off, taking me safely away from his domain.

My simmering rage came to some sort of climax on the journey back into Nice. It was the sort of anger that inspires the rare creative act. Therefore when I saw a sign above a souvenir shop selling postcards and sunglasses in the rue de France stating, '*Chambre à louer*', I unhesitatingly dragged my bags from the car and without a backward glance at Miguel, who had done me no harm, entered the shop with as much force as I could command. Behind the counter stood an elderly man wearing a short-sleeved shirt and a beret. I told him I should like to see the room. He took a key from a drawer, and led me up a flight of stairs somewhere at the back of the shop. Opening off a dusky landing was a room containing a bed, a table, and a chair. 'Cottin,' said the man. 'Aristide.' 'Cunningham,' I said. 'Zoë.' '*Ah, Zoé.*' He pulled aside a curtain and revealed a wash-basin and a gas-ring, with Gaz de France emblazoned on its side. The room was bathed in darkness, a darkness which seemed symbolic. M. Cottin opened the shutters. This made the room seem darker rather than lighter. Fine, I said. Perfect. My one desire was to put down the suitcases. My hands were so sore that I could hardly get the money out of my bag to pay a month's rent in advance. You are a student? I was asked. Yes, I was a student. When I felt the tears rising I urged him out of the room. No one, not even M. Cottin, a complete stranger, should witness my collapse.

The rue de France is a commercial artery of no scenic significance. The end occupied by M. Cottin abounds in shops exactly like his own, catering for the kind of tourists who do not frequent the major hotels. From my window I could see crowds of them ambling by, on their way to cafés or restaurants. I rather enjoyed this spectacle, or would have done had I not needed to buy the sort of commodities crowded out of my mother's bathroom by Tina, for whom I reserved my entire hatred. This hatred was useful; it gave me the impetus to go out and find a chemist. I bought soap, toothpaste, washcloths, talcum powder. I added a bottle of cologne, regretting that I had not thought to do so earlier. It was too late to go to the clinic, but I went anyway, in order to give them my new address. I had not noticed a telephone but reckoned there must be one in the shop. This could be sorted out on the following day, when I should ask to see Dr Balbi. I was now very tired, and not a little confused, in no condition to see my mother, who might be awake. I stole past her room on tiptoe, then, ashamed of my hesitation, knocked and entered. A different nurse, Marie-Ange presumably, sprang to her feet, prepared to usher me out again: this was a day when I was not wanted anywhere. On the bed my mother seemed to have changed her position, or had it changed for her. I explained in a whisper that I would not stop, would return in the morning. Marie-Ange, who was older than Marie-Caroline and had a gold incisor on the right side of her mouth, made hushing noises and gestures. I left my bag of toiletries, went downstairs to the desk, told the receptionist of my new address, and managed to get away before bursting into tears.

I was still in tears in the rue de France, although my room seemed almost acceptable, or would have done had it not been encumbered by two large suitcases which took up most of the floor space. Outside the window I could hear the footsteps of a strolling populace. Night time here would be noisy, and I might be glad of it: I lacked company as never before. But tonight I must sleep, for on the following day I must telephone Mr Redman, and consult Dr Balbi, and assume a confident air with which to console my mother. My tears started again. There was a knock on the door. I wondered whether I had been sobbing out loud, whether my sobs had disturbed anyone. On the landing stood M. Cottin, still in his short-sleeved shirt and beret. He was holding a cup of coffee which he presented to me.

'*Je me suis dit, cette petite dame va tomber dans les pommes.*'

I thanked him, no longer conscious of the tears running down my face. It was the first kindness I had received since leaving London. I drank the coffee gratefully. It was bitter and only lukewarm, but it was the best I had ever tasted. Then I removed the harsh brown coverlet from the bed, took off my clothes, and fell into the deepest sleep I thought I had ever known. Like the coffee the night lacked certain refinements, but when I awoke it was with a sense of renewed purpose which I hoped would see me through the day, and through the days after that.

I took the cup and saucer down to M. Cottin and offered him my truly grateful thanks. He nodded briefly and went back to trundling his stands of postcards onto the pavement. The air was fresh, clear; it would be a fine day. I found a café where, presumably, I should eat all my meals, and had breakfast. As soon as the post office opened I should telephone Mr Redman. Dr Blackburn I dismissed as a lost cause; my work would speak for me, if anything could, but was not to be contemplated at the moment. When this appalling adventure was concluded I would make a reasoned attempt to minimize it, for his benefit, and indeed for my own, and persuade him that I was employable once again. As always, when I was in Nice, London seemed remote, a place of dull skies and inferior weather. I lingered as long as I could, then, with a sigh, set off on my errands. I noticed that the sun was already hot, and once again realized that I was not entitled to enjoy it. This was the mood that had greeted me at Nice airport. It was infinitely seductive, an invitation to forget my obligations, or rather to lay them aside onto somebody else, somebody older, wiser, stronger, richer. Above all, richer. The money in my bag had been sufficient for my rent and would probably take care of my mother's costs for the time being. The telephone call to Mr Redman was therefore my first priority.

At some point I should have to open another bank account to receive the shower of gold from Switzerland. The same dilemma presented itself: Nice or London? Nice, if I had to pay my mother's charges, and also my own. At some further point I would have to go back to London to collect some more clothes, and also minimal household effects. It seemed as if I were destined to stay in the rue de France for at least a month, probably longer. Now that I had found somewhere to eat I did not dislike my room. The bed was narrow and hard, but the table and chair were of fairly good quality, and there was a shelf on which I could stack books, if I had any. It seemed to me a decent enough place in which to work, until I remembered that I had no work. The 'student' who had had the room before me had stuck a few pictures on the walls, stills from Hollywood films cut out from magazines, all of women, sultry temptresses with enigmatic expressions and copious hair. This unknown person, a man, surely, with a young man's tastes, had been formed by the cinema, but evidently preferred the sexual promise of earlier icons to anything he might have seen in the rue de France. I was comforted by this unknown presence, with its reassuring idealism. I had slept well; I was in some way reconciled to spending time here. I decided to telephone Mr Redman every day, to give him up-to-date news of my affairs, and to learn from him if there were any new developments in the way of Simon's legacy. At some point money would be produced; at some point I should have to find somewhere for us to live. And, sooner rather than later, I should have to deal with my mother's state of mind, which would be one of dispossession, of shipwreck, perhaps worse.

The weather was so beguiling that I was tempted to sit down and drink more coffee, but I felt that I had no right to do so. After the brilliant sunshine the clinic seemed relatively dim, for blinds were kept lowered at all times. I found my mother propped up with pillows, sipping orange juice through a glass straw. I hardly recognized this emaciated woman, with huge eyes, and the air of questing for approbation. She smiled cautiously when I approached the bed, intent on holding her glass of orange juice, a little of which had spilled on to the sheet.

'I knew you'd come,' she said. Her voice was low, hoarse, unused. 'Have I been ill?'

'A little, yes.'

'Is that why I'm in hospital?'

'Dr Thibaudet thought it best.'

'Dear Maurice. Did they get off all right?'

I assured her that they had. I was immensely relieved that she had remembered the name.

'Is someone looking after Simon?'

'Mama, Simon is . . .'

But at that point she closed her eyes and sank back on to the pillows. Marie-Caroline rescued the glass before it fell. Once again my mother's face was drained, blanched, the face of one who had come back too fast, from too far, from a place where I could not join her.

Marie-Caroline told me that she might be confused for a day or two, but that I could of course visit at any time. It might help if I were to prompt her memory very gently, but not to deluge her with information which would merely bewilder her. Marie-Caroline herself seemed less cheerful than usual, and it was clear that she wanted me out of the way. I asked her if my mother had been seen by Dr Balbi, and was told that he would be in on the following day, when I could talk to him myself.

'If there is any change we will of course get in touch with you.'

I gave her my new address, and asked her if she expected any change.

'No, no,' she said, with something of her old briskness. This all looked more serious than it was. But then she asked if I had a telephone number at which she could call me, and I knew that recovery would be by no means straightforward, might contain unknown risks, might not be assured. She sensed my alarm and smiled a tired smile. She had been on duty every day without a break; the work was tedious, and she was young enough to find the enforced vigilance oppressive. And she had been excellent from all points of view. It was just that now that the prolonged sleep was drawing to a close she was permitted to weigh up the risks of the rest of the procedure, the encouragement to eat, to walk, to wash, to make the sort of recovery set out in all the textbooks. Once again I thought that it would have been better for my mother to have suffered the shock of bereavement straight away rather than be unconscious of it altogether, leaving it to others to instruct her. Those others, and their judgement, or misjudgement, would determine the future of her mental health. It now seemed that this would be precarious. And how could I, so firmly entrenched in this world, make proper contact with one whose senses had been put to sleep, and who might prefer to stay in limbo rather than rejoin me, with my easy unthinking movements, my physicality, and my eagerness, in calculations for a future in which she could not believe, and would not understand?

I stole another look at the figure on the bed, then leaned towards it, as if determined to unlock its secrets. For more than a few moments, maybe for longer, I wondered whether it might be preferable for her to die now, like this, in the care of kindly supervisors who would know how to dispose of her, whether that return to life were not too much to expect of her, indeed of anyone. For to resurrect a fallen life, one which had been all but destroyed, is an almost impossible task, or so it seemed to me, bending over my mother's sleeping figure, hearing her laggard breath. I even wondered whether there were any way of making my fears – or were they wishes? – known to those in charge, and whether they would regard me as an unnatural daughter, or simply as one who recognized the necessity of solutions. For my mother's death would be a solution of sorts. It seemed to me so near that I lost all fear of it. This did not in any way diminish my love for her, which had never wavered. But her life now seemed mired in a pathos which I found unacceptable. She had sunk so gratefully back to sleep. Was it the mention of Simon's name, the beginning of my warning sentence – 'Simon is . . .' – that had closed down her faculties once again? For somehow she must know what had happened, and for a little while was allowed not to know, preferring this half life in a hospital bed to a full life in the world.

That world would not deal kindly with a woman who had always been too tender, too trusting, and might now be diminished. Her return to life would be further threatened by the difficulties that awaited her. She would have only the clothes I had managed to rescue for her, and which I had packed too hastily into the suitcases now in the rue de France. She would have nowhere to live. Even if she had never liked Les Mouettes it was her home, and a rather enviable one at that. I knew that she had always preferred her earlier home, and had been impatient with this view, but now I saw that for a woman of her disposition a modest way of life, and the company of a child, might be preferable to the challenges of a late marriage. This was not a popular view, nor would it be understood. And if she were to be exiled to one of those outer suburbs so favoured by Mr Redman, would she ever find company again? And would the memory of her life at Les Mouettes seem so bizarre a construct that she would reject it altogether?

'The telephone,' Marie-Caroline reminded me. I must go back to the rue de France and give some account of myself to M. Cottin. I was the bearer of information which no one could share. The sheer desire, indeed the need, to involve witnesses, did not preclude prudence. It would not do us any good to confess the various humiliations which had befallen us. And we had been so recently, so splendidly, endowed that we would not attract sympathy. As a chatelaine of sorts my mother would have been welcomed anywhere. In her present condition she would be avoided.

M. Cottin wrote down the number of the telephone in the room behind the shop, and indicated how I might pay for the calls. We had exchanged no information; he was still cautious. I merely told him that my mother was not well, and that I would only use the telephone as and when necessary. He nodded gravely. A hero among men, whom I might trust. Like Blanche Dubois I would now be dependent on the kindness of strangers, no bad thing in the life I was now obliged to live.

10

The obedience with which my mother submitted to the attentions of Marie-Caroline alarmed me. It was the extreme docility of those struck down by illness or immobility in the course of a process of which they were no longer fully conscious. Her hair was now brushed, her nightdress was clean, her appearance more or less restored. Yet she showed no desire to leave her bed, though a chair had been placed next to it, which she was surely expected to occupy.

'Today,' she told me beatifically, 'I am to have a purée, like the ones I used to make for you when you were a baby.'

'You do know, dear, that Simon has . . . died?'

Her face clouded again. 'I think so. Was it an accident? Was he in the car?'

'He was in the house. You both were.'

'I don't remember. I don't remember coming here. Did he bring me?'

'No.'

'Then you did. What happened?'

'Simon had a fall. You called Dr Thibaudet. Do you remember that?'

'I remember Dr Thibaudet, of course.'

'You don't remember waking up beside Simon?'

A look of extreme horror replaced her earlier expression of slightly infantile acquiescence. This was the change I had been hoping for. Now I was by no means sure that I could deal with it.

'Then he died at home?'

'At Les Mouettes, yes.'

She reached out and clutched my hand. 'I can't go back there, Zoë. I can never go back.'

As gently as I could I disengaged her fingers. 'We can't go back there, Mama. The house has been repossessed, by Simon's nephew.'

She sank back on the pillows, alarmingly pale. I was unprepared for, and despite myself shocked, by her next remark. 'Thank God,' she said.

'But weren't you happy there? Simon was so proud of it.'

'I was happy with Simon. I never liked the house. I should never have thought I could be happy there. I wanted to please him, but really I should have stayed at home. Maybe we could go home now. But are you sure he is dead?'

'Quite sure, I'm afraid.'

Her eyes filled with tears. 'Such a good man. I hope I made him happy.'

'I'm sure you did. And you were happy, weren't you?'

'Oh, yes,' she replied languidly. 'I was very happy. In a way I shouldn't have been. He gave me freedom, and then took it away again. And I missed that freedom. I dare say you think me worthless. Worthless and absurd.'

'It was a new way of life for you. You would have got used to it.'

'No, darling, I never would have got used to it. I was used to being alone, that was the truth of the matter. A very sad truth, no doubt.'

'Don't distress yourself.'

'He was such a marvellous man.' She was crying freely now. 'So generous with his feelings. So unselfishly anxious to make me feel at home. But how could I? He was a stranger to me. And it is possible to love a stranger, Zoë, a great deal, so much so that all I wanted was to make him happy, and to make him think that he had made me happy. He made me lonely in a different way, and I never became familiar with that kind of loneliness.'

'I thought marriage was a cure for loneliness.'

'So did I. And there was a longing in him that made me want to comfort him. He looked so upright, so impressive, but in fact I was stronger than he was. My task was not to let him see that. We had a pleasant life, certainly, but it was like being cast in a play, without an audition. And perhaps I wasn't always as responsive as I might have been. I don't mean . . .' She blushed. 'I mean appreciative. I was always trying to do what I thought would please him. And sometimes I just longed to get out of the house, to be on my own again. I was happier when you were there. You didn't seem to think there was anything wrong with me.'

'There wasn't anything wrong with you.'

She shook her head sadly. 'And now that I have my freedom again I don't want it. I long for that dear stranger, and I dare say I always will, even though I hardly had time to get used to him. Had I known how short a time we were to have together I should have refused him. Maybe I should have done that anyway. It was not right to have expected so much, and then to have rejected it.'

'But you didn't.'

She gave a tired smile. Marie-Caroline shook her head minutely. 'I hope I gave a creditable performance. Do you think he knew?'

'I can't say.'

'I think he did. My poor darling.' She was too exhausted by now to shed more tears.

'Has Dr Balbi been to see you?'

'Dr Balbi will be in tomorrow,' said Marie-Caroline. She advanced purposefully towards the bed. 'If you could come back then?'

'We'll talk about it when you are less tired,' I said. My heart sank. I saw us both in my small flat in London, myself trying to work, my mother idle and dispossessed. My work had never seemed so attractive to me, and so elusive. In those years, for women, work had as much dignity as marriage; old archaic longings had been relegated to the musty attics where they had always lingered. Or perhaps cellars was a better metaphor. These desires were subterranean, out of sight. But no woman can be unaware of them, no matter how persuasive her propaganda.

To deny a right true end is to deny nature, but nature is also, or can be, the enemy. I understood my mother's false compliance, but it evoked little sympathy in me. By an odd reversal she seemed more up to date than I was, able to live without a man, able to live with one, even on his terms, but in the knowledge that what she was doing was consciously willed, a debt she owed to her upbringing, rather than to her inclination. I found this horrifying. In her place I should have behaved differently, I told myself. But how? Was my own desire for love exacerbated by her confession, by her reliance on me? I had no wish to play the man, to be the strong one in an unwanted alliance. Had I been free I should have scorned such weakness as I was feeling in the wake of my mother's somehow shocking explanations. The fact that I had understood them seemed to point to a further weakness of my own that I was not anxious to probe. I should have liked matters to be simpler. I should have liked my mother to have retained her enigmatic reserve. Above all I should have liked to remain a child. This, however, is no longer possible once the age of childhood is past. Any attempt to counterfeit the condition of childhood is dishonest. It is also immoral.

I kissed my mother, whose eyes were closed, and told her that I should be back soon.

'Tomorrow,' supplied Marie-Caroline. 'Now she must rest.'

I left the clinic in a state of some perplexity. I did not

understand, nor was I willing to understand, an illness so subjective, so open-ended, so voluntary. I could understand Simon's demise because it fitted in with the apocalyptic view that any young person has of death. I remembered a dire sermon in the school chapel, in which the preacher had enjoined four hundred little girls to remember their Creator in the days of their youth, and had gone on to detail all the systems that would eventually fail. The windows, he had said, indicating his eyes, the grinders – here he had ground his teeth – the keepers of the house, and here he clamped his hands to his chest as if to show us his lungs. Ignoring the stifled giggles of the congregation he informed us that the grasshopper would be a burden and that desire would fail. A restlessness at the back of the chapel was a discreet signal to him that none of this could be appreciated or understood, but he was not finished. If ever the golden bowl be broken, he said, tapping his forehead with a bony finger, or the silver cord be loosened – here he pressed his hands to his windpipe as if to strangle himself – we should do well to consider such matters. At this point I had found the words so beautiful that I had paid attention, and I was not much dismayed. If this happened to everyone then surely everyone would know how to deal with the decline, or rather, the collapse, that he seemed to know so much about. I imagine that he was in fact a sick man; he was certainly an angry one. He disappeared shortly after that particular warning and was replaced by a nervous youth who told us that Jesus was all-merciful and that the end was merely the beginning. But I had been more attracted to that account of the dissolution of the body. I still think of it as authoritative, and of *Ecclesiastes* as the most convincing book in the Bible. With those matters in mind I could come to terms with the oblivion that awaited me, and awaited us all.

But my mother's sojourn in a hospital bed made me impatient, and also ashamed of my impatience. Surely, with a warning of the inevitable, any right-minded person would cling to life, would fight off the desire to collaborate with any degenerative process? Yet my mother did not seem so inclined. She had suffered a shock and a bereavement, and although affected by the death of her husband, as any woman would be, was strangely willing to look on it as if it had happened to somebody else. Even the relief, to which she could hardly confess, but to which there were unmistakable pointers, should have given her the impetus to conclude the matter, to get up and get dressed, and to prepare to take charge of her own destiny (and of mine). There were plans to be made, and she should show signs of wishing to make them. She was free, as she had never been in her life, free of the burdens of both child and husband. In time, I hoped, she would look back ruefully as she calculated the loss that Simon represented: loss of comfort, loss of protection, of status. For I did not under-estimate the latter. Even if she were secretly glad of her new freedom she must realize that no one is actually free, that freedom is a concept, an ideal, with which everyone seeks to come to some accommodation.

She had, or seemed to have, an unrealistic idea that all could be as it had been before this intemperate introduction into her life of a man who had been her opposite in every way. She had even expressed a desire to go 'home', as if that early home still survived. Her recent home she had dismissed without regret. This was in fact a blessing in disguise: she would not mourn for Les Mouettes as I should; she had walked out of it, meta-phorically, as if released from prison. I wondered at what point I should have to tell her about the Speddings, if at all. As an anecdote she might find it amusing, but only if she had been successfully transferred to a place of safety. She might miss her possessions, but very little; Simon's gifts to her would be counted as fairy gold, not to be turned into common currency. And her brief life in the sun had been, or would seem to have been, an interlude, an entr'acte, whereas the serious business would resume in known surroundings, where the long task of introspection could be undertaken at her convenience. Maybe that task was already underway, and her present inanition a pointer to it.

But she had other duties, other business. It was too much to expect her to tell me what to do, for it was obvious that I was in charge. The fact that we were without a home had somehow slipped her notice. There was nothing for it but to do as she wished, to go 'home'. Yet that home, which to her was real, as Les Mouettes had somehow seemed imaginary, did not exist either, or not in the dimensions she required. That home had vanished when the lease of the flat in Edith Grove had expired; what had followed it belonged to me. Here was where the fantasy broke down, for I did not wish to be dispossessed even by my beloved mother, particularly not by my mother, who might oversee my life as Simon had once overseen her own. At close quarters there would be no escape, no place for the occasional overnight guest. And I had no intention of restricting my life to her company alone.

Before all this could be concluded, if it ever could be, I should have to find some way of lodging her until she was strong enough to travel. I thought the best, indeed the only, thing to do was to find her a decent room in a decent hotel, where I might visit her every day, much as I visited her in the clinic. Simon had always directed potential visitors to the Westminster or to La Pérouse. He was not keen to let anyone stay in the house. Even I must have seemed intrusive at times, although I think he loved me. I now saw that the existence of Adam under his roof represented an outrage, and I blushed when I was thus brought face to face with my own lack of understanding.

Since it was such a fine day, and since I had little to do, I walked along the Promenade des Anglais to the Westminster, which seemed to be filled with healthy, rich, noisy tourists. The season had begun and the hotel was full. My timid inquiries at the desk, after I had tried explaining my story, brought little in the way of sympathy. In addition, an enormous sum of money would be required. I retraced my steps and went in search of La Pérouse, in the old secretive part of town. Here the visitors were more discreet, but even in the foyer I could see that they were wealthy, even if they were not much in evidence. Again I was told that there were no rooms free, but was directed to a small pension a few streets away. This seemed a possibility, but with some kind of resolution in sight I put off my decision for another day. I was tired, I was hungry. I went into a café, ordered a sandwich, and went down to the telephone in the basement.

Mr Redman, in his peaceable way, seemed moderately pleased to give me more news than he had managed to do previously. A surveyor had been sent into the warehouse in Walthamstow and in the course of his work had come across a large iron safe. On Mr Redman's instructions this had been opened with the help of a local safety expert. Inside the safe were a number of documents: share certificates, he told me, and an insurance policy which should be left to mature. I ignored this, and asked him to realize the lot, once my mother's consent had been given, as I knew it would be. Had he found a buyer, I asked him, to be told that two rival concerns were interested, which might send up the price. If I could be prepared to wait . . . I could not, I told him, without much finesse. Had he any news of the account in Switzerland? Ah, that would take a little longer: the Swiss were only willing to disburse the accumulated interest, which would amount to very little. In which case, I said, we were reliant on the stock options in the safe. I reflected how odd it was of Simon to have allocated his interests in this way: the panache of the Swiss account backed up by the secret hoard in a disused warehouse. I told

Mr Redman that the money was needed quite urgently, as I was looking for an hotel for my mother. I might have to pay quite a lot, I warned him, as if the money were in fact his and I was in the business of extortion. His professional calm was, I could tell, slightly disturbed by my tone, but I was finished with politeness, which had not done much for me at the reception desk of the Hôtel Westminster. I also told him that I should telephone on the following afternoon. Then I sat down, ate wolfishly, drank two cups of coffee and smoked two cigarettes. I rarely smoked, since I regarded smoking as an act of defiance, but now I was impenitent. A certain insensitivity seemed to be called for in my dealings with others. I did not like this, but I bowed to the inevitable.

When I returned to the clinic I was told that my mother was less well. She had had a disturbed night; they had been obliged to administer a sedative, and it would be better not to pay my daily visit. Perhaps I could return that evening? The door to her room was shut quietly in my face. Alarmed, I went in search of Dr Balbi. His secretary seemed affronted that I had no appointment, but such niceties were now beyond my reach.

Dr Balbi, at least, did not seem to object to my intemperate entrance. He was seated behind his desk with a folder of notes in front of him: my mother's, I presumed. It was the first sign of clinical activity that I had ever seen in that place. He looked up briefly and signalled me to sit down.

'Your mother had a slight episode last night,' he said. 'This was successfully controlled, but we shall keep her under close observation for a day or two.'

'A slight episode of what?'

'Her heart is not strong. There may have been one or two episodes in the past.'

'You mean she had a heart attack?'

'No, no. An irregular beat, nothing more.' He looked at me more carefully. 'You did not know of this?'

'I knew simply that she liked to live quietly.'

'She will have had some awareness of her condition. Did she not consult a doctor in England?'

'I have no idea.'

I assumed that it was possible. I knew little of my mother's daily life, and of her recent life in France nothing at all. Yet it seemed logical that her extreme passivity was an act of self-protection, and her quietness an attempt to palliate any form of aggression from her body. I doubted whether Simon had known any of this, for she would have wished to protect him as well as herself. That protection extended even to me; her silence was the safeguard of my liberty. Now I saw her as the vulnerable creature she had always been, vulnerable not through loneliness, though that is vulnerability enough, but through an awareness of her own fragility. The only sign of delicacy was her rest in the afternoons. But then women of her kind did rest, in shadowy bedrooms, whereas women of my generation, instructed to assume their independence and to enjoy it, took little rest and despised those who did. Ladylike behaviour had long been renounced in favour of a more militant stance; we were at the cutting edge, fighting for equality. We had no time to rest from our labours, for we owed it both to ourselves and to others of our kind to carry on the fight.

Suddenly I felt very tired of the struggle. My mother had chosen her way of life, one that was certainly anachronistic, and had taken full responsibility for it. I saw her as an heroic figure, isolated, certainly, but with resources of her own which I had not suspected.

'Is she very ill?' I asked fearfully.

'No, no. Hearts can recover quite successfully with the correct regime. But she will require care. Please do not cry. She has you, though you are young, and it may seem a little unfair . . .'

'Yes, it is unfair, but I will do what I have to. My mother is innocent . . .'

He smiled. 'Ah, yes, the innocent place an unfair burden on the rest of us. I know how you must feel. I too had the care of my mother. I loved her dearly, but she took away all my hopes.'

'Yet, here you are, a doctor . . .'

'That was her wish for me. Not mine, not originally. But she made so many sacrifices for me, and would have made more.'

'You rewarded her.'

'Yes, I did. It was important for me to do so. You have found somewhere to live?'

'For myself, yes. A room which I quite like, but which could never be regarded as anything but provisional, until I can get my mother back to London. She will have to go to an hotel, I suppose, until she is stronger.'

I blotted my eyes. I felt unattractive; my feet were sore from all the walking, and my hair needed washing. And he was being kind; he had broken that severe silence which had reduced me to tears. I did not want to earn this man's disapproval, for he too had performed heroic acts. It was easy to imagine him as a poor student, in a temporary room, with no home comforts, and always the memory of that sacrificial mother to spur him on to greater efforts. He spoke with a slight accent, that of Marseilles, although I did not doubt that most of it had been ironed out in the course of his career. Now he was the finished product, a successful doctor, even though he had none of the confidence, even the ebullience, that one sometimes encounters in those conscious of worldly success. There was, if anything, a hint of reserve, even of melancholy, in his manner. His looks were nondescript; he was not an impressive figure. And he was watching me carefully, as if in doing so he might prohibit any weakness of my own from manifesting itself.

'An hotel would not be suitable,' he said. 'And I doubt if you would find one willing to take your mother at this time of the year. Hotels prefer people who come to Nice for pleasure, not for convalescence.'

I looked at him helplessly. He was a man; let him make the decisions. I now craved the strength of another; I felt that without Dr Balbi's resourcefulness I might as well give up straight away.

'Can she not stay here for a while?' I begged.

'That would not be suitable either. Long-term patients become institutionalized, have difficulty in adapting once they are back in the world. You would have a much heavier burden on your hands if we were to keep her here much longer.'

'Then where is she to go? What is to become of her?'

'In such cases I usually recommend the Résidence Sainte Thérèse. It is a place for those who need a certain amount of care and attention.'

'A nursing-home?'

'No, it is what it says it is: a residence, run by lay sisters. Excellent women. There are only twenty ladies there at any one time. Naturally a vacancy occurs when one of them . . . leaves. I believe there is such a vacancy at the present time. She will be quite comfortable; she will have her own room, although the residents are encouraged to mingle in the down-stairs salon, and of course the dining-room. You will be able to visit, and she will have company. There is no need to look so shocked. My own mother spent her last years in such a place, and was, I think, contented.' A shadow crossed his face. 'But then she had had such a hard life that any kind of rest would have signified contentment. But she took pleasure in the friendships she formed. One particular lady took her under her wing, saw to it that she visited the hairdresser, and so on. Your mother will come to terms with such an arrangement. She is relatively young: she will adjust, though she might find it a little strange at first.'

'Will she be in there for life? If so, it's not possible. I mean to take her home with me.'

'Of course you will make your own decisions, though she will need to make a full recovery. I see no reason why she should not go home eventually. You will no doubt be able to look after her yourself then.'

There was no note of interrogation in his voice. I had received my orders. Not only that, he expected nothing less of me. He knew all about obedient sons and daughters, and no doubt also about their sorrows.

'Was your mother very old when she died?'

'Not very, no. But old for one who had never been really young. A widow, with two children. I have a sister, older than myself.'

'My mother too is a widow.'

'I doubt if you have known the same hardship. We lived in a very poor part of Marseilles (I was right), but when I went to study, in Montpellier, she rented a little room for me so that I should feel like the other students. I never did, of course. And I was lonely. We were both lonely. And when I went home there was little to say. That is why the residential home was such a relief to us both, as it will be to you and your mother. And of course I shall look in from time to time.' He stood up. 'If you agree to this I will make the arrangements.'

'What should I tell my mother?'

'As little as possible. You will find that she accepts the change quite well.'

'And when . . .?'

'We shall keep her here for one more week. After that she will be ready to leave.'

Standing, he looked more severe than he had done when seated. I was to accept his ruling or he would do nothing more for me. I felt inclined to accept it anyway, so grateful was I to have our fate decided for us. In due course I should take my mother home, and we would live together, as it seemed to me now more likely that we should have to. We should live in my flat, or in another flat, and I should care for her. I had not made good use of my time, or my youth, and now had little to show for either. Yet as I stood up and shook Dr Balbi's outstretched hand, I almost wished he would entrust me with more confidences, in another setting, so that neither of us need ever speak with more restraint.

'*Dis bonjour à Mémé.*'

'*J'veux pas,*' said the child, twisting away from the lovingly held-out arms of the lady with the crooked face.

'*Voyons, Jean-Claude,*' said his mother. '*Il est fatigué,*' she explained to the attentive circle of ladies who scrutinized every visitor on those longed-for Sundays, when the outside world was allowed into the Résidence Sainte Thérèse for a brief opportunity to monitor the progress of those too frail or too diminished to venture out.

'*C'est normal,*' said the lady with the crooked face, Mme Levasseur, but the light went out of her eyes. My mother laid a consoling hand on the hand which was slowly replaced on the arm of the chair, as Mme Levasseur recovered her composure, which was considerable. So practised was this composure that she was able to summon a smile and to look indulgently on the recalcitrant Jean-Claude, who was sent off to draw at one of the small tables which, together with a selection of unmatched chairs, furnished the salon. The ladies sat expectantly, waiting for their visitors, for any visitors, for the sight of a man, a son, a nephew, even if such a man belonged to another. All would be discussed in the long days and evenings to come, until another weekend arrived to break the monotony of their lives. On Saturdays, in preparation for these visits, those ladies who could still get out went to the hairdresser. For those who were housebound Mlle Jacqueline came in and performed a similar service. There was a clear division between those who had had their hair done professionally, and those who had made do with Mlle Jacqueline, a goodhearted but unfortunately unskilled assistant who undertook this chore as part of her Christian duty. My mother, who was some twenty, even thirty years younger than the other inmates, went to M. Hervé every Saturday morning, although she could have gone on any other day of the week. Consciously or unconsciously, she followed the pattern laid down for the others. Her hair was now quite grey.

The Résidence Sainte Thérèse occupied a once dignified town house in the rue Droite, near the church of Sainte Rita, in the oldest part of the city. It was a pleasant walk from the rue de France, down the Cours Saleya, past the market, to the rue Droite. I had taken this walk anxiously, eagerly, every day, until told that Sunday was visiting day, or, in exceptional circumstances, Saturday. I too had conformed to the prevailing pattern, and, like the reluctant Jean-Claude, had developed a resistance to the evidence of deterioration that was hard to overlook. And yet it was a good place; even I, trying to ignore the smells of cooking and of age, was obliged to concede that it provided a community of sorts for those who, through no fault of their own, had to live with strangers. On Sundays the visitors, particularly the male visitors, manifested every kind of good will, tried not to notice the freckled hands, the swollen feet of those who had once cared for them, complimented those whose hair denoted particular effort, and made the obligatory round of greetings and farewells to those ladies left unattended. In that way a kind of harmony was maintained which had everything to do with gallantry, very little with natural inclination.

The ladies were in fact ladies, or perhaps had been ladies before being struck down by one infirmity or another. They were members of a recognizable class, although they may have lost the distinguishing marks of that class: hauteur, good posture, careful appearance, a desire to uphold status. Now they were like girls again, in a way they could barely understand.

They were cared for by a staff of lay sisters, who wore short blue uniforms, like celestial factory workers, and by the maids, Agathe and Julie, whom they loved. It was these two girls who provided what gaiety there was on those endless weekdays, particularly on Mondays, when they reported their activities with husbands or boyfriends, to the delight of those whose memories could still entertain such accounts. The activities of the girls were eagerly discussed; a certain precedence was formed among those who had received one confidence more than those so generously shared with others. The love of everything young brought smiles to faces which had lost the memory of youth, in the same way that uneasy sons and sombre grandsons held the secret of the opposite sex, so far out of reach now that widowhood was the only condition that many of them understood. They evaluated long legs, jaws rough from hasty shaving, as badges of what was still desirable, even at an age and in a context when such matters were an affair of the distant past; they responded, still, to the sound of a male voice. And the very young, in particular, awoke responses which had once been habitual: the desire to embrace, to kiss, to cherish. The return to normality, when the visitors had left, was the low point of the week.

My mother, after her initial terror, was strangely content, no doubt recognizing the regime as benevolent, as indeed it was. She had a small room of her own, and a *cabinet de toilette*; above her bed hung a black wooden crucifix. I think she would have retreated there, had Sœur Elisabeth not bustled her downstairs shortly after her arrival and introduced her to two of the younger residents, Mme Levasseur and Mme de Pass, both in their late seventies. Out of politeness she had responded to their questions and thus unknowingly passed the test of acceptability. They sympathized with her on the death of her husband, for this was a routine subject of conversation, and if they did not understand how she came to be in their midst did indeed understand that she was recovering from a debilitating illness exacerbated by shock. This was entirely respectable. Of the nature of that death – 'an accident' – and of that illness little was said. Though they would have liked to know more, Mme Levasseur and Mme de Pass were tactful enough to desist from further inquiries. Confidences were voluntary; there was to be nothing so vulgar as interrogation. Thus my mother was permitted to be comfortable with the story that she had perfected for herself, or that I had perfected for her. Conditions had somehow to be met and respected. I was, in spite of myself, shocked at the ease with which she had come to terms with those conditions. It was as if she had been returned to some part of her girlhood, her schooldays perhaps, when the company of those of the same sex was entirely natural. All the women seemed to share this attitude. Only those male accoutrements on the Sunday visitors stimulated some sort of reminiscence. Then eyes would recover their sharpness, hands go up to touch the snow-white coiffures. Men, whether as sons or lovers, would be suddenly, succinctly, remembered.

But the residents were not encouraged to brood. Those who could go out were permitted to do so, preferably in twos or threes, for the streets were steep in this part of town, and excursions were limited. Coffee might be taken at the café on the corner, before the slow walk back for lunch. Sometimes a son or a nephew would propose a short drive in the car, but not often. The Sunday visit, once concluded, no doubt with a sigh of regret and relief, was as much as anyone could endure. The residents, too, were almost glad when they were left undisturbed once more, were tired by the unaccustomed company, and always disappointed by that confrontation with a world which had ceased to be theirs. My mother, who knew only myself, was less affected. I provided continuity of the sort she could understand, and she was able to count on my presence. Her conversation, on those Sunday afternoons, almost entirely excluded me. I was told how Mme de Pass's son was unavoidably detained in New York: this was my cue to have a few words with Mme de Pass. I was told how Mme Levasseur was very disappointed by the way Jean-Claude was being brought up by his mother: this was my signal to send a wave of the hand to Mme Levasseur. The same inquiries had to be made every week, without actually naming the malady that had brought these women to this place. A bad back, to which reference could be made, was the recognized metaphor for any ailment of a chronic or painful nature. It was a matter of dignity, of survival, even, never to refer to parts of the body. My mother never mentioned the stroke that had twisted Mme Levasseur's face. No one mentioned it. Yet it was brought forcibly to mind when Jean-Claude jerked away from the kiss she was longing to give him. Sometimes he relented, but only under pressure.

'*Donne-moi un bisou*,' she would plead, and the child would plant a noisy kiss on her good cheek.

'*Encore un*,' she would plead again, but this was too much to expect.

'*J'en ai plus*,' he habitually flung over his shoulder before preceding his mother out of the door.

Those who had watched this exchange with their usual intentness handsomely pretended to think the child adorable, and congratulated Mme Levasseur on having such spirited progeny. All knew better, of course, had recognized that hatred of the wilted flesh which they knew for themselves, were willing to excuse the child who had squirmed away out of the sheer instinct of his youth. I too felt that hatred, as I shook hands prior to departure. Outside the sun was still bright; the beautiful day denied the existence of age and of decline. It would get dark, but then the streets would be filled with another kind of light; cars would flash by, strains of music would be heard, young people would be released from the duties of Sunday, Mass in the morning, the visit to the relative in the afternoon, and would once again celebrate their freedom from bodily ills before the working week began on the following day. As I emerged from the Old Town I would welcome the brash sights and sounds of the tourist-filled centre, embrace the sheer philistinism of the traffic and the hotels, prolong my wanderings for as long as I could before turning into the rue de France. Then I too would say goodbye to Sunday for another week. The most insistent memories were of those poor hands patting their newly coiffed hair, in the expectation of a compliment which was not, could not be genuine.

It was a relief to return to my landlord, M. Cottin, who was also old but who seemed to have aged in a superior manner, possibly because he was still working. Every morning he surveyed the rue de France from the threshold of his shop, before going back inside to scan the deaths column in *Le Figaro*. If death were on his mind he did not talk about it, at least to myself, apart from referring to his late wife, which he did frequently. The day after her funeral, he told me, in an unusual moment of confidence, he had got up, gone down to the shop, opened up, and carried on as usual. This he had done ever since, wearing what seemed to be the same shirt and beret. From my upstairs window I could see his sparse figure on the pavement, among the postcards. His other confidence, in which he somehow thought we had a common interest, was his modest research into the history of his own family. Since I was so fond of my mother he thought this might be a way of indicating solidarity. The Cottins, he told me, were originally from Lyons. I, being something of a scholar (for to this excellent man all students were scholars), would appreciate how absorbing such intellectual work could be. Yet every morning he would arrange his stock on the pavement in apparently perfect contentment. I believe he was a modestly happy man.

I paid the rent regularly and faithfully, as the months advanced and became less strange. The cost of my mother's room and board was somehow met. I did not see how our stay in Nice could last indefinitely. I should be sorry to say goodbye to M. Cottin, but I was conscious of having too little to do in Nice, apart from my weekly visits to my mother. I began to long for a return to normality.

But normality for my mother was now the Résidence Sainte Thérèse, the church of Sainte Rita, her newspaper, and the café on the corner. In a vain attempt to awaken earlier responses I plied her with questions about my father, to whom I felt vaguely disloyal in those straitened times, when family affections seemed to be a matter of prestige. My mother regarded my questions with a glint of irony, as if she knew that I was attempting to engage her in a therapeutic exercise destined to investigate her memory, and to see if she had any real recollection of her own history. That look of amused scepticism was the only truly adult expression I had seen on her face for months, years, probably; it returned her to adulthood in a way that singularly reduced my own age, as if once more I were a clumsy apprentice, or worse, that reader of fairy tales avid for romance that I had been as a child. It revealed her briefly as a woman with a mind and body of her own, one who, if she cared to, would understand the extent of her present humble mien, and reject it.

My father, of whom I had no memory, apart from that of an undifferentiated face overhanging mine, was someone who preceded and therefore excluded me. I did not even know why he had died, or how, for this was in a curious way a subject too delicate for me to approach. This aura of mystery had kept me at arms' length for most of my life. I understood, without being explicitly told, that it was too painful for my mother to discuss. I respected this, did not even mind too much, but now that our conversation was restricted to exchanges about other people's relatives I felt we should both lay claim to relatives of our own.

My inquiries were routine rather than heartfelt, but I had read an article in a magazine about an enterprise which encouraged retired people to put their reminiscences on tape in the interest of family history. Privately I considered such an undertaking worthless, but I could see that it might have some value if the participants were lonely and old. I assumed that my mother was lonely, if not old: how could she be otherwise? I understood her relief at being in a place of safety, in which her health had clearly improved, but I wanted her to react against her own passivity, which seemed to me disastrously premature. I saw a kind of willed collapse in what was in reality an habitual dreaminess. Because I never spoke of Simon, unwilling as I was to awaken painful memories, I felt that my father must pull his weight, must contribute something in the way of information, might even furnish some conversational appeal on those arid days in the middle of the week when there was no man in sight, other than Jérôme who polished the floors and who averted his eyes when anyone addressed him. A charming story, brought to life again by my diligent questions, might be of benefit to all.

'David?' she said. 'You funny girl. Why do you want to know that now?'

'Well, I never knew him.'

'You were unlucky. We both were. He died too young. We were both young. He was my first boyfriend, and I was his first girlfriend. People don't live like that any more.'

Virgins, I translated. I thought it a poor way to go about the business. Then I felt more sympathy for this unknown David. Simon had been a true father figure, supplying security, money, a beautiful house, whereas my father I saw as a sort of novice, returning every evening to his wife and baby after a day's virtuous occupation in the prelapsarian days of the 1950s.

'What did he do?' I asked.

'He worked in the library of the House of Commons. He loved it, though he was only a clerk. I dare say he would have stayed there if he had had the chance.'

'How did he die?'

'A heart attack. I don't really want to talk about this, Zoë. We loved each other. There's nothing more to say. In many ways my life ended when he died. But of course I had the baby to look after. I think of him a great deal.'

'And do you think of Simon?'

'Not in the same way.'

'Do you wish you had met Simon first?'

'Oh, no,' she said quickly. 'Simon was a different matter altogether.'

I waited for her to say more, but she was rigorously silent, as if I had intruded on a private memory. My role in her life seemed reduced by the legacy of that young husband and of her own younger self. Incredible though it might seem all the women at the Résidence Sainte Thérèse had once been young and ardent, and of that youth and ardour no trace remained.

'One comes to terms,' she said, smiling faintly, as if divining my thoughts. 'Mme de Pass was married three times. I dare say you find that unbelievable. And I have no doubt that she was in love more than once. But you will find that it is not always comfortable to remember such feelings. There is something indecent about old women who talk about their love affairs.'

'You are not old, Mama.'

'I have become old, Zoë. Now let's talk about something else. Where are we to live? When we go home, I mean.'

'I might go back in a day or two. Look around.'

'Do that, darling. Fortunately, we are in no hurry.'

I glanced at her, surprised, and saw that her face had gone

pale again, as it had in the clinic when some subject had exhausted her.

'Would you like to rest, Mama? Have I tired you?'

'I still get these silly feelings of weakness, as if I had come up against something too big for me to take in.'

'Would you like to come out? For a walk in the sun?'

'No, dear.' With an effort she waved goodbye to a man with a small girl, who waved back. 'Violette,' she said. 'A darling. I'll just go to my room until dinner. I feel a little tired. Sundays are almost too exciting.'

Here she smiled, with something of a return to her original irony. But the light soon went out of her eyes. I kissed her and prepared to leave, as that was what she wanted me to do. One or two ladies nodded to me kindly. They were all kind, had learned to tread a careful path among dangerous subjects. I had no doubt that they would be tactful, would make no reference to her change of colour. Dinner on Sunday evenings would be a quiet affair, since all emotion had been newly found to be exhausting. By Monday defences would be once more in place, and life would be resumed. The maids would come back and their youth would be acceptable, not yet endangered by illness and by the shadow of times forever concluded. Then it would be possible once more to propose a short walk, a cup of coffee. Some kind of balance would be restored, and it was one to which outsiders could be only briefly admitted.

She had forgotten, or seemed to have forgotten, my approaching birthday. Whether this was a simple oversight or a genuine desire to arrest time seemed to me equally significant. Simon would have made a fuss; he set a great store by family celebrations. Such celebrations were now inappropriate, and in the circles in which I now moved I could expect no congratulations. Even at the Résidence Sainte Thérèse birthdays were not celebrated, for all knew the downward path they now traced. Muted good wishes would be offered and received, but the ladies would have to wait until Sunday to acknowledge that triple kiss that signified that a son, a grandson, a nephew had remembered the date. And what were birthdays, or indeed any celebrations, without a man? I was fascinated, despite myself, by the persistence of this attitude, which was more than an attitude, an article of faith.

The young doctor who had assessed my mother when she arrived to take up residence had been regarded with a kind of contempt by the other ladies, for his eagerness, his boyishness, or rather his girlishness. He was good-looking, had all the components of masculinity, bright eyes, brilliant teeth, a lithe deference, yet he made as little impression as the man who came to polish the floors. Was he too assiduous, too anxious to please, too, in a word, kind? It was as if a man needed, to preserve his autonomy, to be respected. Those ladies, whose experience was, after all, authentic, would respond more to embarrassment, even to a kind of surliness as long as these were accompanied by proper male qualities: independence, a suspicion that women would overrule them if given half a chance, the sort of instinctive wariness that so often defeats women, even more than a desire to annexe, to conquer, to seduce.

I remembered that Adam had tried to explain this and had done so rather badly, but I retained from that conversation the idea that a certain resistance was called for on both sides if a love affair were to be experienced as truly powerful. Poor Dr Lagarde had shown none of this and had thus failed some elementary test. Women would submit to his professional care without embarrassment, judging him inadequate for any other kind of exchange. They would recognize that he was probably a good son, a faithful brother, but would cast him in these subordinate roles and abandon him to his fate, as though he were doomed to be forever eager and forever unimportant.

After his ministrations he was usually dismissed kindly, but without special appreciation, as if he were some kind of servant, for he lacked that essential quality that would have enabled them to regard him as a proper man.

I had been brought up to regard men as potential saviours, guardians, preservers, but this attitude was no longer viable. Perhaps it never had been. Those doughty French ladies, now reduced to quasi-impotence, knew that love was a battle-ground, on which territory had to be won, and were quite happy with this knowledge. That was why they were still so susceptible to male reluctance; that was why they so instinctively understood the resistance of Jean-Claude, the little boy who evaded his grandmother's embraces, not only from disgust at her old age but from an altogether masculine withdrawal from unsought ardour. And this was what the other women had understood. They had excused the child with a smile, and had no doubt cast a complacent backward glance at their own strategies of enticement. The confusion so unfortunately manifested by Mme Levasseur in the circumstances would be sincerely regretted on her behalf, but it would be instinctively condemned. They would take all the more care to receive their own offspring with the detachment, the worldly smile, that would signify not only to others, but also to themselves, that no pride had been relinquished in the course of their long incarceration, and that they were still capable of responding to a man in a way that the man would find acceptable. Yet with what keenness would the touch of a masculine cheek be received, and be remembered in the eventless days and evenings until the following Sunday, when the same good manners would prevail! What memories might be evoked by those long legs striding so confidently out of the door when the magic hour was over!

I was now caught up in this web, albeit only as an observer. I sometimes thought that I had much to learn from these women, or rather that they had nothing to learn from one such as myself. A daughter was not worth as much as a son in their eyes, and although they applauded our devotion to one another, my mother and I understood that, in the absence of a man, we had both undergone some process of diminution. The friends of my youth would have despised such an attitude, but I was uneasily aware that it had some validity. I was more aware of this on Sundays, when I witnessed the superb arrogance with which those filial kisses were received, as if, in the war between men and women, certain tactical victories were still *de rigueur*. My mother, in her perpetual innocence, was unaware of the complexities of this particular commerce. Her account of my father had not inclined me in his favour. No doubt a marriage in which each partner respected the innocence of the other was a marriage of true minds, but in my view it did not amount to the real thing. No fairy story would persuade me now. I required more in the way of artfulness, which is not a fairy attribute. And I would reject any pilgrimage which was content merely to anticipate a happy ending.

On Sunday evenings, I re-entered the noisy streets as if I had been freed on probation. Nice was never so shamelessly sexy as at that hour. Some visitors still find the winter season preferable, but the true Niçois came alive in the intemperate heat, the long days, and the even longer nights. From my room I could hear laughter into the small hours. At times like these I could even envisage maintaining a permanent foothold in Nice, or, if that were impossible, of returning at regular intervals, much as if Les Mouettes were still available to me. Instead of this I must re-evaluate our possibilities, if possibilities there were, of either remaining or returning. In the Cours Saleya I could still smell the aroma of the market, of the vegetables that had been crushed underfoot. The pâtisserie, where the Sunday gâteaux were bought, was still open, though its shelves were now bare. Cafés were full: the visitors were now in command, over-excited, over-tired, but beautiful in a way they would never be at home. It was impossible not to applaud their enjoyment, even if one were denied such enjoyment for oneself. Tomorrow would be a working day, yet something of that effervescence would remain. My own Sunday observances had left me tired, and my solitary cup of coffee was a mere gesture towards the fact that I was on my own again. I should go back to London for a few days, and on the following Sunday I should reacquaint my mother with news of 'home', her home, and no doubt my own in the days to come.

12

London was full of children, on their long summer break, and also of tourists, ambling slowly, clutching maps. 'Been away?' people inquired of each other, as if going away were the whole point of staying at home. My eye encountered brick house fronts and shady domestic trees which seemed to me utterly strange. This strangeness extended to the flat, which I remembered as from long ago. I felt little affection for it, but saw it quite objectively as a place which would accommodate two persons only with difficulty. The small second bedroom, which would be mine, was sparsely furnished with a single bed and a chair positioned near the window. The window looked out on that famous courtyard which the estate agent had so admired, but which kept the room in semi-darkness. At some point I must have gone out and bought that bedcover, which now struck me as intolerably jaunty; in a brief moment of optimism I had had an architectural engraving framed and hung on the wall.

Now it all seemed quite mute and alien, as did the kitchen with its dripping tap, and the sitting-room, with the books I no longer read. Those long winter days which were spent indoors had been banished, as if for ever, by the fierce alien sun which I now accepted as my birthright. But they would come again, and with them a proximity to my mother that was only half desired. She would be comfortable; I could see to that; but how would we fare in the dark days when we were obliged to scrutinize each other, for want of other company? My life would be hedged in by duties, most of them of an unwanted nature, most of them inherited from other guardians who were more competent than I could ever be. And my mother's longing for home might prove illusory once the reality of the small flat in the quiet street was seen as less reassuring than had been her distant view of it. Moving carefully around each other we should be polite, accommodating, yet uncomfortable, for nothing could revive those days of child-hood when such companionship was second nature to us both. Now events had intervened, had altered us; we might find ourselves to be strangers, and that would be the saddest outcome of all.

Conscientiously I went back to the estate agent and told him that I needed a bigger flat. He looked at me incredulously when I mentioned the price I was willing to pay, based on the sale of the flat that was still mine. 'There's a housing boom,' he told me. 'Prices have gone through the roof. My advice would be to sell your flat and rent somewhere. It's a short-term solution, I know, but I don't see how you can do otherwise.' He then showed me some details, and it was my turn to laugh incredulously. Every available property was out of our reach, or rather out of my reach, for I did not know exactly how much money my mother had had in her account. We were living on the sale of those policies in the safe in Walthamstow, sufficient for our present needs but no more. Our only hope was the Swiss bank account, but that seemed as far out of reach as it had ever been. We were needy; there was no other view to be taken. We could afford our present arrangements, we could even afford to live in my flat, but the future would depend on what I could earn.

And with this in mind I contacted Dr Blackburn, who supplied me with such work as I was able to undertake. He too was incurious, as incurious as M. Cottin. There was an index to be prepared, he said, for a thesis accepted for publication. It was what I wanted; it was work that could be done at home, either in London or in Nice, but it was not a prospect that filled me with pleasure. I had become used to spending my days out of doors, either on the way from the rue de France to the rue Droite, or, restlessly, in the late afternoons, among the crowds and the traffic of the Promenade des Anglais. It suited me now to be something of a vagrant, wandering at will, returning only very late to my room. Even in my bed I was reassured to hear the footsteps of passers-by, their snatches of conversation, just as I was reassured, on my visits to the Résidence Sainte Thérèse, to know that there were other conversations in the background, as my mother and I attempted to renew our intimacy after so many upheavals.

To sit alone in my room all day, in either of my rooms, whether in Nice or in London, no longer suited me. I wanted noise, company, above all company. It appealed to me to be rootless, as if in this state I might be available, at a moment's notice, to change, to expand, to divert my energies. And my energies were now considerable, for I was better fed, and in good health. The cataclysms that had brought me to this juncture had receded into the background. I no longer viewed them as monstrous, dangerous. What seemed much more dangerous now was the silence that threatened me, both physically and metaphorically. I collected the manuscript from Dr Blackburn and arranged to return it when I was next in London. When would that be? Oh, very soon, I said. I could always come over for the day. And then of course I might soon be home for good.

The one advantage the flat possessed over my room in the rue de France was that in it I could listen to music all day. Music was in fact an essential component of my working life, enabling me to concentrate on my current task and keeping me company in the quiet afternoons, when the street was silent and footfalls infrequent. Kind people said good morning, good evening, and finally goodnight, and I was thereby soothed into a sense of community. And these nice people had the tact not to interrupt the music for too long, so that the day was presided over by agreeable voices, by beautiful harmonies. I resolved to ask M. Cottin if I might have a radio in my room. I was spending so much money that I did not see why I should not benefit in this particular instance. M. Cottin would almost certainly say no, but the request would be carefully made, promising no music after lights out, and no pop music at all, ever. I could not live as austerely as M. Cottin, who seemed to manage with only his own company, and that of his customers, but he would surely acknowledge that the needs of the young were different. He approved of me because I made no demands, introduced no visitors, did not come back in the small hours, or indeed disturb him in any way. He was the ideal landlord, the missing link in our non-existent family relationships. There was no one to pass on family secrets, or to whom we might have recourse in times of greater trouble. This greater trouble I could foresee only too clearly. All the more reason then to make this strange interval more agreeable, for once back in London my life would be hedged around with restrictions which the outside world would do little to mitigate.

My two days in London stretched to four, and would have stretched to five had I not been troubled by the loss of contact with my mother. Not that I saw her more than once a week, but I could be reached by telephone should I be needed. M. Cottin was also relieved that I did not make use of the telephone, which was closely guarded. There was no need for me to do so, for I longed to be out in the air, and would make my way to the Résidence Sainte Thérèse early every morning, merely to say hello to the sister on duty and to inquire whether my mother had spent a good night. She was unaware of these daily visits, nor was there any reason why she should know about them. In truth they were not necessary, but it reassured me to pay my respects in this way, after which I was as free as I would ever be. With a radio, if I achieved one, the work I

137

would bring back with me would be possible, and more than possible, a pleasure. I reminded myself that the money I earned, pitiful though it might be, would help to pay for our requirements. At the back of my mind was the prospect of transporting my mother, together with those belongings I had managed to rescue for her, not to mention her fears and frailties, from a place of safety to one that depended entirely on my resources. It was not something on which I cared to dwell.

When I left the Résidence Sainte Thérèse after those unofficial morning visits and went out thankfully into the bright air I had an ache in my throat, as if I had consigned my mother to her fate as an inmate, a *pensionnaire*, an ageing schoolgirl, with a schoolgirl's limited choices. My own freedom to move about seemed to me to constitute a disloyalty. At the same time I was grateful that I could discharge duties which I should at some time inherit. I knew that we were coming to the end of the present arrangement. I could see that my muted London neighbourhood would be suitable for gentle walks, such as the tentative walks she already took in the steep crooked streets of the Old Town in Nice. I could see that the change would benefit her; I could also see that she would lose some of the stoicism she had absorbed from her French acquaintances, would become timid and valetudinarian with only myself for company.

I had to face up to the fact that the present circumstances suited me well enough. On the other hand I could not bear my sadness when I thought of her, and pictured her carefully reading her newspaper until it should be time for another meal, another interlude of cordiality, before the long afternoon began. The distance between us was growing. She spoke French now, attended the church of Sainte Rita, had her grey hair unbecomingly dressed by M. Hervé. And yet she longed for home. It would be her home rather than mine, the home she would reach at the end of the long parenthesis which had been her life in Nice. And if this should prove a disappointment there would be no going back. She would be as safe as I could make her, but that would be all . . . She would not be happy; neither would I. But I would assuage the habitual ache that somehow dominated those days in the sun, when I wandered, directionless, until it grew dark. At the end of the day I was glad to hide myself in my room. Yet the following morning I would retrace my steps, for no other reason than that of allaying my anxiety, my sadness. I am here, those visits seemed to say. I shall never leave you.

I shut up the flat with a lassitude which only slightly masked a feeling of dread. My dread was of my mother's growing disinclination to think for herself. She had, as I had been warned, become institutionalized, though this had indeed happened long ago. What courage it must take to grow old! And she was growing old in exile, as I should, in exile from our own lives. I knew that I should have to bring her home, as she always referred to it, if only to counter her inchoate longings. We should keep each other company, as if this had always been intended. No word of love, other than our own, would be there to lend support. And yet our fate seemed ineluctable. Normality was, or could be, London, my work, my dusky flat. And maybe she would recover her autonomy in these almost familiar surroundings. And maybe, in time, I should be strong enough to leave her.

Back in the rue de France I felt steadier. Maybe it was the clarity of the French language that lent some definition to my thoughts; speaking French made me feel braver. I laid out my work on my table and sat there, looking at it. I made a plan: we should go home in the autumn, when the next instalment of rent for our respective rooms was due. I should acquaint her of this when I visited her on the following day, Sunday. In that way she would have a little time to get used to the idea, which should not present too many difficulties. This decreed, I felt a sense of relief, but it was only the relief of having come to a decision. The future was now a manageable prospect, begun in extravagant circumstances, and now strangely, but misleadingly becalmed.

I went downstairs to M. Cottin and asked him whether he would object to my having a radio in my room. Not only might I have a radio, said M. Cottin, but he could get me a discount on any radio I cared to purchase. It so happened that his cousin, Louis Gros, had an electrical shop in the Baumettes district, and that on receipt of a letter from M. Cottin, would let me have a very advantageous price. In any event they owed each other a favour; this would serve. He summoned me into the room behind the shop, donned a pair of wire-framed spectacles, and sat down to write a letter to his cousin. This took some time. My presence, indeed my existence had to be explained; news had to be exchanged; the times had to be deplored. My eye followed the pen's spidery progress. I felt once more, as I had felt all day, that my life was being infinitesimally impeded, though with all the good will in the world, on the part of others. My profuse thanks struck me as excessive, but had the effect of bringing a rare smile to M. Cottin's face. I renewed my thanks and backed out precipitately into the shop, where I knocked a pair of sunglasses to the floor. Not to worry, he gestured: he was glad to be of service. After such an exuberant exchange it was a relief for us both to part company.

Out in the street the light seemed harsher, brassier, as if there might be a storm brewing. I was now obliged to visit M. Gros's shop, although it might have been wiser to stay indoors. It seemed a long walk under an unfriendly sky, and the Baumettes district was less reassuring than the rue de France, less amiable, less commodious, more functional. I found the shop, and waited until M. Gros had read his cousin's letter. He then showed me several radios of fairly hideous design and demonstrated their power. I bought the least expensive, which was also the biggest; it made a cumbersome package when wrapped up, and the plastic bag in which it came to rest was oversized. When I emerged into the street it was to a darkening sky and a rumble of thunder that sounded as if someone had dropped a metal tray. As heavy drops of rain began to fall I dived into a nearby café, my plastic bag banging against my leg. I was shown half-heartedly to a table, although the place was relatively empty, and it was too early for regular patrons. I ordered hastily from the menu, annoyed that I had been caught up in Mr. Cottin's designs. The kindness of strangers also had its disadvantages. The rain was now falling heavily, and I was without a jacket. I ate gloomily; it was only when I was drinking my coffee that I was able to sit back and look around. The few people who were eating at that early hour had seated themselves in shadowy corners, as if they were ashamed of the fact that they were obliged to eat alone. I lit a cigarette, resigned to waiting for the rain to end. Across the room I singled out a familiar face. Not that Dr Balbi was entirely familiar. But his was the only presence to which I could lay claim.

I marched resolutely over to his table, my uncouth bag marking me out, as if nothing else did, as an unwelcome presence.

'Miss Cunningham,' he said warily, laying down his fork with some resignation

'What a strange coincidence,' I remarked. 'I did not expect to see you here. But I am very glad of the opportunity to talk to you . . .'

'You could always talk to me at the clinic.'

'You know I never like to bother you. Dr Lagarde answers most of my questions. But as we are both here, in this rather bad café . . .'

'I am not in this rather bad café in my professional capacity. I have been visiting a friend in the neighbourhood.'

He seemed put out, from which I deduced that the friend was a woman, one of those discreet liaisons which take place off limits, and to which there are no witnesses. I even wondered whether Dr Balbi's friend were a prostitute, which would account for the reserve with which he viewed my intemperate presence.

'I am sure we are both anxious to be on our way,' I said suavely. 'I just wondered whether I might have a few words with you about my mother. I am not happy about her. We shall be going back to London soon, and I should like to know how much care she will need.'

'Your mother will always need some degree of care. I am not unduly anxious about her.'

'But you haven't seen her recently.'

'I am in touch with Dr Lagarde. He would have advised me of any change.'

'I have very little confidence in Dr Lagarde. And the other ladies don't seem to like him.'

'That is because he is young and they are old. There is nothing that I, or anybody else, can do about that.'

'She seems so vague, so passive, so patient. Like an invalid. Not like my mother any more.'

'You are not going to cry again, I hope?'

But I was. There was something about this man, his severity, his melancholy neatness, that reduced me to tears. I wanted him to take over, in a general rather than a particular sense, and tell me that I need have no concern for my mother. This he was clearly unwilling, or unable, to do. And I was being a nuisance; I had breached the only code of manners he was willing to understand, with himself on one side of a protective desk and the supplicant on the other. Instead of which I was untidy, unseemly, and I had caught him out at a bad moment. On his plate was a half-eaten millefeuille. I bent down as a passing waiter knocked over my bag and surreptitiously wiped my face. When I sat up again it was to see him regarding me with a fixed and by no means friendly expression.

'Aren't you going to finish that?' I said, indicating his plate.

This was another gaffe. He wanted no witnesses to any of his appetites. He pushed the plate away from him and held up his hand for the bill.

The rain had stopped, and had been replaced by a hectic burst of sunshine which held no conviction. There would be more rain that night. By now I had no desire to go back to the rue de France. What I urgently wanted, and was not to receive, was some sort of direction, which Dr Balbi resolutely refused to give. I felt some anger with him, even more with myself. I had been seen at my worst, as a crybaby, whose tears could not beguile. I felt my cheeks grow warm with the consciousness of how unattractive I must look. Yet I had no thought of persuasion in mind; I did not expect to sway him in my favour. I did not think him a worthy object of my interest. He was not tall, although his extreme thinness made him seem taller than he was. He gave the impression of having worn a double-breasted suit from a tender age, part of his disguise. I remembered his few remarks about his mother and her sacrifices. These seemed to have dried up his sympathies, the sort of sympathies with which Dr Lagarde was so prodigal. Dr Balbi probably, though not consciously, compared all his women patients with his sacrificial mother, to those patients' disadvantage. He seemed both righteous and self-righteous, an unpromising combination of qualities.

'You have your own man in London, of course?'

'I don't know. I don't think my doctor is competent . . .'

'You seem to have a very poor opinion of the medical profession. Most doctors are competent, though they vary in temperament.'

'Will you see my mother before we leave?'

'There is no reason for me to do so. I shall have a word with

Dr Lagarde, though he has expressed no particular anxiety on her behalf. Those ladies receive the best of care. They are in a protected environment. In many ways it would be better . . .'

'We can't afford it,' I said flatly. 'We have very little money . . .'

He regarded me with some scepticism. 'Would it not be better to let your lawyers take care of that?'

'I should have to be at home. I can't deal with it by telephone.'

'No.'

There was a silence. The interview seemed to be over. I leaned down and retrieved my poor radio. In the course of the afternoon I had forgotten why I had wanted it. I wondered whether I might ask Dr Balbi for a lift back to the rue de France, then dismissed the idea.

'Thank you for your time,' I said.

I stood up, feeling ten feet tall. The handles of my plastic bag had got twisted. And now I should have to thank M. Cottin all over again. He had shown me a dangerous kindness, and that had weakened me into desiring kindness from others.

'Goodbye, doctor,' I said. 'I'm sorry to have spoilt your meal.'

He stood up and held out his hand. 'Goodbye, Miss Cunningham.' He did not tell me not to worry, as an English doctor would have done, nor did he tell me to keep in touch. He did not tell me he was there to help. I knew exactly where I was with him, which was nowhere.

As I made my way home I realized that I was seriously annoyed. I thought that I should have been shown more courtesy. Yet he had been perfectly correct. I had interrupted his meal; I had taken advantage of him in an unprofessional setting, and he had as much right to be annoyed with me as I had with him. It was that mutual annoyance that had led us to square up to each other like antagonists. In other, more favourable circumstances this would have been unimportant.

But I had been seen as unattractive, and that was what I could not forgive, and for which I held Dr Balbi partly to blame. I was tired of being polite and tactful, as my lowly status now decreed. I should have preferred a furious argument with someone, anyone: I should have preferred all sorts of flamboyant behaviour, on both sides. It was not that I particularly admired him. I simply wanted to be recognized as a woman. My life was cast now among old people, for I saw my mother as old, as she did, and they were old people who dismissed my youth as an irrelevance. I could not join in their conversations, because my experience, in which they had no interest, was so different from theirs. Dr Balbi was nearer to my age than anyone I currently knew. I thought he must be in his early to mid forties, but in fact he looked no age at all. He had been seen by me in a setting and on an errand which belied his professional standing. Yet I was the more exasperated.

My mother seemed to have acceded to the prevailing belief that a daughter was of lesser value than a son, which was why I was so eager to attach a masculine presence to my own. She would have listened respectfully to Dr Balbi, who at least impressed one as a man, unlike poor Dr Lagarde, whose assiduity somehow diminished him. There seemed to be an unspoken consensus that his recommendations need not be followed, since he offered them as an option rather than as an order. His flirtatious manner, which should have been thought to work with the elderly, was viewed with a sceptical eye; my mother's new friends would only respond to a certain masculine rigour. And as they thought they knew their own ailments rather better than he could, they were in no sense dependent on him. Given the chance they would certainly have been dependent on Dr Balbi, which was probably why he did not intervene. Had he been in evidence they would have looked up to him; his severity might have reminded them of masterful men in their own distant pasts. Prudently he made his own inquiries to Dr Lagarde, whom he seemed to trust. Whether he did so or not was his own affair.

On the following day, Sunday, I told my mother that we should be going back to London in due course. 'How lovely,' she said, but she was more interested in Mme de Pass's son, who had arrived back from New York. All the ladies were interested, for this was the sort of man they could understand: robust, even brutal, but knowing his duties. He had a word with each lady in turn, adopted an attitude that was almost caressing, as he kissed hands, patted shoulders, joked. They looked at him worshipfully, laying aside their habitual toughness, smiling, even blushing. They accepted the fact that he was able to spend only a short time in their midst, for real men had important business and could not delay any longer than was necessary. His departure was almost as tempestuous as his arrival had been: he would be a subject of conversation at dinner. Mme de Pass, for all her three marriages, was obviously in love with her son, this big man who had once been a little boy. She would receive congratulations and would accept them as her due. When he left the emotional temperature dropped noticeably, and faces were turned once more to those who sat patiently beside them. He was their type, as the rest of us were not.

My mother differed from the others only that her response was one of interest, of respect, as if she were now on the far side of a sexuality that had proved only intermittent. Yet when M. de Pass left the room her colour faded, and she relapsed into the gentle dreaminess that I had always known, but with one important difference. She seemed to know that she could no longer join in, had no part in the world's business. The other ladies were tactful: for all her relative youth they understood her to be more at risk than they were themselves. They were used to her obvious frailty; she had gained their affection, rather as a younger relative might have done. An occasional sharp glance was directed at her in those moments of weakness, but no officious concern was expressed. They were all face to face with mortality, and their own took precedence. That was why it was so important not to give way, even to the extent of asking her how she felt. That was my job, and I discharged it badly. I was always glad to leave her on those Sunday evenings, and to be out once more in the beautiful streets. At such times our homecoming seemed to be a matter of dire necessity, and also a more hazardous outcome altogether.

13

Mme Levasseur, the lady with the crooked face who had befriended my mother, suffered another stroke and died. She had been found at the foot of the stairs while attempting to go up to her room, and transported to Dr Balbi's clinic, where she did not survive the night. I learned all this on one of my morning visits, slightly earlier than usual. I had been eager to get out into the bright day, eager to have the visit behind me. I had thought it to be routine, no more than a brief contact which would then leave me free. Instead I encountered anxious whisperings, and Sœur Elisabeth trying to control and reassure a group of ladies who had gathered in the foyer. The news had travelled swiftly; rightly or wrongly – and I think rightly – it had been thought preferable to announce it straight away.

The sisters obviously had a friendlier attitude towards death than those for whom it represented a dread reality. Voices were lowered, expressions doleful. Yet Mme Levasseur had not been much liked. In other circumstances the ladies, having repaired their morale, would have regarded her demise as evidence of further incompetence, on a par with her intemperate quest for kisses from her grandson. But this was the very early morning and the death had taken place too recently for attitudes to have been perfected. There was even muted discussion, a desire for company. Yet they could not reassure each other, for all were vulnerable. The 'accident', as they called it, was regrettable. It would take some time for them to come to terms with it. An effort of will was called for, and in the early morning, after an unusually disturbed night, they were not quite able to summon up the requisite determination. This was the ugly face of the

Résidence Sainte Thérèse, a place where people lived out their remaining lives before being claimed by the sort of event that had overtaken Mme Levasseur.

As a special concession I was allowed to see my mother, who was naturally distressed. I found her in bed, under the crucifix, two spots of colour burning in her normally pale cheeks.

'Zoë,' she cried. 'Have you heard the news?'

'They are talking about it downstairs.'

'I was very fond of Madeleine,' she said, still in a slightly loud voice. 'The others didn't like her. She was not popular.' Again the school parlance. 'They thought she was common.' Another word from the past. 'But she was unhappy, you see. She felt out of place. Well, we are all out of place. But she wanted to go home, to live with her son and daughter-in-law. And to see her grandson every day. Of course, they didn't want that. And she was frightened.'

'What frightened her?'

'Everything. She felt unloved, that was what frightened her. As well it might.'

'Have you had your coffee, Mama?'

'I don't want coffee. I want tea! Oh, for a cup of tea!'

'You shall have tea at home. In those big cups you always liked.'

She smiled gladly. 'I got them at Peter Jones. Is it still there?'

'Of course it's still there. It won't be long now. You remember what I told you.'

'I remember. Is it true?'

'I promise you. But you must make the best of it here, until we leave. Is there anyone else you might sit with?'

'Mme Lhomond. That silly woman. A sweet nature, but rather slow-witted. When we go out together she drags on my arm, talking all the time. It makes me feel very old, though I shouldn't mind it.' She sighed helplessly. 'I feel out of my depth, Zoë.'

'That's quite natural. And it won't be for much longer. Won't you come out and have coffee with me? I haven't had any breakfast either.'

In reply she pulled off her nightdress, in a way that shocked me. Yet she did not seem to be afflicted with any particular shyness, having evidently forgotten that she was an ageing woman face to face with someone who was still intact. I helped her out of bed, took her into the adjoining *cabinet de toilette* and left her there. For a terrible moment I thought that she might expect me to wash her. I shut the door resolutely and wandered over to the window, aching for a glimpse of the outside world. But there was nothing to be seen from here, only a corner of the courtyard, several empty boxes, and a row of dustbins. In the distance I could hear the sound of a van, come to deliver the day's supplies. Only the ardent sky served to remind one of the season, which was high summer. In contrast the room seemed dark, as would all interiors deprived of that light. The sounds of splashing ceased; a smell of soap replaced the odours of the night. I noticed them, as I noticed them every morning. However rigorous the efforts, and I did not doubt that they were rigorous, nothing could quite disguise that miasma, which was of women living together. It would have pertained to any school, any convent. It served to remind one of the desirability of other arrangements. Here, among women, efforts would be made, but such efforts would be nugatory, for however great one's care one would recognize in others that negligence that time bestows and which is time's sad legacy.

Dressed, my mother looked more like herself. I placed my hand under her elbow and guided her down the stairs. In the foyer Dr Lagarde and Dr Balbi were attempting to console a red-faced man who was trying not to weep. This was Levasseur *fils*, I presumed, and I could see why his mother had been thought of as somewhat inferior in rank. Any tiny distinction would have been seized on with alacrity in this place where there was nothing to do. Mme Levasseur had confided in my mother, and in no one else, that her son was in the construction business, as I might have observed for myself from his footwear, massive dusty trainers of the kind worn by men on a building site. He was apparently a successful entrepreneur, able to afford the best of care for his mother, but preferred not to visit her too often, leaving that task to his wife and the boy. Yet he seemed so sincerely affected, struggling against his tears while being assured that his mother had suffered no pain, would have been unconscious at the time of her death. This glimpse of an adult man newly deprived of his mother moved me strangely. I ceased to think of my own condition, and felt a desire to reach out, to comfort. A woman would have managed better, I thought, than this poor fellow, who now resembled no one so much as his son, Jean-Claude, source of pleasure and of pain.

My mother laid a hand on his arm and murmured condolences, which occasioned more tears. He was a graceless sight, a fact registered by both the doctors, seen here at a natural disadvantage since they had failed to prevent death from taking place. My mother told the son how she had found a friend in Mme Levasseur, who had been so kind to her when she had first come to take up residence. He listened eagerly, smiling from time to time as he allowed her to take over. This she seemed willing to do, even too willing. In a moment she would ask him if he had a handkerchief, and would generally soothe him into acceptance of the inevitable. This might have been touching, but I did not wish to see it.

'You are going out?' questioned Dr Balbi, who had observed these manoeuvres with a faint smile.

'We have not had our coffee,' I told him.

'There is a place on the corner. It should not be too busy now.'

I looked at him in some surprise. This solicitude was new, but maybe he too was affected by the death of this unknown man's mother, of any man's mother. I was slightly irritated by this, and yet I had seen the man's tears, had registered the softening of Dr Balbi's attitude, although it was Dr Lagarde who seemed uncharacteristically gloomy. He too was a mother's favourite son, as his normal behaviour proclaimed to the world at large. His mother's preference had not made him a hero, as Freud had said it would, but had turned him into a sexless acolyte for whom his mother would always come first. He hovered at Dr Balbi's elbow, as if Dr Balbi were Jesus and he merely one of the disciples. And like the disciples he was outclassed, not able to give a good account of himself. Yet with such a charismatic teacher he would eventually amount to something. His slow climb to man's estate was, fortunately, something we should not be here to witness.

M. Levasseur shook my mother's hand wholeheartedly, and at last I was able to guide her out into the sun. The café was empty, for the usual habitués were on their way to work, and the later visitors not expected for a couple of hours. She preferred to sit inside; that was where she had sat with Mme Levasseur, the fact of whose death and absence was just beginning to crystallize.

'Had you met the son before?' I asked her, curious as to the origins of her briefly authoritative behaviour.

'No. I recognized him from the way she described him. Poor man; he will go home to a wife who will be relieved to have the matter over and done with. There will be little comfort there. And the boy hated those visits. She was so unhappy on Sunday evenings. I was of little use to her then.'

'Eat a croissant, Mama. And drink your coffee.'

'I don't think I can. I don't want anything to eat.'

'The coffee, then. And tell me about Mme Lhomond. You might as well have some company while you are still here.'

She smiled. 'I have you, darling. Mme Lhomond is a good-natured silly woman who is too naïve to be malicious or unkind. That, alas, does not make her more interesting.'

She brought her coffee cup to her lips, then abruptly put it down again. 'I don't think I can drink this after all,' she said, bewildered.

I looked at her. The brief hectic colour had faded from her face, the unnatural excitement of recent events had deserted her, leaving behind a mournful impression of disaster. I went to the counter and paid the bill. Both our cups had remained untouched, though I was now hungry and would have lingered. But then had I been on my own I would have stayed outside, in the light, not sheltering from a day which was already radiant. Had I been alone I should have made my way to the market in the Cours Saleya, where I could feast on the colours and smells, the evidence of appetite, of nourishment, of life itself. The women there would be robust, noisy, ample; they would shout without embarrassment, embrace one another, give every sign of rude health. No inhibitions there, no circum-spection; they were as lavish with their insults as with their greetings. And there would be no hurt feelings, for the common currency was boldness, and those who did not possess it might just as well stay away.

Instead of that ideal boldness I accompanied my mother's slow steps back to the Résidence Sainte Thérèse, alarmed and puzzled by her sudden loss of vigour. She had begun the day well, and apart from that careless act of undressing, had shown her usual delicacy of feeling, particularly with regard to M. Levasseur. Now she looked haggard, even slightly unkempt; a strand of her grey hair blew gently against my cheek as I attempted to take something of her weight. We reached the end of the street in time for her to recover slightly. Nevertheless her hand went to her heart, as if to still its rapid beat.

Dr Balbi was still in the foyer with M. Levasseur, who did not seem anxious to leave. For all his hefty build he was just another disciple in attendance. Dr Balbi, a man of few words at the best of times, was clearly finding his presence onerous. He looked up with something like relief as we entered, shook M. Levasseur's hand with finality, and motioned one of the sisters to take him up to his mother's room to collect her sad possessions. This was no job for a man. I imagined more tears as he faced the pitiful evidence of her clothes, her abandoned necklaces. But there would be no need for fortitude among these relics, for this was the proper place for tears. And when he went downstairs again Dr Balbi would no longer be there, having made good his escape, and leaving Dr Lagarde to deal with further distress.

But Dr Balbi was still there after I had seated my mother in the salon, which was almost empty. Many ladies were resting in their rooms or perfecting their appearance after the events of the previous night, when their sleep had been disturbed by the sound of precipitate footsteps, muted exchanges, all the paraphernalia of an emergency. I thought it better for my mother to have company, even the company of Mme Lhomond. I went in search of one of the maids, to ask if she might have some tea.

'Tea?' questioned Dr Balbi. 'But you have just had coffee.'

'She didn't want any.'

'And you?'

'I don't seem to have had any either.'

'Then you will have some now. As I will. It has been a long night.'

We went back to the café, where the proprietor seemed to know him, know what he wanted. All I wanted was coffee, though the smell made me feel slightly sick. Dr Balbi ate decisively, motioning me to do the same. I took a croissant from the basket and nibbled it, then found that I was hungry after all. I drank my coffee, in no hurry to leave.

'That's better,' he said. 'I thought you were going to faint.'

'You speak very good English,' I remarked. 'And no, I am not going to faint. I have never fainted in my life.'

'I had a year in Southampton.'

The consonants slightly eluded him, but the accent was excellent.

'In a hospital?'

'Of course in a hospital. It was an exchange. I hated it.'

'Why?'

'The work was, as always, interesting. But it meant another horrible room . . .'

'You missed your mother.'

'. . . in a terrible little house, with patterned carpet on the stairs. I preferred our building in Marseilles. It was noisy, but you knew there were other people around, all in the same boat, with the same degree of poverty. Yes, I missed my mother.'

'How did you find this house?'

'One of the nurses at the hospital lived there with her mother. That, as you can imagine, was frustrating. In the end I had to marry her. It seemed the only thing to do.'

I was shocked. 'Didn't you love her?'

'One has the lovers one can afford. And I wanted to get her away from there. I thought that once we were at home, once she was with my mother . . .'

'And of course they didn't get on.'

'And she was homesick.'

'For Southampton?'

'Apparently.'

'Are you still married to her? Did you divorce?'

'Yes, we divorced.'

'And then you returned to your respective mothers. What a sad story.'

'Yes, it is. I am fully aware of that.' He patted his mouth with a paper napkin. 'Miss Cunningham.' It was a conclusion rather than a preamble.

'Do you live alone?'

'Yes, I live alone. Quite near you. I sometimes catch sight of you in the early mornings, or in the evenings. I know you are concerned, not only for your mother, but for yourself. My advice is to use your energies while you still have them. You have friends?'

'I have no lovers, if that is what you mean. I had them once, but that was when I was free.'

'One is never free. One only has the illusion of freedom. One is never free of obligations, whether explicit or implicit. The latter are the worst.'

'That poor man . . .'

'Levasseur? There you have the tragedy of a man who knows he will never see his mother again.'

'Even though he avoided her when she was alive?'

'When she was alive he was a man. When she died he became a child again. I will walk you back, if you are ready.'

'You will see my mother?'

'For a few minutes only. As you will. And you will not return until Sunday. The sooner matters return to normal the better it will be for her. For them all.'

Dr Balbi's relative loquacity had taken me by surprise, as had his confessions, which were made without any apparent reluctance. If this were a subtle form of treatment I was grateful, for it had worked. I had been jolted out of my nervousness by the sort of exchange that was normal between a man and a woman. My mother too brightened when we made our entrance together. There was an empty cup beside her, and she had her newspaper to hand.

'Has she eaten anything?' she asked.

'Yes, she is quite all right. She will see you on Sunday, as usual.'

'You have been very kind. You know we are going home soon?'

He patted her hand. 'Yes, I know all about it. That is why I want you to rest while you are here. You will need to be strong.'

'Oh, I shall be. Go home now, darling. I don't want to spoil your day.'

Dr Balbi appeared to endorse this. I saw that she would do whatever he told her to do. I kissed her and left, but lingered outside in case he wanted to talk to me. Yet when he came out he strode off in the opposite direction, without looking round. From that I deduced that my particular consultation with him was over.

I think I knew then, at the precise moment at which I saw his slight figure disappear into the distance, that my mother was doomed. I owed this insight not to her condition, to which I was accustomed, but to Dr Balbi's tact in diverting me to a story of ordinary love and disappointment. I knew it; Dr Balbi knew it; the only person who did not know it was perhaps my mother. The fiction we all entertained of the return home was simply that: a useful fiction, to which she clung as I had once clung to those fictions I had pursued in the days of my early reading. Such reading was optimistic; that I saw now, though I had once not thought so. The illusions, or delusions which I had so eagerly accepted, would no longer serve. Neither would the guileless trust I had had that there was a right true end to every endeavour. I felt a childish disappointment that I had been deprived of my happy ending, that I would be obliged to struggle on without that assurance. Nothing had changed, and yet everything had changed. My task was now to let my mother believe that her hopes, wishes, fears were all in my care,

157

that whatever came about would be within my competent grasp. I must show no misgivings, no hesitations. I would transform myself into the sort of useful fiction that beguiles one on a dull afternoon and is remembered faithfully, even when a harsher truth should prevail.

I did not intend to have any far-reaching discussion with her. The time for honesty was past. I blushed when I remembered my clumsy questions to her about my father, though they had seemed to amuse her. If they did it was because they were out of place, because her life had given her too much time for reflection, because she needed no reminders from me of events which she had internalized so thoroughly. The flash of irony that had greeted those questions was an indication of my immaturity. She knew what I wanted, another touching fiction, which she had refused to provide. That was the last time that I had had any sense that she was an adult and that I was her child. But the position was too difficult to maintain. All the time she had really craved the alternative: no thought, no memory. Hence her curious acquiescence, her contentment, even, in the company of Mme Levasseur, of Mme Lhomond. For my visits she put on a show of interest. That interest, I now saw, was limited. Her lack of curiosity about how we should live was more significant than I had realized. What was to be managed, I would manage: she would have no part in it.

I was grateful for Dr Balbi's finesse, his generosity in reminding me that a world existed beyond the one I was now obliged to inhabit, even if it meant plundering his laconic secrets in order to do so. Yet he had not seemed reluctant. He was a successful man, but even he had succumbed to the lure of conversation. He had no particular liking for me: if anything I was a nuisance who appeared at the wrong time in the wrong places. He had seemed unnaturally alert after his sleepless night, perhaps because of it. He was more authoritative than I had given him credit for, aware of the dilemmas of others, even if he refused to indulge them. I thought of him in that suburban house, with the patterned carpet, of his frustrations as a young man, as a young husband. He was now as he had perhaps not intended to be: dour, self-sufficient, powerful. His power seemed to come from all sorts of negation. I saw the perverse strength that lack of intimate satisfaction can bestow. Quite simply, he had left his youth behind. I should now have to do the same.

I should also, at some point, have to go home. Homecoming is a theme around which many useful fictions have been built. One thinks of Ulysses, but he had Penelope waiting for him. Penelope herself had the suitors to distract her. My mother had been right all along. The home she cherished was devoid of realistic details; it existed in limbo, perhaps in memory. She believed in it as an act of faith, which is the opposite of reality. For as long as she did so she was becalmed. The details could be left to me, for I had become the narrator of that particular story. Magical thinking would do the rest.

My own homecoming would be not the end of exile but the beginning of it. I felt as if I should be saying goodbye to the natural world, and to my own memory, which was of those early days at Les Mouettes, when my movements and my impulses were unrestricted, and were allowed to be. We never mentioned Simon now. By common consent he had been relegated to the past, a past which had been brought to an abrupt conclusion, like an episode from another life, or from someone else's life. The people who had existed in that life had been healthy, untouched, with nothing to fear. With Simon's genius removed – and I saw now that it had been a kind of genius – we had acceded to a world of accident, of illness, of poor company, in which it was no longer possible to think of a good outcome. For the good outcome had presented itself, had been embraced, and had then been lost. Even if my mother had not been entirely comfortable in that context she had accepted its reality. I remembered her shy pleasure at Simon's initial approaches, her awakening to new possibilities. How then had she turned so completely into this unknown woman, who accepted other women as her natural companions?

In the rue de France I switched on the radio, listened for two minutes to a winsome contemporary string quartet, and switched it off again. The radio was redundant: a displacement activity. When I left I would give it to M. Cottin, as well as all the other modest paraphernalia I had managed to collect. I would need no reminders of this life, which would always register as a life I had lost. Home is a closed world, with its own rules and customs, lived mainly indoors, with the usual obligations. I thought that I could deal with absence of company. I had grown so used to my own that it seemed entirely natural to spend days communing only with myself. The visitors to the Résidence Sainte Thérèse all fell into a sort of heartiness that denoted an effort being made. I had thought I had managed to avoid this. With my new perception of the day's events I saw that such artificiality was a useful stratagem. The affections were still there, but rendered harmless by a carapace of self-protectiveness. If one were to survive one must wear a mask, for to go through the world without one was to court disaster.

My task now was to wear such a mask with my mother, in order to protect us both. I should be the competent daughter, and if I felt any uneasiness, as those dutiful sons so obviously did, I should dismiss it as an unenviable necessity. In time I should develop the same sort of heartiness, so that all the residents would be comforted by the prevailing mood, and no one should be left out of that collusive company. I had seen the relief on the faces of those visitors as they left, the smile fading, the nod of recognition to others in the same boat. Only the following day would restore them to themselves. The company of the able-bodied would reassure them once again that nature was on their side, and if nature needed a little help from time to time, needed to be postponed, or relegated to a dark corner, there was no harm intended. Surely it was more honourable to joke and to encourage than to cast oneself, weeping, at the feet of a parent now in ruins?

I would tackle my work some other day. For the moment I would go out and walk until I was too tired to walk any further. I had not eaten, but was not hungry. I wanted space, light, air, and all of these were more imperative than food. I had no fear of the night; indeed I had no fears at all when I was out of doors. I walked down to the shore, and stood for a while listening to the rattle of the shingle as the sea sucked it down, only to return it with the next wave. The light had faded suddenly, as it did here. There were few other walkers, sometimes the occasional couple entwined, pensive now, the last day of the holiday approaching.

I looked about me for somebody familiar, though I knew no one. Dr Balbi had said that he lived not far from me, but had prudently given no details. He had added that he saw me sometimes, from his car, presumably, may have known something of my habits. He lived alone, as I did, but could call on company when he needed it. At that moment I was not unhappy. Not, that is, until I turned to make my way back up the shingle to the steps that would restore me to the street. The light had been so subtle, the sounds so beguiling that I had thought of waiting out the tide. Then some sort of common sense prevailed and I prepared to make my way home. Glancing up I saw a figure watching me from the Promenade. This figure was in darkness, yet that slightness, that sparseness: surely I had seen them before? The figure moved away, melted into the surrounding gloom. I gave no hint of recognition, neither did he. Yet I did not doubt that Dr Balbi, perhaps taking an entirely coincidental evening walk, perhaps not, had seen me, had even followed me, and had nevertheless remained out of sight. I thought, with some timid feeling of comfort, that this event might be repeated. I should not refer to it. Neither would he. But if it did happen again, as I hoped it might, we should acknowledge it, accept it, as something that had been prompted by nature, and not yet disguised by an appropriate mask.

14

The men I had known, in particular Adam, had been charm-
ingly evasive, mocking my sincerity. I would take care not to
be so sincere again. But it would be difficult.

I took to walking in the very late evening, sometimes after
nightfall. Instinctively I would make my way to the shore, from
which I imagined I could survey the huge crescent of the Baie
des Anges. I could not, of course, but I liked the feeling of
infinity after a restricted day in my room poring over my texts.
Behind me cars kept up their rushing speed along the Corniche
road, but on the water's edge it was possible to capture silence.
I would look round from time to time to see if anyone was
following me, but for two nights nobody was.

The second time I saw him I approached him with surprisingly few misgivings.

'Dr Balbi.'

'Miss Cunningham.'

Yet I found that without sincerity there was little to say. I
tried my best, although my technique was poor.

'You too like to walk in the dark, then?'

'I have always liked the dark. It is flattering, particularly to
an ugly man.'

'You look quite personable in this light.'

'I dare say. Do not let that deceive you.'

'Oh, I shan't.'

There was a brief silence. We had come to the end of our
opening gambits.

'I will walk you back,' he said. 'You should be in bed. It is
late.'

'What happens now?' I asked.

'I am not prepared to think about that.'

'Are you opposed to me on principle?'

'On principle, yes.'

'Your position . . .'

'My position.'

'I have never been very good at this,' I said. 'I frequently find myself at a disadvantage, trying to guess what the other person is thinking, or even wanting. But the other person rarely says, or not in words I want to hear.'

'Why do you think you are not very good, as you say? Most people want the same thing.'

'Then why can't they say so?'

'It is very alarming, the sort of declaration you say you want. One finds one has given too much away. And been poorly repaid.'

'I only want what could be freely given. And should be freely given.'

'You place too much emphasis on freedom. There is no such thing.'

'Yet I have known that sort of freedom. You must have known it too. Your mother . . .'

'Yes, that love was a sort of freedom. You have it with your own mother. But, as you have discovered, it turns into something more tragic. One is obliged to care, to take responsibility, just at the time when one's own life beckons.'

'And yet one is left with that memory, that imprinting . . .'

'One cannot remain in love with one's mother for life.'

'Yet, that sort of love remains the ideal.'

'That is the love of an infant, a nurseling. We cannot go back.'

'I want to go forward, not back.'

'How do you see yourself in, say, ten years' time?'

'That is what I can't do. Once I leave this place, as I shall have to do eventually . . .' He nodded. '. . . I see myself leading a very dull life, doing very dull work, waking up each morning in a panic, wondering how to fill the day. I shall be living automatically, artificially, pretending to be like everybody else. I shall fill the day somehow, shop, cook, settle down with my books, perhaps walk in the evenings . . . No, I shan't walk in the evenings. By the evening I shall be frightened again, wondering how to pass the time.'

'Does this life you describe contain no other people?'

'There are friends, of course, the friends I have left behind, and whose activities I hear of long after they have taken place. I could not emulate their lives. They seem so busy, planning holidays all the time. And the strange thing is I think they envy me here. To the unknowing the South of France means leisure, pleasure. The holiday syndrome, all over again.'

'Whereas you see it as a place of . . . what?'

'Sadness, I think. Above all, sadness. I am here against my will, yet I cannot bear to think of my eventual departure. That will mean the end of everything.'

'You may marry.'

'No. I shall never marry. I don't seem to have the knack.'

'Most people marry. Even I married once.'

'But you would not do so again.'

'No, that is true.'

'One thinks of marriage as the end of the story.'

'There is only one end to our story.'

'You mean . . .?'

'Yes, I mean that.'

'Are you warning me of something? Is there something I should know?'

'At this stage you know as much as I do. Whether you know it as consciously I cannot say.'

'So that one day I shall leave empty-handed. With very few stories with which to entertain my friends.'

165

'What stories would entertain them?'

'Oh, love, of course. Women lose interest if you deprive them of this sort of exchange. They think you are concealing something. Or else that you are a crashing bore.'

'Do women count on love to such an extent?'

'Of course they do. Don't men?'

'Oh, sometimes, I dare say.'

'You are very cautious.'

'Well, it is my job not to rush to conclusions.'

'But don't you get lonely?'

'Naturally. Most people know loneliness. Even with a partner one can know loneliness.'

'Mme Levasseur was lonely when her grandson refused to kiss her. I saw her face. I never want to look like that.'

'The rejection of a child carries a shock. But one knows that the child means little by it, except petulance, distaste.'

'Rejection by an adult is worse.'

'We have all known such rejections. They are not always significant.'

'But I think they are.'

'Your circumstances are perhaps extreme. You see everything from a vantage point of isolation.'

'Strangely, I mind less and less about the isolation. But I know that this will increase in ways I am beginning to appreciate.

'You have no other family?'

'No, we were always together, my mother and I. I remember two women coming to see us when I was quite young. They were some sort of connection on my father's side. They were sorry for my mother, which annoyed me; I thought that they were trying to take her away. They were delighted when she married again. They thought that that was a natural conclusion. Instead of which the marriage changed her life for ever. And mine.'

166

'I believe she is not unhappy.'

'She should be.'

'You talk like a young person. I have observed this process for much longer than you have.'

'This process. Is that what it is?'

'Oh, yes. We shall all know it one day.'

'Who can console one for one's own death?'

'Ah, that is a very big question, one nobody can answer. The choir of angels, the company of saints? That is what the sisters believe. In many ways they are to be envied. Such trust has kept them young. They could not do the work they do if they were not convinced of eternal life.'

'What a prospect. I only want one life.'

'That is all you will get. Come, I will buy you a tisane. Then you will sleep. There has been enough talking for one night.'

'I always feel that when a man spends money on you it is some sort of concession.'

'It is only a few francs.'

'Maybe that is all you can afford. Emotionally, I mean.'

'Quite.'

He led me down a side street, away from the traffic and the noise. My one regret at that point was that I might not be able to find it again. Yet even this was only a passing reflection, for I felt, whether rightly or wrongly, that the time for contrivance was past. Those anxious moments I had experienced with other men, the fatal question – 'When will I see you again?' – had faded from my mind as though they had never existed. That not quite accidental meeting had allayed old fears. This fact alone made me quiescent, although quiescence in itself can be a danger. We sat at an ordinary table in an ordinary café, and I obediently drank the faintly nauseous decoction that he had ordered for me. I sensed that any further discussion would be unnecessary; a silence had intervened which it would be difficult to break. Dr Balbi drank coffee, in spite of the late hour. I did not think it appropriate to comment on this; his habits were his own affair. So were his appetites, for they did not seem to include me.

In other circumstances this would have alienated or alarmed me, but now I did not seem to mind. For that short interval I was content to obey his rules. His conditions had been stated; he had a stern professional conscience, and to him I was, if not a patient, the nearest relative a patient could have. He seemed beyond desire, and briefly I was the same, content to register the evening as one of the best I had ever spent. What conferred this realization was Dr Balbi's absolute calmness, which had a similarly hypnotic effect on myself; my habitual agitation had fallen away, leaving behind an impression of benevolence, not the right true end of my childish imaginings, so much as of circumstances which might be permitted to turn in my favour. I was in no way attracted to him. He was not an attractive man. He had authority, and it was to that authority that I was willing to submit. I wanted to ask him whether he had been looking for me, or had been merely taking a walk on his own account. I did not, for I had the sense to realize that this might expose him in a moment of weakness, and I had no desire to do so. I sipped my tisane and looked ahead of me, at the few passers-by still enjoying the evening. It was very late, near to midnight, but neither of us seemed in a hurry. Finally he signalled the waiter for the bill, and turned to me.

'Your main concern at the moment is your mother,' he said.

It seemed both a prediction and a promise.

'You will see her again?' I asked.

'As I have explained to you, she is in the care of Dr Lagarde.'

'But at the clinic . . .'

'The clinic is where I work. The Résidence is where Dr Lagarde works.'

'Yet, I should like to feel that I could call on you.' Consult you, I should have said, but it was too late. 'Does the clinic belong to you?' I hurriedly asked, aware that the question was unseemly.

'I have a controlling interest. The owner is Dr Thibaudet, whom I think you once knew.'

I nodded, aware that I had not contacted the Thibaudets, as I should have done. My mother had reported one visit, which had not been repeated. This had rather surprised me, though on the whole I was relieved that they had not seen her too often in these reduced circumstances. Besides, Simon had been their friend; their hospitality had been for Simon, only incidentally for his wife.

'He always asks after her,' Dr Balbi continued. 'He is a good man. I am glad to say that he is enjoying his retirement. One never knows.'

'So the clinic belongs to you both?'

'It will be mine eventually.'

'Is that what you wanted, all those years ago in Marseilles?' For I was as familiar with his childhood as I was with my own.

'I believe it was, yes. Or almost. With one significant difference: I wanted to help poor people. My patients at the clinic are comfortably off. I wanted to help the sort of people I had grown up with. But I was ambitious, I suppose, so I followed a certain path.'

'I might even have met you at the Thibaudets' house,' I remarked.

'We do not mix socially. He regards me, still, as his assistant, one to whom he issues advice and directions. Our professional relationship depends on my showing respect. Which of course I do. Are you ready to leave?'

Yes, I was ready. I was suddenly tired, a fact which Dr Balbi had registered before I had. I got up painfully, like a much older woman. He did not offer his hand, merely watched me, as if checking an earlier impression. I would have welcomed an arm to lean on, but recognized that any request would seem out of place. The walk home lost something of its charm, the charm it would have possessed if I had known that I should see him again. Nor could I invite him in; that was out of the question. I still believed that he had matters in hand, though he seemed to be regretting his earlier confidences. I could sense a new awkwardness emanating from him, a regret that he had taken leave of his habitual reserve. How did this man ever relate further to a woman? By seeking out professionals? I felt a disappointment on both sides. He too was aware of gaffes: talk of the clinic had been a mistake. It had been a mistake to mention Dr Thibaudet, for that too took me back into territory which had been closed off. I had no desire to resurrect the connection with Les Mouettes. If Simon had brought us, my mother and myself, to this place, he had also deserted us, leaving us to fend for ourselves. Of Les Mouettes nothing remained. We might have been interlopers all along.

Brought back once more to a realization of our very real neediness, I felt a certain resentment towards Dr Balbi's easy acceptance of the situation. This increased the distance between us, and left me feeling angrily without resource. Dr Thibaudet had not sought me out, had merely consigned my mother to this unknown man who had been professionally bound to exercise some duty of care. Then he too had discharged the obligation on to Dr Lagarde. I saw this as a form of dereliction, of indifference, where I would have welcomed anxiety, ardour, even, on my own behalf. Particularly on my own behalf. For there was no further indication that Dr Balbi had any interest in me beyond my weak connection with his professional colleagues. I was a case, but a case without a history. I was therefore of no great interest. The courtesies had been observed, as they always would be, but perhaps no more. I blushed when I considered how eagerly I had expressed my willingness to know him better. He had dealt with it expertly, having no doubt had to deal with it before. Women would respond to him precisely because he was impervious to them. And yet, as I supposed, he had come to find me on the beach.

At my door I shook hands firmly. I did not ask him whether he would take a similar walk on a similar evening, and although I was pleased with myself for my inhabitual reticence I felt a desolation, as if I had foolishly denied myself comfort. I wanted him to give me a sign that the evening had been a pleasant one, but he was determined to give no such sign. Possibly he regretted having been seen in such a place at such a time, alone, and, as he thought, unobserved. Almost certainly he regretted my approach, though at some undisturbed depth of his own he may have wished for it. He had confessed to loneliness, but in a worldly manner which divested the condition of its real hurt. Whereas I was lonely in a quite specific sense, lonely for company. The inequality of our situation resided in the fact that whereas he could find company of a sort when he desired it, I could find none. Women are at a disadvantage in this sort of situation, for to state one's desire for closeness, or indeed for further closeness, is to give away something that should be kept in reserve. And this is always registered as a weakness. Which, of course, it is.

I resented my being returned to a condition I had known before. Whether I liked it or not I had gained a certain hardness from being on my own, particularly in such circumstances. I had grown to rely on myself, had not once succumbed to the temptation of throwing caution to the winds. Until now. Towards this man I now felt some of the enmity that all women feel at some time towards all men. This unequal business, as hazardous as war, divides men and women more than it unites them, so that any eventual partnership bears the scars of what might have gone wrong, nearly did go wrong, just as all failures to achieve parity leave one with a lasting feeling of shame. The politest of rejections eats into the soul, destroying the trust that might have existed, the friendship that might have survived. I saw now that I had been put in my place, or rather returned to it, and I admired the tact with which it had been done. Nothing had been stated, or even implied, and yet I knew that I had been unwise in expecting anything more than a banal and possibly accidental meeting. He had not needed to warn me; his polite noncommittal stance had done that for him. Whether or not this was an all-purpose disguise there was no way of knowing. I thanked him for the tisane. He did not wait to see me safely indoors. In the way I already recognized as characteristic he was on his way down the rue de France by the time I had shut the door behind me. I put this down to a faulty education. His mother, for all her undoubted virtues, had not taught him to care for a woman. I hesitated to acknowledge that this indifference might have been his own affair. I had had more than enough insights for one evening.

Yet on the following day, when I visited my mother, Mme Lhomond, who was sitting with her, remarked, '*Mademoiselle Zoé est en beauté aujourd'hui.*' Fortunately there was no need to reply to this, as she was accompanied by her daughter, also called Mme Lhomond, not because she was married to any son of the authentic Mme Lhomond, but on account of her long-standing liaison with an exceedingly wealthy man. That this was a union of some significance we had been left in no doubt, for it was boasted of by both the mother and the daughter. The other ladies also appeared to approve of it, since it represented a sort of victory for women. Virginie Lhomond always made an effort for her mother, as her appearance was ready to testify. This was regarded as honourable behaviour, and she was accorded some of the respect normally reserved for Mme de Pass's son. Today she wore an extremely tight-fitting white crêpe suit, which bore the stamp of the Chanel boutique; this was noted by the other ladies, to whom Virginie Lhomond sent a cheery wave of her plump hand. Her powerful scent helped to vivify the atmosphere, overlaying other scents, so that the salon became a kind of salon once again. Her various outfits were closely studied, although they bore a family resemblance: all were tight, worn to flatter her opulent figure, and accompanied by the appropriately expensive bag, the high-heeled sandals, the gold necklaces, and the useful tips she left for the maids, conveyed to her mother in a scented envelope, to be disbursed by her on the following morning.

It was surprising how little resentment there was of her obvious wealth. This if anything created a climate of admiration, pioneered by both Mesdames Lhomond. The mother appeared to think that her daughter had done extremely well for herself. As for the daughter, she pulled her weight manfully, or rather womanfully, by frequent references to the yacht in the harbour at Cannes, ready to entertain business acquaintances, or the car and chauffeur at the door. This was regarded as true filial behaviour, particularly as visits to her mother involved taking a suite at the Negresco for the weekend, something that few other offspring would have been enabled to do. What was disarming about Mme Lhomond junior, who had acceded to married dignity without altering her *état-civil*, was the fact that she acknowledged the craving for luxury that could rarely be expressed by the mostly middle- and upper-class inmates and satisfied it. 'Are you expecting your daughter today?' one of the ladies might ask of Mme Lhomond. She would swell with satisfaction, for few such inquiries came her way. She too had had an adventurous youth, my mother had told me, though little remained of it now. There was no harm in her; one had only to see her clutching her box of marrons glacés, also supplied by her daughter, and staring into space after such a visit, to register her complete absence of anything resembling character. Her love for her daughter supplied whatever moral values she possessed. Fortunately her daughter responded in kind.

There was an almost palpable feeling of disappointment

when Mme Lhomond junior announced that she was taking her mother for a drive. Only my mother abstained from this corporate sentiment, as if she would be relieved when they both left. Virginie Lhomond conducted the exit to their satisfaction; that is to say she smoothed down her skirt, patted her hair, twisted her rings, and then performed the same services for her mother. That all these gestures were vulgar gave additional pleasure. The pleasure was not entirely malicious; there were echoes here of former behaviour, though on a more muted scale. There had been an unmistakeable undertow of generosity in Virginie Lhomond's display; she knew she was supplying an interest, and that it would be one to inspire future reflection.

Not that these austere women would or could emulate such self-satisfaction, but they had not always chosen to be so austere: austerity had been thrust upon them and they had dealt with it as best they could. Virginie Lhomond provided the sort of entertainment they might derive from a lavish television production, in which extravagance supplied most of the plot. And she had had the sort of indifferent goodwill that made her a welcome presence. Though she did not remember their names – the only thing that might have been held against her – she smiled and nodded to them all in general, if not in particular. It was a visit from a local celebrity, leaving in its wake the sort of gratification that attention from a celebrity bestows. They all felt better for her visit, although their normal good manners would, unfortunately, prevent them from discussing her in any detail. Having been out of the world so long, they had no idea how much money she represented, but all privately concluded that it must have been a great deal.

I was intrigued by this performance; not so my mother, who seemed irritated and forlorn. I think she thought that I might be offended, having in mind the obscure life she rightly imagined me to be living. It was in fact she who was offended, as if aspersions had been cast on her own virtue. Maybe she thought that virtue was paying poor dividends. She had been polite, acquiescent, a well-brought-up girl who had made no particular plan for her future. And I, in imitation, had done the same. Now we had both seen the alternative, the altogether more agreeable evidence of the wages of sin. She minded for me, but I think at that moment she minded more for herself. In contrast to the two plump Mmes Lhomond she looked older than her years.

'Did you not go to the hairdresser yesterday, Mama?'

'Didn't I? I must have forgotten. Not that it matters.'

'Of course it matters. You saw what a lot of care went into Virginie's appearance.'

'Oh, yes,' she said wryly. 'I saw. I could hardly help seeing.'

I was faintly shocked by her evident rancour.

'But surely there was something rather splendid about her?'

'I don't mind her. It's her mother who drives me mad. She talks all the time: and now she will talk even more . . .'

'Naturally she was pleased to see her . . .'

'. . . whereas I should be talking about my daughter, the one good thing I have achieved in my life.'

'But there's not much to say about me.'

'No,' she agreed. 'I'm afraid you take after me in that way.'

For a moment we contemplated our destiny, which was to live out our lives in the best possible taste. I furiously denied this possibility, but I thought it unwise to expose hurt feelings. We were both hurt. I believed that my mother preferred me as I was, a comfort and a support. I was shocked by this, an additional sadness to add to all the rest. Or was it merely a confirmation of her habitual and disastrous innocence?

'Get your jacket, Mama. I am taking you out for coffee.'

Obediently she rose. 'I won't be a minute, darling. I'll just tidy my hair.'

It was quiet on that particular Sunday. There were fewer

visitors than usual, the weather being too good to sacrifice to elderly relatives. Outside the big windows of the salon the sun blazed, the late sun of high summer. There were few voices from the street; everyone had congregated in the cafés and ice-cream bars, where the tourists were spending the last of their money. The contrast between youth and age had never been so sharply defined; even Virginie Lhomond counted as young, though she must have been in her mid to late fifties, not much younger than my mother, who was an old woman by comparison. I had no sense of my own comparative youth: I had become part of the furniture. Only the unsettling recollection of the previous evening served to remind me. But that evening had ended so inconclusively that I felt returned to a state of non-being, almost at one with the ladies of the Résidence Sainte Thérèse. They too were disappointed: there were few distractions for them on this afternoon. The smiles were tired. They could not wait now for the day to end.

When my mother appeared, after a rather long interval, her hair was just as it had been when she had left me to go to her room.

'I don't think I want to go out, Zoë. I'm a little tired. You go, darling. I'll see you next week.'

'Are you all right, Mama?'

'Yes. Go, darling. I'll rest for a bit.'

She sat down thankfully. With an effort she put up her face to be kissed. When I turned round at the door her eyes were closed.

As usual I felt an immense relief when this visit was over. Maybe it was the sheer physical relief of emerging into the air; maybe it was the relief of getting away from those old people. But, shamefully, it was the relief of consigning my mother to the care of others for the space of a week. As my love for her grew more poignant and more threatened my impatience and my weariness grew. Unwittingly she had come to represent a way of life that horrified me: a faded regretful life in which one's own desires counted for so little that they could be easily ignored. By contrast I felt myself becoming rougher, tougher, on these Sunday evenings, ready to blame, to admonish. But how to blame the blameless? My mother's present circumstances were hardly of her choosing, and her condition, which mystified me, should surely evoke concern. Yet I felt the resentment of one whose own health was being undermined. On Sundays I felt impelled to take some violent action, yet all I could do was walk until I was tired. I rejoiced, as always, in the sun, the crowds, the blaring traffic, yet at the back of my mind was the ineffaceable image of my mother sitting back in her chair, with her eyes closed. The gratitude with which I embraced the light had something feverish about it. In many ways I felt less burdened at night, when the darkness would be universal, and I could count on sleep to efface the memory of the day.

Except that I could no longer count on sleep, as I had once been able to do. Sleep had begun to evade me, so that it was easier to stay awake, to work, to go out. I was not tired. I deduced that I was being kept in this state of wakefulness for a purpose. This purpose had to do with my mother, but also with myself. On this particular Sunday I set out and walked for a couple of hours, not paying much attention to where my steps were taking me. Late at night I found myself, as I knew I should, on the beach. The air was calm, the night particularly beautiful. It would have been entirely possible for me to walk out into the sea. That I did not do so was the result of a sense of duty to myself. I wanted to know the rest of the story, however it might turn out. I turned and scanned the Promenade for the sight of a known face. But Dr Balbi was nowhere to be seen.

15

I liked to think that the Baie des Anges was once inhabited by angels. I could visualize their phosphorescent descent, see them performing a brief spiritual dance on the shore, before heading inland to stimulate the economy. That economy was now thriving, but at night, on the edge of the sea, it was still possible to imagine a different sort of tourist, an unearthly visitation at one with the elements. These angels would have been entrepreneurial, with an eye to expansion. Their brief vacation on the shore before shouldering their duties would have been the only trace of their otherworldly origin. Within a very short space of time they would have transformed themselves into a limited company, leaving behind only the beautiful appellation they had bestowed on a large area of pebbles. There are no angels in Nice today: their activities have passed into other hands, those of M. Cottin, of Sœur Elisabeth, even of Dr Lagarde, who was so resolutely angelic that he invited the snubs of those less finely wrought.

I was obliged to rely on all those people, and they did not let me down. Even when Sœur Elisabeth told me warningly that my mother was not eating and sometimes refused to leave her room I placed my entire trust in her robust disapproval of such weakness. I dismissed from my memory the sight of my mother politely accepting a marron glacé from Mme Lhomond and of her trying to eat it. Or rather I tried to dismiss it. The image was too painful to be retained; it had to be dismissed as an unfortunate lapse, one of those unwise and unbecoming instances to which we are all prone. It was more than this, of course; it was a sign. I was in no position to disregard that sign, nor did I manage to do so. I merely relegated it to a time of future contemplation which had not yet come about. I placed my hopes in the superimposition of a more cheerful image, a smile, a greeting resembling her loving greetings to me in the past. Yet the smile and the greeting were mine, growing more vivid, more eager, as her own response grew more faint.

The major shareholder in the angelic enterprise was Dr Balbi, whose immanence was unmistakeable. That he was immanent rather than present I put down to his professional obligations, which placed us in different geographical locations for most of the day and rarely allowed him out in the evening. I saw him only occasionally, and after nightfall. There was no more subterfuge: if we registered each other's presence we did not always speak, but passed on with merely a discreet signal of recognition. The fiction that we both took a late walk had become a reality, but then it had never entirely been a fiction. The tisane incident was repeated once only. It was an immense relief to have managed this, as if it marked a significant development in our relationship. Yet it was disappointing in every other respect. Dr Balbi, having made this concession to my presence, seemed determined to treat me like a patient. This was quite comfortable in its way, but it was also baffling. Behind his professional reserve lay vast areas of personal reserve which had to be protected at all costs. By nature laconic and sceptical he preferred to be seen as formidable, unapproachable, perhaps unaware that such a stance was an open invitation to marauders. I liked to see him battling with his nature, or with nature in general. Only the occasional, very reluctant smile was any indication that he had registered me as an adversary. He was clearly both willing and unwilling to do so.

His was the only narrative I now cared to follow, though he managed to make it as opaque, as uninteresting as possible. I admired the technique, having been unable to acquire it myself. It is a defensive strategy, the object of which is to make the terrain safe from invasion. Thus I got to hear about his sister, whose fate he compared to mine. She had stayed at home to look after their mother while he pursued his studies. I concluded that she had been sacrificed to the brilliant son, who was thus given his chance to make his way in the world.

'I sympathize with women,' he said. 'My sister never married.'

'I shan't either.'

He made a deprecating gesture. 'I always felt badly about leaving her. But my mother wished it. And I wanted to get away.'

'Where is she now?'

'She is staying with me.'

'She lives with you?'

'No, she still lives in Marseilles. She has a flat there. She comes to stay once or twice a year.'

'She must be very proud of you.'

'That is almost the worst part. Though I think she is quite happy.'

I doubted that. A woman who has been sacrificed is never happy. And although such sacrifices may be involuntary they are also instinctive, so that there never has been, and never could be, any choice. The flat of one's own is the only symbol of upward progress. My own flat loomed larger, would soon have to be faced.

Dr Balbi's verbal camouflage, to which I meekly assented, marked the limits of our contract. Although the exchange of information is never without its purpose I saw that this was of more value to Dr Balbi than it could be to me. It was easy to imagine him with his sister, eating together in the evenings under a centre light, returned to their early days in Marseilles. He would have been the protective brother, although she would always be the older sister, anxious about his health, proud of his progress. I was aware that this was a burden to him. He would fear the regression that such closeness implied. No doubt they would enact, or re-enact, those earlier days. And he would be uneasily aware of his own guilt, which he would have been able to surmount when faced with the evidence of their poverty. For they had been poor, of that there was no doubt, and he would have been dismayed by a reminder of that early poverty in his sister's behaviour. I had no desire to meet the sister, nor did it seem likely that I ever should. She seemed to be a family secret, and as such belonged to him alone. This was implied by his determination to come clean: it was as if our conversation could not continue until she was out in the open. I admired the purity of his motives, but wished rather that our conversation would take another turn. It was I who suggested that it was late, that I should go home. As always he walked me to my door and disappeared before I had locked myself inside. I tiptoed up the stairs, aware of M. Cottin sleeping somewhere above my head, and of Dr Balbi walking steadily away from me.

I began to perceive the advantages of living in more than one room. I had had a strange dream, which had alarmed me. In the dream I had been consigned to a small room, not unlike the room I currently occupied, but with one essential difference: it was in an advanced state of dilapidation, with strips of paper hanging from the walls. I was delighted with this room, thanked the owner effusively, until I noticed that there was a breach in one of the walls, rather like a cat-flap, covered with yet another strip of wallpaper, but of a different pattern. Once I had seen this I had become uneasy, but the urgency of my mission, the mission that had brought me to this place, dictated that I must be about my business, and that I must issue out into the day to fulfil my obligations. This, in high good humour, I was willing to do. There was one disadvantage. At some point I should have to return to the room, with its gap in the wall, and await the outcome of whatever it had in store for me.

I awoke from this dream in a state of horror, with the details still vivid in my mind's eye. I could even see the contrasting patterns of the unmatched wallpapers, hanging in strips which no one had thought to repair. I knew that the owner of the room was well-meaning; I also knew that I was not fully conversant with the custom of this place, which was in Nice. As ever the relief with which I encountered the light and air of everyday was profound.

Perhaps for this reason, or out of a longing for normality, I determined to go to London. My current work was finished and must be delivered. There was an additional reason: my childhood friend Mary was getting married and had sent me an invitation to her wedding. There was to be a small reception at the Basil Street Hotel after the ceremony at the Register Office. I loved Mary; we had once been close friends, though that closeness had been eroded by my long absence. If I left on the Monday, attended the wedding on the Wednesday, and left again on the Thursday I could be back by the end of the week. This seemed to me a perfectly reasonable objective. It would mean interrupting my various routines, but that might be no bad thing. And I should see my mother on the Sunday as usual. And Mary would be glad to see me; she may have been a little hurt that I had been such a bad correspondent. I had not wanted to burden her with such strange information, and therefore my letters may have struck her as evasive. They were deliberately so, for there was another fiction in play, namely that my stay in Nice was voluntary, even rather dashing. I saw how impossible it might be to destroy this fiction. Attendance at the wedding could be used to test my ability to adapt. The attempt should be made before it was too late.

I told Sœur Elisabeth that I should be away, gave her my London number, but said that I should in any case telephone every evening. I boarded the plane with a distinct feeling of relief, which shocked me. I was used to my duties, and this excursion seemed frivolous by comparison. But I had the alibi of my work, and of the quest for further assignments. Both were genuine but felt false, as did the familiarity with which I noted various features of my former life, still bewilderingly in place. Only the weather had changed: leaves were falling, for this was now early September, and the children were enjoying their last days of freedom before going back to school. I saw them in the streets when I went out to buy milk; they seemed strong, invincible. In the cupboards of the flat my clothes looked staid, unfamiliar, out of date. I had been absent for so long that they might have been bought by somebody else, for a purpose I could no longer remember. There was no money to spend on further adornment. Even the fee for my work was earmarked for a more serious purpose, for those modest supplies on which my mother depended, the soap, the talcum powder, the hand cream. They were little enough to contribute; they were a symbol of intimacy rather than intimacy itself. They were a means of exchange that soothed us both, and there was no question that it might be foregone.

Dr Blackburn was away. I handed the work to a secretary whom I did not know, and told her that I should be in touch. I was almost glad of his absence. I registered fatigue, not the fatigue of the journey but of remoteness, of being out of touch, of no longer knowing my contemporaries, of not being in context. My isolation was emphasized by the activities I could sense in the background and to which I had no access. There was no place for me here, had not been for some time. What work I did – and that was little enough – made no impact on the wider scene. It may have been useful to someone, but I had no sense that it was useful to me. I had become removed from what had once been habitual. My long absence had taken root, and I was no longer at home.

This sense of isolation increased at the wedding, as I knew it must. Mary's look of pleasure was my only reward; otherwise the occasion was something of an ordeal. Many of my former friends were present and exclaimed with astonishment when they saw me. I must have seemed something of a revenant. I was aware too of other discrepancies. These friends were now successful professionals, assured, even wealthy. Girls with whom I had been at school had become adults, a different species, while I was still serving my apprenticeship. I was told how well I looked. 'France evidently suits you,' said Mary. 'But when are you coming home?'

For everyone went home eventually. The truth was never more self-evident as I surrendered to the English atmosphere, louder, less well-behaved than I was used to. I was used, too used, to my slice of *pissaladière* and my bottle of mineral water at lunchtime to appreciate the glistening complicated food and the abundant champagne. I found it difficult to make the transition from my quiet way of life to the slightly ribald atmosphere of a wedding. I found the conviviality forced, as it may always be on such occasions. It was, in any event, difficult for me to break my long habit of silence. Silence, I thought, should only be interrupted by significant exchanges. The onus was on me to talk vivaciously, something I could no longer do. I appreciated the company, or rather I appreciated the idea of the company, the fact of the company, but found myself longing for other conversations, for other concerns. I would readily sacrifice occasions such as this for the rare hoped-for encounter, however tentative this turned out to be. I was newly tentative myself, and by now could hardly be otherwise.

As I knew I should, I saw my former lover, Adam Crowhurst. He was still handsome, insolently so, though he had put on weight. Now he looked like a man, rather than a graceful youth. I studied him for a minute or two, as he did me. He was in the City, he told me, a trader with an old-fashioned and highly regarded firm. He loved the work, loved the money, about which he was unapologetic, even loved the pressure. Sometimes he managed to get away for a weekend, but this was becoming increasingly rare. He had a flat in Bayswater, was getting interested in contemporary art, had purchased one or two pieces of sculpture. Might even change tack eventually, he said; one never knows.

'And you,' he said. 'I know nothing about you now. Are you married?'

No, I told him, I was not married.

'Neither am I,' he said. Then he hesitated. 'We could have made a go of it, I suppose. Only you were a bit difficult, as I recall.'

'Oh, I was always difficult. Much too difficult for most people. You were no exception.'

He looked at me uncertainly and decided to assume that I was joking. His expression cleared as he greeted a girl on the other side of the room. Did I know Sophie? He would introduce me. As he veered off in her direction I escaped into the blessed anonymity of the street. It was already late afternoon and the light was beginning to thin, to lose its vigour. I deplored my recent performance, my attempts to respond to those friends whom I still treasured. They had not appeared to mind the fervent smiles and fragmented sentences to which I was reduced. It had been essential to conceal the seriousness of my concerns, and this at least I had managed to do. This was the full extent of my social success.

Later, in the flat, I thought not of the wedding but of my strange dream. Once between the clean sheets, in my own bed, I pondered its significance, for I did not doubt that it held some meaning for me. My initial gratitude for that derelict room had been overtaken by bewilderment, as I contemplated that gap in the wall, which was nevertheless too small to be of any use. No one could enter through it, nor could I use it to get out. Yet it was unmistakeably a feature of the room, as was the urgency of the business that had brought me to this place. Half open, under the fluttering strips of wallpaper that revealed rather than concealed it, it was the room's most salient feature. As I had woken from this dream I had been impressed by the feeling of dread that must accompany any return to that room. No good could come of my presence there, even less of my absence. The room was my destiny, and the gratitude with which I had initially warmed to it was the most dreadful feature of all.

I returned to Nice a day earlier than anticipated, for I had nothing to do in London. Again the journey was a relief, and I wondered whether I should seek refuge in aeroplanes in the unguessable future. This return would be problematic. I had no work, no reason to stay in my room – my real room – and no real reason, save one, to be out of it either. I took M. Cottin the packets of biscuits he liked, and I thought his thanks less fervent than usual. His expression was grave, as if I had somehow displeased him. Then he told me there had been a telephone call from the Résidence Sainte Thérèse that very morning. There was no message, but perhaps I should call back? The telephone was at my disposal. No need to leave any money.

'*Mademoiselle*,' said Sœur Elisabeth. '*Votre maman est au plus mal. On vous attend.*'

This, then, was the dread, not the room with the gap in the wall, the significance of which was now clear to me, as was the nature of the business which had brought me to this place. My business was, and always had been, my mother; however much I repudiated the idea it refused to go away. That was why my own hopes and plans had been so tentative, so nebulous. My life had become a stasis I was unable to alter in any direction; that was why every other enterprise seemed beyond me, beyond even my eventual possibilities. My timid affections remained timid for that very reason; they were prevented from moving forward, for I was a prisoner in that room, and until the gap widened I could not proceed. And my fear was that the gap would yawn so wide that the whole wall would collapse, and the room with it. My life was that poor room, with its enigmatic opening, the purpose of which was not to let me out but to have me contemplate it for so long that I could no longer relate to the rest of life, even though that life was my own.

I found my mother in bed, under the black wooden crucifix, and I was struck by the beauty of her expression. Her eyes were open, but her head was turned slightly to one side, as if she were listening to inner voices. One of the sisters had dressed her in a clean nightgown, prior to her being taken to the clinic, for the rule was that no one died at the Résidence Sainte Thérèse, at least not on the premises. The incongruous pink nightgown sat lightly on her slight frame, and I saw how thin she had become. She looked neither sad nor frightened, merely preoccupied, and I did not immediately see the reason for Sœur Elisabeth's telephone call, her note of unmistakeable urgency. For my mother was surely resting: her eyes were not even closed. Her arms lay quietly on the sheet, and from time to time one of the sisters would take her pulse. Dr Lagarde, I was told, was in the office, on the telephone, making arrangements for the transfer.

'Mama,' I said. 'Mama,' for these brief childish syllables were now the only ones I had to offer.

I tried not to watch as the attendants lifted her from the bed. I had no sensation of the ride in the ambulance, though it evidently took place, for within half an hour of my arrival I was installed in my mother's room, by her side, her hand in mine. Her eyes were now closed, as if the effort of leaving the Résidence Sainte Thérèse had exhausted her. From time to time a nurse, not one of the ones I remembered, would come in and palpate her wrist and throat. Then her hand was returned to mine. I longed for her to speak to me, if only to murmur my name; I longed for a sign of recognition that she knew me, knew that I was there, that I would never leave her again. Once she stirred, and I bent over her, but then she was still again. Someone placed a cup of coffee in front of me. When I looked up I saw that the sky beyond the window was quite dark.

The vigil lasted all night, as I had known it would. It seemed fitting that it should do so. At no time did my mother appear conscious of where she was, yet I had the impression that she knew that I was with her. The eyes opened from time to time, but closed thankfully once more. It was clear that she would not speak: her concentration on what was taking place was too great. Yet she was not, or did not seem to be, in any sort of anguish, which I should have expected to be part of the process. She seemed to rest her head so lightly on the pillow, turned slightly towards me, as if she could see me, or would see me, once she summoned the strength to do so. Then her eyes closed for ever, and I knew that of the two of us I was the more alone.

I must have slept briefly, for when the door opened and the nurse came in, the room was once more filled with light. Dr Lagarde was summoned to certify that death had taken place. He had the sense, or the tact, to say nothing, merely laid a hand briefly on my arm, and gave instructions in a muted voice. The nurse shocked me by opening the window, by moving noisily about the room. Beyond the door I could hear the ordinary sounds of early morning. Once more a cup of coffee was put before me. These people were never less than kind.

Dr Balbi, I was told, was absent, but if I cared to wait in his office Dr Lagarde would come and talk to me. I sat down quite calmly in the accustomed chair, as if waiting for further news. My mother's illness, though technically attributable to heart failure, seemed to me more than ever an affair of the spirit, of a spirit too easily broken. Dr Lagarde seemed to be of the same opinion. He was crestfallen, until I warmly expressed my gratitude, at which he was plainly relieved. He explained what arrangements had to be made, unless I wished to take her body back to England. At this point I must have changed colour, for I found him at my side with a glass of water in his hand. I assured him that I was quite composed; what I wanted was for him to go away and leave me in communion with the events of that long night. Yet I felt nothing but a deep sense of preoccupation, as if there were no end to this mystery, although the end had already come about. When I looked up again the room was empty. I was free to leave.

And so, to borrow David Copperfield's words, I lost her. In the street the weather was unclouded; there was a smell of coffee and washed pavements. At some point I should have to go back to the clinic, if only to pay the bill. This could be done later in the day, for I had no patience for such contingencies, no capacity for them either. The distractions of the past few days had merged into one major distraction and into one unanswerable question: how to live now? I needed no friend to whisper insidiously that life would be simpler, for I already knew that. Life would be simpler, but it would not be better. The world would be a lonelier place, and no amount of rationalization could alter this. At the same time I knew that this was a rite of passage which all must undergo, and there was even a sort of relief in acknowledging that this experience was part of the human condition. What hurt most was the realization that I must return to her room and collect her belongings, for the room was already earmarked for another. The pitifully small suitcase I had packed for her to take to the clinic was still in Dr Balbi's office, for I could not bear to confront the fact that it would no longer be needed, could not bear to pick it up and walk out with it, as though setting the seal on the inevitable. I wanted to be empty-handed on this fine morning, to be out of touch, to be unavailable. Despite the pressing decisions that awaited me I wanted to be alone. Even now various busy persons, people in authority, were expecting me to tell them what I had in mind for the funeral. This was laughable. Any funeral would be irrelevant. Therefore any funeral would do.

In the rue de France M. Cottin came out from behind the counter of the shop when he saw my face, sighed, and shook my hand. I found that I could not bear to be in my room, although it was recognizably an ordinary room, not the room of the dream with its gap in the wall. I needed no one to explain the meaning of the dream, the symbolism of that exit – for it was an exit rather than an entrance; I saw that now. The walls of my real room were intact; the room was shadowy, as it had always been, but it contained no hidden surprises. Its very blankness signified that it had served its purpose and would shortly be returned to anonymity. For I should have no further use for it, should take my leave of M. Cottin, and go home, the home that my mother had professed to long for, or so she said. Now I wondered. She had not been homesick; she had been displaced. This was the condition that so perplexed her and which seemed to continue to perplex her even when death itself was overtaking her. For she had known that death was near. The open eyes had looked beyond me, as if there were matters of greater interest to absorb her. That was why after speaking her name once I had said no more.

I believe I spent the day in the garden of the Musée Masséna, as I had once loved to do. I found my usual seat, and must have stayed there for several hours. Only when I felt faint did I realize that it might be wise to eat something. I found a noisy bar with a radio playing and ate the two stale croissants that had been left over from early that morning. Instinct told me that I would need all my strength for the days ahead. I went home and washed myself thoroughly, as if preparing for some ultimate ceremony. It was evening once more when I emerged, as ready as I should ever be for what lay ahead.

The disappearance of the sun saddened me, as it always did. The painter's pronouncement – the sun is God – still held good. Creativity seemed called for, though I had none to offer. I had no sense of a possible future, only of the innumerable tasks that lay ahead. I now had to do caretaker's work: there were arrangements to be made, people to be advised, explanations to be offered to those who might be kind enough to inquire. Life was hugely complicated, as it had not been when my mother was alive. Then my steps had taken me from the rue de France to the rue Droite, with very few deviations. Of my evening walks I preferred not to think, or of that strange freedom, that inevitability with which I recognized a known face. That inevitability had been an illusion. I had registered as interest what had been no more than a taciturn kindness. Wanting more I had gained less.

Though I knew where I was going I lingered in the emptying streets, longing for any sign of life, of recognition, to help me through the night I would have to endure. I even delayed my arrival at the clinic, for the business was now finished and I knew that no one awaited me. I should have been there all day, I now realized, should have wept, have asked anxious questions to which I already knew the answer. Instead of which I had spent the afternoon like a tourist, and now, like a tourist, must take up my life again. The sight of the clinic alarmed me, so that instinctively I turned into a café and sat down at a table. I ordered coffee, though my heart was beating strongly. I put my hand to my throat, as I had seen my mother do, as if I were ready to join her in whatever malady had caused her physical death. For her spiritual death had taken place some time ago. Her removal to unfamiliar places, one after the other, had so undermined her that only a memory of home, or an illusion of home, had kept her intact for a while. That illusion had not lasted, and even the petty irritants of the Résidence Sainte Thérèse had become threatening. It had been, in its way, a death foretold, and for better or for worse we had both known it.

When I looked up, and wiped my eyes, Dr Balbi was sitting opposite me. 'You have heard?' I said.

He nodded. 'I thought I might find you here.' But this was the preamble to another sort of encounter, or even the beginning of a prepared speech, one that might prove to be out of place in the present circumstances. 'Do you want to walk?' he asked.

'No. I have done all the walking I shall ever do. You will not see me on the beach again at night. Do you know that I always looked for you?'

Now I had embarrassed him. There was no sign that this day would ever end, that I could say goodbye to sadness and confusion.

'You knew that she was dying?' I asked.

'I thought so, yes. As you did.'

'Did I? I suppose I did. Yet I rejected the idea so thoroughly that I managed to believe the opposite. Or I thought I did. Did you come looking for me? Not now, before. I wanted to believe that you did. I had no one else, you see. I'm sorry if I was a nuisance. I didn't mean to be. I wanted to be self-confident, even a little high-handed, as if you were merely some sort of functionary, someone who was paid to carry out certain duties. I am so very sorry, sorry that I failed to be that person. It would have been so much easier to say goodbye, easier too for you to dismiss me, as you must have been yearning to do . . .'

'No,' he said.

'I just don't want to turn into the sort of person my mother had become, dignified, but essentially helpless. And this is what

I seem to be doing now, only without the dignity. I would rather be defiant and rather nasty, eager to censure, to hand out blame. But there is no one to blame, is there? You cannot be blamed for anything, not even for not taking me seriously.'

'No, I cannot be blamed for that. If you are ready we will go and see your mother now. Before she is taken away. Dr Lagarde has been expecting you.'

We walked slowly out of the café, up the steps of the clinic, and took the lift to a basement room, where my mother was lying on a small bed. The light was kept low, for which I was grateful. She looked calm, untouched.

'Please do what has to be done,' I said. I kissed her and turned away.

In his office he opened a cupboard and took out her small suitcase and her bag. The bag contained a card giving details of her name, address, date of birth, her bank in London, and the telephone number of a firm unknown to me, but presumably known to the staff of the Résidence Sainte Thérèse: in brackets were the words *Jourdain, Pompes Funèbres*. There were no letters; she had received none. Nothing from home except a photograph of myself as a small child. On the back of this was written, 'My darling girl'.

Dr Balbi moved quietly about the room, giving me time to recover myself. This was not easy, yet I had gone through the day relatively tearless. And I would be tearless again, on the following day. I would be that managerial person I always intended to be, nodding wryly in the direction of the fates, or the furies, or whatever agencies had brought me to this pass. It was just that one's resolve slackens at night. This worldly conclusion was my first step to becoming that other person. Yet the transformation was not yet within my grasp. As I broke into tears once again I felt two hands on my shoulders.

'Dr Balbi,' I began.

The hands tightened on my shoulders. 'Antoine,' he said. 'My name is Antoine.'

16

The ladies were all present in the salon when I went to the Résidence Sainte Thérèse to collect the rest of my mother's possessions. They were formally dressed, although this was not a normal visiting day: they were observing an occasion which none of them wished to observe, for the death of one of their number was a matter on which they did not care to dwell. The tributes were led by Mme de Pass, who could not entirely manage to conceal an expression of disapproval. It appeared that my mother was at fault in some way, first by being so much younger than themselves, and second by dying in so inconclusive a manner. There may have been a third reason: she had not appeared to mourn her husband, or at least to reminisce complacently about her previous life. This they could not forgive: they had perfected the art of editing their own lives in such a way as to make them acceptable to others of their kind. My mother had offended against the prevailing code by being both heartbroken and so obviously relieved, so that the heartbreak had to be attributed to factors in the unknowable past, to which they were not privy. I doubted whether such invisible wounds were much to their taste. Their widowhood had been turned around, from bereavement to a sort of satisfaction: they had survived. Yet my mother's survival had been so compromised that her previous marriage, of which they knew little, was either more memorable than their own or so entirely dreadful that she preferred to offer no information about it, let alone the complacent accounts which they all colluded in offering to the public gaze.

'*Elle n'avait pas la santé, la pauvre Anne,*' said Mme de Pass.

'Je lui disais, mais il faut réagir! Mais elle n'avait le cœur à rien.'

It was true that she had no heart for anything. I was impressed, against my will, by the strength these women had accumulated along the way, so that they had managed to accommodate their reduced way of life in a manner which they thought fitting. True value was placed in what remained: their own carefully monitored health, their children, their appearance, the routines they had devised for getting through the day. I suspected that they were sorry for me, not because I was an orphan, but because I was unmarried myself and would have no emotional capital on which to draw. They did not envy me my new appalling freedom, and they were right not to do so. I did not value it myself. They may even have suspected that I had once longed for such freedom, whereas they had learned the value of community, even the community of their peers. I stood more or less helplessly as, one after another, they came forward and pressed my hand. Mme Lhomond was in tears, and that too was out of order. The correct stance was one of dignity; there were forms of behaviour to be observed, and they had perfected these in the course of their long lives. Anything less temperate than dignity was to be deplored.

I responded as best I could, though I am sure my inexperience showed. They thought I was to be pitied, as my mother had been, but for the wrong reasons. I must have struck them as being deficient in a sort of gravitas which they themselves possessed. Just as Mme Levasseur's son had given offence by weeping so extravagantly I gave offence by not allowing them to finish their carefully prepared condolences, and also by failing to reassure them that I too was a survivor.

I escaped to my mother's room as hastily as I could, although I knew that this too was some sort of a lapse of dignity. I should have stayed with them until Mme de Pass had given the signal: then I should have thanked them all in turn for showing their friendship. Instead of which I had cut short the proceedings, leaving them free to discuss me and my inadequate performance for perhaps an hour or so. This would have strengthened them in their own beliefs, their own self-sufficiency. Yet I did not doubt that they were shaken. Their lives were constructed on a bedrock of determination, the sort of determination necessary if one is to weather those last years. My mother had not obeyed the general rule: she had absconded. Though they knew that she had a weak heart they did not see that this was sufficient reason for an early eclipse. If anything such a condition should have stimulated her to more vigorous efforts on her own behalf. As Mme de Pass had stated, she should have reacted. But she had, if anything, collaborated in her own decline, and this they could not allow.

In my mother's room the bed had been stripped. Another, larger, suitcase stood ready to receive the last of her meagre possessions. I found myself unwilling to handle her clothes, her shoes, her hairbrush, and ended by bundling them out of sight into the case, which I should have preferred to leave downstairs in the courtyard, with the other discards. This again was not to be considered, though I could not discern any clear reason for the prohibition. I had no one now to disapprove of me, for the only possible leavetaking had already taken place in the salon They pitied my freedom, my unsought freedom, as I did. They did not see how one could live without attachments, and neither did I. They were more prescient than I was, but only just. I saw now that the sort of freedom I was obliged to embrace brings in its wake intolerable anxiety, for there are no permissions and no sanctions. I also saw why it was not quite appropriate to cite freedom as an absolute. This had been pointed out to me by Dr Balbi, when I had known him as Dr Balbi. Perhaps I always should; in my present circumstances kindness was not unusual. In any event he was absent, and I must get used to all kinds of absence. I too should be absent, for it was clear that my presence in this place was no longer required.

The Résidence Sainte Thérèse had been a beneficent institution, and it proved strangely difficult to leave it. When I went downstairs again I looked into the salon to offer final thanks to those present, but the salon was empty. The conventions had been observed, and now the incident could be consigned to the past. I did not doubt that heads would be shaken when my mother's name was mentioned, nor did I doubt that they had been genuinely fond of her. But she had worried them, and of this they preferred not to think. I could not fault their attitude. Indeed so robust was it that I found myself in sympathy with their disapproval. My own loss was, and would be, irrevocable, yet I too had been alienated by my mother's passivity. I should have preferred her to be more actively unhappy, more confessional, more open to persuasion. Then I could have comforted her and satisfied my own conscience. I would have wished her to be one of those complacent widows, all previous failures satisfactorily disguised, a resolute face presented to the outside world. And if she had not appreciated being a wife for the second time she should have managed to conceal the fact not only from others but from herself.

That there was something shameful in her failure to do so I could see for myself, just as there was something about my own misgivings that I preferred not to contemplate. She had tacitly refused the life that had been offered to her, or had come to do so, whereas I should always see it as idyllic. I wondered if I had wronged her in coming to this view. It was entirely possible that she had been as happy as she had initially appeared to be, that the marriage to Simon was a success, although in her eyes a mistake. One lives uncomfortably with one's mistakes; one never entirely comes to terms with them. Simon's death had in some ways compounded the mistake. He had not given her enough time in which to know him. And the manner of his dying had left a permanent feeling of horror, which had come to envelop the whole episode. Her desire to go home was a desire for a place of safety, where extravagant lives and deaths were unknown. Horror had never quite been banished, as I had seen from her relief in not being allowed back to Les Mouettes. It had persisted throughout her time in the Résidence Sainte Thérèse, so that she had pursued a policy of silence in an effort to conceal her wounds. Never once had she asked me about my own life, my own activities. Maybe she thought my loyalty depended on my having none. This was in fact the case.

I left the Résidence Sainte Thérèse without looking back. I wandered down the Cours Saleya, inhaling the smells of the market. Once again, I was weighed down by a suitcase, which I was resolved to leave by M. Cottin's dustbin. The clothes, which I could not quite bring myself to discard, would find a place in my own cupboards as soon as I got back to London. For there was now little to stop me from returning home, except the emptiness that awaited me there. Similarly there were no reasons for me now to remain in Nice. My return seemed as obligatory as it seemed undesirable. I should have preferred, once I had got rid of the suitcase, to have wandered down to the beach, although it was no time of day for a half-expected encounter. I felt shame that I should still be preoccupied with such encounters: I had little to offer. Nor had any promises been made, any pledges of further meetings. I should have to eschew such fantasies. But they had not quite been fantasies, at least not on my side. They say that love is the antidote to death; they even say that love is more powerful than death. I was willing to believe it, even anxious to do so. But in the absence of a lover this is not entirely possible.

I should have to cure myself of this habit of wandering and speculating. Such activities belonged to the dark and I was now obliged to live by daylight. Yet the day seemed to pass without my noticing it. I did one or two sensible things: I put a notice of my mother's death in *Le Figaro*, where the ladies of the Résidence Sainte Thérèse would expect to find it. I could satisfy them on that score as on no other. The matter of the suitcase I decided to shelve for the time being. I stowed it under my bed with a view to leaving it there until I vacated the room. This, fortunately, was not a matter of urgency. The rent was paid until the end of the month, for I had foreseen a longer vigil than the one that had taken place. I had grown fond of the room; I should be sorry to leave it, yet I could think of no good reason for remaining in it now that my business in Nice was at an end. I knew that it would never be entirely at an end, for I had felt so much and so deeply in Nice that it seemed to have witnessed my entire life, a life whose shadowy beginnings in London might have been little more than a setting of the scene, after which the main drama could unfold.

Even now the sun blazed outside my window, as if nothing of significance had taken place, as if exits and entrances were part of normal currency, and as if mourning were an act of profligacy out of step with the real profligacy of nature, which was our true endowment. I leaned out of the window for the luxury of witnessing humanity, ordinary movements, ordinary gestures. Below me M. Cottin stood on the threshold of the shop, hands clasped behind his back, surveying his domain. It had become my domain as well; in a little while I should eat a meal in my usual modest café, greeting the proprietor as I always did. These people had been good enough to accept me, and to accept me without question. Delicacy, or a genuine indifference, had kept our exchanges to a minimum. I knew nothing about them, yet they were part of my life; they did not expect me to give an account of myself, did not know of my anxieties, would not presume upon my apparent disposability. I think they saw me as one of their own, laborious, frugal, self-sufficient. That was how I liked to think of myself, while knowing intimately that at any minute I might collapse, implode, and know the despair of one whose life is lacking in several essential components. That this burden could be shouldered by no one but myself was part of my freedom, which I now saw as an existential tragedy. But to peer into that abyss was to court further disaster.

On a sudden prompting I determined to keep the room until the end of the year. While making arrangements in London for my future life there I could prolong the memory of Nice by retaining a foothold in M. Cottin's establishment. My presence was not required in either place, but at least in Nice there was that everyday busyness that tempted one out into the sun, the flux of life that compensated for one's very real solitude. Even now, in the disarray of recent events, I began to hanker for my usual wanderings, which, now that they might end, began to assume an exalted significance. There was no need for me to remind myself that nothing had come of them, no apotheosis, no conclusive explanation, or declaration. What I had felt might have been the full extent of what had been enacted on the shore of the Baie des Anges, in shadow, without witnesses, and therefore not on record. It was pointless to speculate about another's feelings, particularly as that other was not present.

I wondered about that. I must have hoped that Dr Balbi would come looking for me, would have neglected his patients in my favour. A moment's thought showed me that this would have been entirely out of character. Nor would such extravagant behaviour have convinced me. I was now fearful, conscious of the limits of our association; it suited me to keep it at arms' length, as if it were a mistake that I had made in assuming it to be real. On this radiant morning it seemed like a bargain into which only I had entered. I was too affected by loss to see that I was confusing one loss with another. It would be preferable to rely only on facts, for the dangers of delusion had never been more apparent. It might therefore be wise to pay no more rent than was due. I might hanker after my life in Nice, but to linger when I was no longer expected would be a solecism I need not commit. It would be enough to know that the room was mine for a short stretch of time, for my time must now be used for practical matters, for envisaging a future which I must negotiate alone. I flushed at my belief that it might be otherwise. Such fantasies were no longer appropriate.

I arranged for the curé of Sainte Rita and for *Jourdain, Pompes Funèbres* to perform a brief and discreet ceremony. This was done decently, under a quiet blue sky. It was an interment of which no one need be ashamed. After it had been completed my movements were uncertain, even to myself. How then could I convey news of them to others?

I returned to London, where several further tasks awaited me. The first was to clean the flat and to prepare it for my eventual installation. This took the better part of a day, or rather I allowed it to, for I had no pressing engagements. In fact I had no engagements at all, and this absence of motivation disconcerted me. When I had swept and mopped and polished I made up the bed with clean sheets, and consigned the old ones to the laundry basket, to be dealt with at some future date. Then I washed my hair, but when I looked in the mirror I was alarmed at my appearance. Pale, and with wide eyes, I looked like my mother. This must be rectified. Disregarding my wet hair I went out and found a hairdresser, had my hair cut, and my neglected nails manicured. Then I went to the bank, where the contents of my mother's account, to which I now had access, were made known to me. It contained a useful sum of money which would assure my future until this could be supplemented by my own earnings. I paid several bills, which had accumulated in my absence, and wrote a letter to Dr Blackburn announcing my permanent availability. My mother had left no will; at least none had been deposited in the bank. As far as I knew she had never consulted a solicitor; her affairs had been subsumed under Simon's, which meant another visit to Mr Redman. Nothing further came to light. The only news was that Simon's Swiss account was empty; he had drawn heavily on it during the years at Les Mouettes, no doubt to fund a way of life that would eventually have had to come to an end. Purchasers had long been found for the remaining property in Walthamstow. All in all I had no immediate worries about money. I thanked him for his help in the past and went back to the flat. As this had been accomplished in the space of a single day I was now faced with the problem of filling my time. In the end I went to bed at a ridiculously early hour and consequently lay awake all night.

The next day, Sunday, was the day I had been dreading, for this was the first visiting day when I should not be in attendance. It is possible to miss occasions which one has observed resignedly, or with reluctance, and this I did. The worldly Mme de Pass and the lachrymose Mme Lhomond had retreated into a distant sphere of influence. I should miss the visit of Mme Lhomond's daughter, although we had never exchanged more than a few words of greeting. There would be no more slow careful walks to the café on the corner, though these had become rare. I dismissed from my mind, as best I was able, the image of my mother applying herself to a cup of coffee, and thankfully relinquishing the task. I was beset with all sorts of doubts as to my own conduct. I should have brought her home, as she had initially desired, although we had both known that this would be difficult to accomplish. In the end I had connived at her weakness, had allowed it to become a determining factor. She herself had come to realize this. Had she not refused to go out, when it was still possible for her to do so? And do not all lives end badly, or at least not as we would wish them to end? My mother's death had been inevitable, and as deaths go not particularly terrible. Yet I knew that her expression, as she lay dying, that look of absorption, of preoccupation with an overriding mystery, would haunt me for ever. I understood those people who try to get in touch with the dead. Their desire is not to exchange news, or even to receive a comforting message, but to hear a first-hand account of what the process revealed. How had it felt to die? This was the news that no one was available to tell. Hence the entire business remains unknown, and must remain so until it is one's own turn to confront it. Then perhaps one would conclude that it is indeed a mystery, and one that no living person, the person so helplessly in attendance, can imagine. One would be more alone in death than one had ever been in life, and that would be the worst outcome of all.

I returned to Nice to pay the final accounts. At the Résidence Sainte Thérèse I was received rather more favourably. I had done the right thing in some way. '*On a vu l'annonce dans* Le Figaro,' I was assured, for I had thought to follow the wording that these ladies would find acceptable, even adding '*Priez pour elle!*' to the meagre facts of her name and age. I had no doubt that one or two of her former companions would offer a prayer, and that comforted me more than anything else could have done. The rest was up to God, in whom I had no belief, but they might have fared better. I hoped so, for their sakes, as well, rather shakily, for my own. I paid the bill and thanked everyone again, but by now I was an unwelcome reminder. It was my duty to disappear. The obituary notice might have been my last useful manifestation. There would have been constraint on both sides had I lingered.

At the clinic I paid the bill. I made my way instinctively to Dr Balbi's office until a kindly hand diverted me to the seat of commercial operations. I could hear snatches of conversation in the corridor outside, but none that were familiar to me. I lingered over the business of writing the cheque for longer than was necessary, but none of this was of any use; it was clear that no one would disturb me. I asked the secretary to convey my thanks to the nurses and to Dr Balbi. I was assured that this would be done. On my way out I heard a familiar voice somewhere in the background, untraceable. I thought I could hear the voice growing louder, a door opening and shutting. Then, overcome by the futility of my behaviour, I left, letting the front door swing slowly behind me, just as I imagined the footsteps approaching me. I was out in the air before they could overtake me. I knew that they would not follow me into the street.

Since leavetaking seemed to be appropriate I thought that I had better pay my respects to the Thibaudets, something I should have done earlier. They might have been expecting me to keep in touch; on the other hand they had not visited my mother more than once, though Dr Thibaudet may have been aware of her progress. Certainly he would have been advised of her death. But he was retired now, and had been for some years. I did not know whether he continued to take an interest in the affairs of the clinic, or whether he had been thankful to relinquish his former duties. An entirely formal visit on my part might make up for my long absence, though this was regrettable. It was regrettable, but it was not entirely regretted. I had not returned to the district since I had been so summarily ejected from Les Mouettes. And it was possible that the Thibaudets had made their peace with the new owners, as prudent neighbours always must. My presence might be something of an embarrassment after so long an interval. Yet they too would have seen the notice in *Le Figaro* and would be expecting some sort of a gesture from me. I reminded myself that they had not known where to find me. But they had known where to find my mother. It was as my mother's daughter that I would present myself, their fault cancelling out my own. In that way the rules of good behaviour would be observed, with no blame attaching on either side.

In the event I was able to avoid any possible awkwardness, for the Thibaudets were not at home. Their housekeeper told me that they were on holiday, a fact for which I was grateful. Already on the bus, the bus that had taken me home so many times, I had regretted this gesture. They were better and more practised than I was in consigning the past to a region it would be better not to disturb. Simon's death lay between the Thibaudets and myself as an event on which it was no longer proper to dwell. They might see it as somehow fitting that my mother too had disappeared, so that their former friendship belonged to history. The Thibaudets were old; they might not care to be reminded of what lay in store. I left my name, and an assurance of my affection. This was not entirely false. They had been witnesses to a time when I had been happy. It does not do to neglect such people, for if they care to examine their memories such memories may supplement one's own.

I wandered back down the road to Les Mouettes, as I knew I should. The white villa blazed red in the setting sun. I stood behind the hedge of tamarisk that shadowed the side entrance, the one nobody used. Visitors, such as we had had in the past, entered by the conservatory, the doors of which were opened on such occasions. There was some sort of party in progress. I could hear voices, hear too the sound of a glass being shattered. High-pitched laughter was interrupted by male shouts of welcome, as cars drew up and stopped in a spurt of gravel. Great attention was paid to these cars, small knots of men congregating to examine them, to congratulate the owners. Less attention seemed to be paid to the women who occupied the chairs on the terrace, their conflicting scents pungent in the evening air. There was no possible way for me to take a last look at the house, as I had hoped to. It had passed finally out of our possession, its epitaph a cocktail party attended by noisy strangers. I walked away, not caring too much if I were noticed. My right to be there was in doubt, but that seemed a minor offence. The right of those other people to be there seemed to me much more questionable.

They were of course perfectly entitled to amuse themselves; even I was willing to concede this point. It was just that my thoughts had been so sober, so fearful, for so long, that I had no notion that such entertainments could be, almost certainly were, entirely innocent. It was just that I disliked leaving the house to be despoiled in this way. The raised voices, the intrusive scents had seemed so out of place compared with the quiet manners of former times. Once more I saluted Simon's memory. He had created a domain out of what was in reality a misappropriation, and had done so with something like dignity, a dignity that might have escaped him in previous incarnations. To me he would always be a part of my life. The house would signify an enchantment, though it had never been more than a sort of fiction. But it is the duty of fictions to supply other lives, and this Les Mouettes had done. That is why the house, and the brevity of our tenure, had something of the finality one recognizes when closing a book. I should never attempt to recreate the fiction of our lives there. I was the only one of the three of us to have believed the fiction to be fact. Both my mother and Simon had known the truth of the matter, and had dealt with it in their respective ways. Simon had believed in his own ability to sustain it. My mother had admitted to herself that she was not safe. Hence her longing for a home built on less dubious territory. I doubted whether she knew of the existence of the rightful owners, had indeed known that there were owners other than Simon. Yet her instincts had told her that there might be a reckoning of some kind, that all was as temporary as her marriage had seemed, even more temporary than she had suspected. The end, when it came, was a perverse relief. And my mother was never at all comfortable unless living in the light of the truth. Although she had once been an avid reader she had never made the mistake of confusing fiction with fact.

I decided to walk back into town, a distance of some five or six miles. The intense heat of the day persisted, but with something disturbed in the atmosphere: there might be thunder later. A new moon made a brief appearance before being engulfed by cloud. I made no wish, turned no money in my pocket. The adventure was over. Dr Balbi had not pursued me, as I thought a man should pursue a woman. I had not rid myself of my childish imaginings. I doubt if one ever does. I was as near to doing so as I should ever be, and a certain peace descended on me as I realized this. There would be no happy ending. I should have to live without such consoling fictions, as most people do. The disadvantage was that the fictions exert such a power that one comes to accept them as revealed truth. But they were always fictions, and must remain so. And one's powers are limited, for that is the unarguable truth of the matter. That was the whole point of the fairy godmother in the Cinderella story. That is why one longs to believe in some kind of intervention, divine or otherwise. That is the wish lurking behind all songs of praise, even in the hearts of the righteous, the obedient, the well-meaning. To live with unalterable truth is a very hard discipline, though one may receive many reminders of it along the way. Those who manage to do so are to be congratulated. Such acceptance is not within the competence of the indifferently endowed. Yet that was the path I must now follow.

It must have been very late, but I was not tired. I was now so short of sleep that I seemed to have passed into a different state, a state which imposed its own laws of what seemed like normality. Sounds were muted, perhaps because of the approaching rain. I was prepared to walk all night if need be:

the day had already been so long that it might just as well merge into the next. No one would note my absence, which now seemed a matter of little importance. Warning signs, the sudden feeling of faintness that I had come to recognize, prompted me to sit down and eat a meal, or rather to drink several cups of coffee in lieu of a meal, for in this incorporeal state I doubted whether I could digest food. The shutters were being pulled down as I left the café. Night had thickened, aided by the now menacing clouds, which could be felt rather than seen. I was still reluctant to go home, made my way, as I had not intended to do, down to the beach. I was without volition, merely being moved along by memory. I was familiar with this procedure. I was devoid of intention; it was merely a fitting way to end the day. I should be glad when it was over, yet did not seem able to bring it about. When a few heavy drops of rain began to fall I turned and made my way back over the sliding pebbles. It was so dark that I nearly missed the pale disc of a known face, or should have done had Dr Balbi not come forward to meet me. We stood for a few seconds in the rain.

'I saw you,' he said. 'Why did you not wait for me?'

'I thought that I might find you here. Or that you might find me.'

'As I have,' he said. 'As I have.' Then he led me away.

17

October is a beautiful month in Nice, and November is equally benign. By that time the tourists have gone, and the streets and cafés have been restored to their normal inhabitants. I am usually there in October, as I am in May and July and December. The rest of the winter months I spend in London, working as a copy editor. When the light changes I am anxious to be on my way. My return to Nice has come to represent a true homecoming, and I would not have it otherwise.

I unpack my bags in my room and take my usual present of tea and biscuits downstairs to M. Cottin. He has come to accept me as his permanent lodger, and sometimes we have a cup of coffee together before he opens the shop. He also appreciates the radio which I presented to him when I realized that I had no further use for it now that other voices fill my evenings. These voices belong to Dr Balbi, Antoine, and his sister Jeanne, whose visits increased in frequency as soon as she suspected that his affections were divided. I understand this, as he does: he is a faithful man, and would regard any defection with distaste. I have worked mightily to repair the breach which she must have feared, and have probably succeeded. She is an envious woman, who bears the marks of her early privations, suspicious of my presence but making heroic efforts to be welcoming. She is naïve enough to let her suspicions show, but I have become adept at defusing them. The days usually end with the three of us sitting together in their dark dining-room, our hands on the table, discussing the day's events.

She manifests an inordinate interest in my work, hoping that it will soon take me away again. There is no pretence that I am just a friend; on the other hand no uncensored words or gestures disturb the harmonious atmosphere. They are my family now, and I am careful to defer to them both. Occasionally Jeanne will succumb to her earlier love for her brother and extend that love to myself: a favourite dish will be produced for dinner, at which there will be smiles all round. I thank her fervently, knowing what such gestures must have cost her. She is there most of the time now, and this must be accepted. It is their home, after all, and perhaps it suits the three of us when I exclaim at the time and announce that I must return to the rue de France before M. Cottin double-bolts the street door. She is relieved to see me go, but manages to be gracious enough to say that they expect me on the following evening. 'As usual,' she says, with a gallant smile. Such smiles represent true sacrifice, and also immense relief. In that way the conventions are observed. Antoine finds this appropriate: he is not a man for indiscretions, for breaches of good manners. He spares her feelings in this way, as I do, although I have no taste for hypocrisy. But then I have no taste for giving offence, and I think I have the better part of the bargain.

Jeanne is well aware of my restraint, though she would forgive her brother anything. But her hurt goes very deep, and this humdrum pantomime of normal life is the factor that maintains her equilibrium. As for Antoine, he is grateful to us both for preserving the decencies. This is how we conduct our lives together, and there is no particular cause for regret: voices have never been raised, objections never voiced. In time she will come to accept me more wholeheartedly, knowing her brother to be as much in my care as he is in hers. We all know this. She may even volunteer a kind of love for me, rather than the eagerly disguised resentment she habitually experiences. I feel for her, as I should feel for anyone in her position. I have seen bewilderment before, seen it too often not to sympathize.

Our time together is thus limited, but is all the more intense for that reason. He drives me to Aix or to Montpellier, and we spend a few days in a quiet hotel. Our cover story is his interest in photographing architectural curiosities. I am the navigator on these occasions, a task I enjoy, for these excursions are real: it would offend him to tell a lie. In those out-of-the-way hotels we have come to know each other, to witness each other's intimate life. It surprises me to realize how effortless this process has been, and how heartfelt. Little is said: I respect his silences as he respects mine, for, like him, I have become taciturn. Thus there are no tedious confessions of past affections, no digressions from what is truly our affair. We know each other so well by now that there is no need to ask questions, to offer explanations. Even our returns to Nice are devoid of regrets. We turn to each other with a reminiscent smile before he sets me down in the rue de France. He does not ask when we shall see each other again, for he knows that I will always come back to him. I know this too, for at last I have a certainty in my life. He is my certainty, and I am able to accept the fact that I am his.

He is a busy man, a prestigious man, with multifarious professional obligations. I am his secret life, and perhaps one day it will become less secret. Soon we shall begin to travel together. He has mentioned conferences in Geneva, and in Atlanta. This will truly be a new life for me, but for the moment I am happy with the present arrangement. This is a love affair, not the rapturous kind I once loved to read about, with a definable conclusion. It is more of a lifelong occupation, and I am surprised to acknowledge that it suits me perfectly. When I am in London I can imagine no other, and when I am with him no other is so desirable. I would say that the very slowness of the process has revealed me to myself if I were not wary of such rationalizations. In fact what is so precious about this friendship – for it is a true friendship – is that it has involved no change of character, no effort to meet the other's requirements. We find each other acceptable as we are, and thus there is no room for any possible comparisons. There is no pretence either: that would be anathema to both of us. Equally there are no protestations of happiness. These would be redundant.

After so many upheavals I enjoy the regularity of my life, its predictability, the assurance that is there in the background. I even enjoy my work, which brings me into contact with writers, but not, fortunately, into close contact. I even enjoy those winter months when I am entirely alone, for I know that when the days lengthen I shall be in another place. I pity those people who plan strenuous holidays, just as they pity me for my hidebound routines. They know that there is someone in my life, but no more than that. They have come to accept my reticence, as I have, for I acquired it from an expert. When I am in London I am able to imagine the three of us in that dark red dining-room, presenting a picture of harmony which is not entirely deceptive. I know that Jeanne Balbi is frightened that I might take her brother away from her, just as I know that Antoine is aware of this. But I have no wish to hurt her, no wish to disrupt their lives. There must be some validity in that image of the three of us at the table, like a picture seen long ago in a remote gallery which I do not remember. In time Jeanne and I will be friends, as we pretend to be now. This is not an urgent matter. I have spent so much time in the past months, years even, trying to argue fate into some kind of acquiescence that I am now content to surrender such efforts, such initiatives as I have tried to undertake. In the end they proved useless. Far be it from me to argue in favour of a higher power. If anything there may be a sort of inevitability that demands our patience. That patience I now possess.

Strangely, I do not have a sense of difficulty, although I know that difficulties exist. The problem of Jeanne will not be easily solved. She will not return to Marseilles, or not for long, for she must monitor her brother's affections. I appreciate her unhappiness, as who could not? I do not make the mistake of pitying her, for that would be reductive and insulting. She is still locked into the drama and wistfulness of her early years, and one must respect her yearnings. One must also respect the fact that they are with her for life. Yet I think she believes that I am benign, that I wish her no further suffering. In that way she will eventually accept me as an ally in the great enterprise of wishing her brother well. It is on such a basis that I hope we will grow old as friends.

As a woman approaching middle age I know that certain changes are inevitable, that I may not always be as adaptable as I have so far proved to be. I shall grow tired, cranky, inclined to insist on a life of my own. The lives of my friends have become expansive, filled with children, houses, dependants; secretly they deplore my lonely status, though that is not what afflicts me. I miss children, as all middle-aged women do if they are childless. I see them in the streets around my flat, on their way to school, chattering blithely to their mothers. Latterly I have found myself lingering in supermarkets to watch them running heedlessly past the shelves. I know that such a life is not for me, has never come within my grasp. I accept that in that sense nothing has changed. What I have instead may have been denied to those happy harassed mothers: I have that terrible freedom of which others are justifiably afraid. I now recognize its deep seriousness. I am free to live my life without restraint, and again without witnesses. This is not always a joyous procedure. On certain cold evenings, before the winter has turned into spring, I look out of my window and feel a sudden loneliness. I tell myself that this is due to the absence of the sun, and that once I am back in Nice the loneliness will vanish. My moments of cold sense disconcert me, for so far I have managed to maintain my resolution to live as I have chosen to live, transfixed by what I have assumed will be permanent when in fact it may be no more than temporary.

At such times I picture the brother and sister without me. They are seated at the same table, under the dim centre light, and they are discussing me. This is a conversation from which I am naturally excluded, yet I am sure it is entered into with some regularity. Antoine will have the difficult task of remaining loyal to us both, and will do so by virtue of his habitual discretion, but his sympathy, I fear, will always be with his sister. She is not a strong woman, as I appear to be; she is dominated by her nerves, and is not shy about showing her fears. Strangely, her fears are the same as my own; they are the fears of what happens to a childless woman as she grows old. I doubt if such fears are quite formulated in her somewhat incoherent mind, but she knows instinctively that she must hold on to those affections she already possesses. When I am feeling very brave I face the possibility that she may become ill, may regress, demand protection, demand sacrifices, as the sick so often do, extort promises, and even reveal an antagonism which she does not yet acknowledge. Then, I know, it will be time for me to do one of two things: to stay behind and look after her, or to take my leave of Antoine and come home for ever. It astonishes me that I can even contemplate this. Yet I know that I too may succumb to weariness, may in the end prefer my own isolation, consigning Antoine to his. I know that we shall always be lonely without each other, but will be wise enough to know when the situation has become unsustainable. Then old age will truly begin.

For the moment this is in the realm of speculation. For the moment I am content with the compromises I have made. It is enough for me to remember my life before Antoine – the life of a hapless daughter – to exult in the present. Admittedly this is easier to do in Nice than in London. In Nice I have the simulacrum of a family, a history. I have those evenings round the table, Antoine smiling faintly as Jeanne deplores my poor appetite. Then, just briefly, I wonder how long we can maintain this politeness. I begin to anticipate my return to London, discuss my work, watch Jeanne's expression relax as I do so. Then I make a pretext of an early night. Antoine will offer to see me home, an offer I will accept. Jeanne will start to clear the table before I have even said goodbye.

This almost impalpable disaffection does not last. I am too aware of what might be lost to allow it to continue. With a little practice I can repair the breach almost immediately, for what use is a woman of my age if she still clings to the fantasies that should belong to youth? Before I leave Nice, having said two separate goodbyes, one to Jeanne, one to Antoine, I try to spend a day alone. I wander down to the beach, as I used to, but now I do so in the full blaze of noon, having returned the night to its rightful place. And it is at such times, in the late morning or the early afternoon, before catching my plane, that I am reminded once again that I have been fortunate, and that my continued good fortune depends on tact, on discretion, on clearsightedness. These qualities are not beyond me. I am not without resource, should it become necessary. For the moment all is well. The future is, in a sense, taken care of: it is in another's hands. And in mine, perhaps, but I decide not to think ahead. I prefer, at such moments, to feel the heat of the day, to let my thoughts become as evanescent as the ambient air. The sounds of the traffic at my back hardly impinge on what is in effect a restoration of goodwill, of joy. I do not make the mistake of ascribing this joy to any superhuman reminder of the brevity of life. I am aware once more of the force of nature. And at such moments I experience the fullness of nature and of its promises. Life has brought me to this condition of acceptance, and at last I understand that acceptance is all. I succumb to the genius of the place, and know true felicity. The sun is God. Of the rest it is wiser not to know, or not yet to know. The plot will unfold, with or without my help. It is my hope that there will be a place in it for all of us, for Jeanne, for Antoine, and for myself. Under the promise of that cloudless sky it seems that our lives together have only just begun. In that sense our story will run its course, and I realize, with a lifting of the heart, that it is not yet time to close the book.